Knight Quests

Books by C.C. Wiley

Knights of the Swan series

KNIGHT SECRETS
KNIGHT QUESTS

Knight Quests

C.C. Wiley

LYRICAL PRESS
Kensington Publishing Corp.
www.kensingtonbooks.com

LYRICAL PRESS BOOKS are published by

Kensington Publishing Corp.
119 West 40th Street
New York, NY 10018

All Kensington titles, imprints, and distributed lines are available at special quantity discounts for bulk purchases for sales promotion, premiums, fund-raising, educational, or institutional use.

Special book excerpts or customized printings can also be created to fit specific needs. For details, write or phone the office of the Kensington Sales Manager: Kensington Publishing Corp., 119 West 40th Street, New York, NY 10018. Attn. Sales Department. Phone: 1-800-221-2647.

Lyrical Press and Lyrical Press logo Reg. U.S. Pat. & TM Off.

First Electronic Edition: July 2017
eISBN-13: 978-1-5161-0101-6
eISBN-10: 1-5161-0101-4

First Print Edition: July 2017
ISBN-13: 978-1-5161-0104-7
ISBN-10: 1-5161-0104-9

Printed in the United States of America

Chapter 1

"Thief! Thief! Stop them!" The coarse voice, like nails scraping over cobbles, echoed through the alleyway.

Merde! Brigitte ran, skirts lifted, dodging the garbage tossed from the windows above. She tightened her hold around Piers's wrist and tugged the little boy past the refuse on the streets of Harfleur.

The place where the merchant's boot had struck her ribs squeezed with every ragged draw of breath. The throbbing promised an impressive bruise by nightfall. Instead of giving in to the stinging bite, she ran. Her throat burned. Another pull of the fetid air into her lungs made her want to gag.

"Bee!" Piers dug his heels into the cobblestone. "I can't go any farther—"

The urge to shout at the boy's foolishness soured her blood. It was his fault they were in this mess. She turned, giving him a cutting glare. They could not afford to give in to hunger, to make foolish mistakes. The others waiting in the Nest depended on them. Fear clutched her heart. By the looks of the boy's flushed cheeks, they didn't have much time before he fell over in exhaustion.

"*Oui*," she said. "We have no choice. I will not let them take us."

Piers jerked his head in a nod. The trust in his almond-shaped eyes urged her to move faster. She tucked away the harsh words. The tirade could wait until they were in the safety of their bolt-hole.

She prayed it would be soon and lurched forward. The corner of the brick building loomed in front of them. An opening to the alleyway might allow them enough time to lose the soldier.

"Bee!" Piers stumbled over the uneven stone in the alley. "Please!"

Brigitte glanced over her shoulder. The watchman following them had been more persistent than usual. But of course, the baker had been most adamant they catch the thief. His wagon had been pilfered three times that week. They must have been watching like a cat waiting to pounce. This time, the man had caught the little mite in the act of lifting a loaf of bread. And the soldier had come running with one yell.

"Bee." Piers's wet cough tore through his sobs. "I'm sorry. I won't do it again."

"Hush." She pushed down the pity that threatened to make her weak and blinked away her tears. The dingy alley was getting darker with every twist and turn. Panic roared through her veins. The sound of hobnailed boots striking the cobblestone came closer. A loud curse echoed against the buildings. She spun about, hooked the boy under her arm, and ran.

"We're going the wrong way!"

"Hush, *enfant!*"

She ducked into the shadows and let the child slide from her hip. The pain in her ribs bellowed with each breath. They stood, pressed against the wall, amid rotting garbage from the kitchens and piles of human refuse. *How has my life come to this?*

Maman would be horrified to see her thus. But then, Maman was no longer with her. And Maman's plan to secure their future had failed as soon as her lover, the mysterious Monsieur le Faire, turned his back on his mistress. For years, her beautiful Maman had had the skill to keep her benefactor deliriously happy. Even after she'd delivered him a babe. The three of them had been a family. But then, as most things are wont to do, the happiness faded away. As did the sparkle in Maman's eyes.

Brigitte's stomach growled.

How long since their last bit of food? Judging by Piers's state of weariness, it might have been even longer for him. Master Alexandre had become miserly with the scraps for his fledgling thieves.

She tested the pain in her side by taking in a breath of air. Then drew in more. No broken bones. She would survive another day.

Piers pressed against her leg and looked up at her. Shadows deepened the sunken half-moons rising above his sharp cheekbones. He gripped her fingers as if she were the only thing standing between him and the evil chasing them. Snuffling, he hiccupped softly. She drew him close. His head rested on her hip, reminding her of his youth.

Brigitte swallowed. Though barely out of the nursery, he had already begun the task of thieving for the Nest. He should be too young to know gnawing hunger. Too young for the magistrate to order that he spend his life in prison. Or worse. With one quick stroke of the quill pen, Piers could be sent to his death. She had to find a way to feed the children and keep them all safe from the soldiers. And from the master.

Like so many abandoned children, until she had found the Nest, she had been without protection. But over the years, the pull for more power had been a heady drug, and Master Alexandre had become more willing to put the Nest in danger. All for a few coins. A fat purse.

Brigitte stroked Piers's head as she listened for the strike of hobnails against stone. The child's shoulders began to sag. His breathing was less ragged. The soldier's hobnails never came.

Only the telltale sound of scurrying rats cut through the alleyway's quiet. When the rodents returned to foraging, scratching and fighting for their stake, it would be safe to leave the shadows. When they came out, it would be safe for all.

The faint sound of hissing, the loser's squeal, signaled it was time to move. Brigitte picked her way along the stones. She took the second turn to the left. The lighting of the lanterns had begun. The streets bathed in their glow were brighter, making them more dangerous for people like them. It would take twice as long to work their way back to their nest, but Brigitte was not about to put the rest of the children in danger.

She stopped before entering the public square.

"Wait, Piers." She pulled out a piece of linen and lace, soiled and gray with age. "We mustn't let anyone notice your tears."

He nodded stoically and held still while she dabbed at his eyes and nose.

Satisfied with her work, she tucked the cloth in the pocket of her apron. "Now then, *mon cher*, please explain to me how you ended up in the market by yourself. Where is Master Alexandre?"

The boy scrunched up his nose and frowned. "I don't know. He told me to fetch the bread. I need to pay for myself. Since I'm small, no one would notice me." He sniffed and his head dropped down. "But they did."

Brigitte feared the tears were about to start again. "I will speak to Master Alexandre as soon as we return home. He should know better than to send a lad your age for something as dangerous as gathering our supper."

Piers shook his flaxen head as hard as a pup shaking off water. "Oh, no. Look here." He nudged the flap sewn into his shirt. Inside lay a slightly bent loaf of bread.

Brigitte fought the mixture of pride and fear that bloomed at the sight. He was so young. Younger than she had been when she found herself caught in Master Alexandre's refuge for waifs and pickpockets. He had ordered everyone to call the place the Nest. She kept waiting for the day when he decided to kick her out. Or let her leave.

Southampton, England ~ August 1415

Drem gripped the arms of the chair and grimaced. He fought the desire to demand to hear what was being said behind closed doors. Though demanding would do him little good. Now, thanks to his father's participation in the plot against King Henry, most of the men crammed in the Cottage by the Sea considered him a threat.

Drem thumped his fists on the armrest. Over the years he had made the most of his situation, learned all he could from the king and his knights, utilized his skill, and become the king's friend and confidant. Now, thanks to his father's treasonous acts, everything he'd fought for could be wiped away.

God's oath. For years he had protected his friend and king with his bow and arrows. He had fought by his side. He would freely sacrifice his life to protect Henry.

Even now, bandages covered the fresh burns that proved his willingness to protect both throne and king. The smoke from the fire aboard the king's ship still clung to his hair and clothing. The burns on his head and hands stung, reminding him how close the reaper of death had brushed against him.

He had been trusted. Only recently had the Knights of the Swan been explained to him. They had allowed him a glimpse of the inner workings of their secret brotherhood. He had to believe that at least his sister's beloved knight would step in. Mayhap Sir James would sway them to examine his history with King Henry.

The door swung open, bounced against the wall. Sir Darrick strode across the room, avoiding looking him in the eye.

Drem's skin crawled with a mixture of anticipation and fear. It was a toxic brew that came upon him right before the heat of battle. If they had allowed him the freedom, he would have dearly loved to pace the floor. Instead, he remained bound to the chair, awaiting judgment for a paternal mistake. Betrayed by his father. Outrage squeezed against his skull.

"Ye raven-headed bastard," Drem shouted at Darrick's back. "Do you think to shun me now?"

He flinched when a heavy hand touched his shoulder from behind. "Drem, he worries about the march on France and our friend's safety."

Drem twisted in his seat to see his face. "Henry was my friend before he was made king. Do you think I'd hold a grudge this many years?"

James came up and added, "Your father has."

"And I've told you, I'm not Dafydd ap Hew. Nor would I have abandoned my child to seal a bargain."

"I have myself to blame for not stopping it then." Sir James Frost squatted in front of him, his blade in his hand. The lantern's light caught the steely edges.

Drem tensed. His sister might have given her heart to the man, but the knight could easily slit his throat. Mindful to show no sign of fear, he snorted. "Then you're a bigger damn fool than I thought."

James looked up at him. His brows beetled. The dagger rolled in his palm. "That so?"

"Aye. When plans are put in motion by the nobles, there is naught one can do to stop their roll of power." He let his head drop, his chin resting on his chest. A stretched and bare neck would make an easy target. Less pain in the end. And yet, he could not silence the final jab. "To prove my point further, you left my sister waiting for your return. You dare not make her cool her heels much longer. Otherwise, our Terrwyn will find a new place to send her arrows."

Nathan chuckled. "Drem has the right of it, James. We've all heard of your woman's skill." He nudged his shoulder. "Best deliver your message before she finds you in her sights."

All humor washed from James's eyes. His mouth flattened in a thin straight line. He gave a quick nod.

The dagger hovered too close for comfort.

"Drem ap Dafydd, you are hereby released from bondage."

James sliced at Drem's wrists. The rope split. Then the hemp braid holding each ankle to the chair was cut, freeing him with a whisper of the knife.

Drem cleared his throat. "And after you've finished with your carving?"

James rose silently and stepped back. The smile he had worn mere seconds earlier had not returned.

Nathan nodded to the men who began filing out of the hidden chamber. They surrounded him in a circle.

Drem searched their expressions for understanding. Then he searched for the nearest means of escape.

"The council has voted," James said. He sheathed his weapon. His cool gaze cut across the men. "There are a few who are not convinced of your complete innocence."

Sir Darrick held up his hand for silence. "However, given the most recent events of the Southampton plot and the execution of Sir Thomas Grey, the majority is persuaded that you, your sisters, and your brother are innocent pawns in your father's greedy plan."

"The others in the plot—they were captured?" Drem asked.

"Executed. Cambridge is buried in the chapel of God's House. As for Scrope?" Nathan shrugged as he held his gaze.

There was pain there. Drem recognized the pain in the taking of another life.

"There are but a handful of traitors who have not been found," Nathan said.

Sir Darrick added, "Drem, your father is among that handful."

"Aye." Drem swallowed, unsure of how they would use him. "I feared as much." Thoughts of his family raced through his head. Somehow he would find a way to protect them and right the wrongs his father had created.

"Drem ap Dafydd." James's smile had returned. "Not only are you no longer in bondage to that chair, but Henry releases you from your position as king's archer."

Sir Darrick stepped closer. "What say you, lad? Do you wish to leave King Henry's side?"

Drem struggled to comprehend the freedom he had been given. 'Twas something that occasionally entered his dreams as a child. He watched the men. Their demeanor spoke of things not yet said. "I thank you both for saying your piece to the council. And I accept the freedom I've been given. I'd be a damn fool not to." Noticing the tightening of their shoulders, he quickly added, "But I'll not thank you for removing me from attending to Henry's protection. If I have no other choice, I'd rather stay with the troops. You'll need as many archers as you can muster when you take France."

Nathan, the auburn-haired warrior, towered over Drem. He cleared his throat and folded his arms across his chest. "'Tis not an option now."

"God's bones!" Drem drew himself up. Standing gave him confidence. His height matched Nathan's and gave him the courage to stare down the knight. He turned, searching the men remaining in the cottage. "Who among you feels there are too many soldiers to see to the king's safety and bring victory to England?" He thumped his chest with his thumb. "Best archer he has. I challenge any one of you to stand against me. Discover for yourselves the type of man I am who stands for our king."

"Steady, Brother," James said. "We cannot leave you in the position you once filled because it goes against Henry's wishes."

Drem stepped forward, closing the space between them. "Spit it out . . . Brother . . . Where does my king order me to serve?"

"For God's sake." Sir Darrick pushed his way through the throng of men. "Quit playing with him."

Drem remembered the knight had held him with a critical eye ever since the role his father had played in the plot against Henry had been discovered. He waited. If anything, this man would cut to the truth, straight and clean. Or to his heart. ·

"Henry wishes you to carry an extra burden. One that will change your life." Sir Darrick hesitated.

"Speak it," Drem urged.

"If I should speak it, you'll have no choice but to accept. For it'll be as King Henry ordered."

Drem looked about the cottage. Everyone in the room had their attention on their conversation. These men held one thing in common: Their love of king and country brought them together as Knights of the Swan.

Drem nodded slowly. "Aye. Go on with it. Speak it and make it so."

"There's much you have to learn to be a Knight of the Swan."

Drem searched for the chair he had been so eager to leave and sat down. The words struggled to work their way through his brain. "Knight of the Swan. Truly?"

"Yes." Something sparkled behind Sir James Frost's blue-gray eyes. Terrwyn's beloved, and Drem's brother by marriage, added a warning. "'Tis not for the fainthearted. Best prepare to have your arse handed to you from time to time."

"Your training begins at once," Darrick ground out.

"But first," Nathan said, "instead of a hanging, 'tis call for a bit of celebration."

The men came, surrounding Drem with solemn good cheer and a pitcher of ale. He shook his head, praying he'd heard correctly. Somehow he would find a way to return the favor his king had shown him. Even if that payment involved the life of his father.

Left to his thoughts, Drem knocked back the last gulp of ale and set the mug down. Seagulls called from the bay as they circled over the king's fleet. James had already returned to Terrwyn's arms. The newlyweds would soon be headed to the Welsh borders to cut off any intrusions from the west.

Drem was hit with the realization that he had no idea what was to come next. He did not even know where he was to lay his head for the night. The hearth, though casting warmth from the fire, looked about as comfortable as sleeping in armor.

He groaned inwardly as Sir Darrick strode toward him. He fisted two mugs in one hand, a pitcher in the other. Drem itched under his scrutiny. He could tell, king's edict or no, the knight did not trust him.

"A word or two," Sir Darrick said.

"Aye?'

Sir Darrick poured a healthy portion for both of them. "You need to understand. You are not a knight yet. Not until Henry has performed the rite." He held out the filled mug and took a sip from his own. "Despite the trust we've placed in you, you'll be watched closely."

Drem forced down the outrage that began to pulsate through his blood and pound in his temples. Despite being taken from his home, had he not been a good and loyal servant? "God's blood," he ground out. "On my oath as a Knight of the Swan, I will protect my king or die in the task."

"'Tis because of your new position that your father may make contact." Sir Darrick tapped his mug to Drem's. "We are a secret brotherhood. And yet our enemies know of us. I can't help but wonder how that is, and how I can put a stop to it."

Sir Darrick rose, the pitcher and mug forgotten. "There is a cot in the corner. You may use it for tonight. Come morning, you may return to your lodgings above the tavern. We'll give you time before we begin preparations for France. Sleep well, young Knight of the Swan."

Chapter 2

Brigitte slipped inside the door. The makeshift bedchamber didn't hold the luxury of a single cot. Instead, the children, cast-offs from the people of Harfleur, slept on pallets made of extra bits of clothing.

"Bee, get over here," Master Alexandre barked.

The master of the Nest swung his arm overhead. Sweat stains coated the armpits of his leather jerkin and clung to the gray linen of his undertunic. He had obviously had taken time from his busy training schedule to dampen his hair and slick it back. The red satin ribbon tied around the knob of hair stood out like a streak of blood against his blond hair.

Brigitte released the latch she held in a vicelike grip and forced her legs away from the door. "*Oui*, Master Alexandre," she said, careful to keep her voice calm. It never served anyone well to let their fear show.

She moved closer to his great chair, keeping enough distance to remain out of arm's reach. Despite the twenty or more children milling about, the room became quiet, their lack of chatter stifling. She took a step forward.

The smell of bad wine wafted up and met her nose. His dark eyes glittered back at her. She had seen that look before.

Once, the night when she and her mother had been set out on the street. And when the stranger came to their home, threatening Maman and her scrawny brat. And when Maman's lover had turned his back on them, the owner of the establishment had chased them out of the seaside town. But not before taking what he could. He took all but the brooch her mother had hidden. "For when the days have lost their luster," mother had whispered.

Brigitte masked her fear, forcing her expression to remain calm and passive. It would do her no good to give away the hiding place of her few treasures.

"*Oui*, Master Alexandre," she repeated.

Now, more often than not, the master of the Nest felt threatened. The rages came more frequently. What had displeased him this time?

"So!" He slammed down his empty mug. The table beside him wobbled at impact.

The children in the corner of the room began to shuffle and whimper. Brigitte flinched when he bolted from his chair.

"You guaranteed you'd train the new children personally. Instead, I hear that you bought Piers's bread. You even read to them from the public notices." He moved closer. The graceful steps belied his need for a cane.

"He is not suited for this."

"His training is incomplete. You've been warned before, Bee. You cannot save anyone from what they are. From what you are."

Alexandre's flushed cheeks brightened with his temper. She braced for his rebuke and hoped he would understand this time. She once had called this man her friend. They had found themselves lost, abandoned by society. He had taken her in and shown her how to survive. There had to be some small portion of the kindhearted young man who had held her hand and led her to safety so many years before. "The children deserve a chance for something better."

"Stupid cow. They deserve no more than the rest of us." He leaned both hands on his cane to steady himself. His eyes narrowed above his pinched mouth. "Where is it?" he snapped.

His red knuckles were white around the joints. Brigitte stepped back. Often his cane became a weapon. "What do . . . do you mean?"

Alexandre lurched toward her. "I told you the only way I'd keep my promise was if you lifted a heavy purse." He jerked his free hand out to her. "Put it in there."

Brigitte eyed his palm. *Step into my web, said the spider.* Meeting his gaze, she held it without batting an eyelash and smiled. "Oh, why didn't you say so before?" She plopped the gentleman's purse into his hand.

"Well, well, what have we here?" Alexandre wrapped his long, pale fingers greedily around the pouch. "Though not as heavy as I'd hoped."

"It should pay for Piers's food and lodging for another week or two." She searched his face. "Our bargain fulfilled. As promised."

His full lips lifted at the corners as he tucked the purse into the hidden pocket inside his jerkin. "Daring chit. Are you telling me my business?"

His cane shot out, rapping her on the arm.

Brigitte sucked in a breath as pain seared through her body. Her knees gave way under her weight. She knelt on the dirty floor, afraid to turn her gaze from his cold stare. She closed her ears to little Piers's cries of distress.

Still holding Alexandre's stare, Brigitte reluctantly released her throbbing arm and slowly wiggled her fingers. No broken bones. He would know exactly how hard to bring her to her knees without putting her in a sickbed. 'Twas not an option. Her skills were too valuable to the Nest. Without her, they would struggle to read the banns and learn which homes were left vacant. Or which lady or gentleman might be carrying more gold than usual.

"You steal from me." He pushed the cane down on her shoulder, digging into the sensitive flesh covering the bone.

Brigitte gasped in surprise.

"I want it all."

Shivering, Brigitte nodded and rose from her knees. She slid her hand under her skirts, gripped the small pouch she had hidden earlier and yanked it free. The bag ripped open, spilling a few coins over the wooden plank floor.

"Piers!" She tossed the remaining coins in the air. "Run!"

The lush countryside laced along England's backroads flashed by in a blur of the morning sun. Drem yawned and shook the weariness from his head. He could not allow his concentration to stray from the task at hand. If he did, he knew he would have already turned his mount around and headed for the nearest tavern. Instead, he followed the road to Dunstable Priory.

The note he had tucked into his jerkin seemed to sear his skin. The damned thing must have been delivered to his room above the tavern while he slept the night at the Cottage by the Sea. It was lying on the table beside his cot, waiting for him to see it first thing. He could not ignore it. The words had stated it was a matter of life or death. He swore under his breath. *God's bones. Mayhap my own death.*

Sir Darrick would gladly kill him if he learned of his absence. Though Drem was now a free man, there were enough strings attached that he felt like a prize hart. He had a day, maybe a bit more, before anyone noticed he had made his departure.

On the other hand, if this wild chase led him to his father's whereabouts, he would use it to his advantage to regain Henry's complete trust. It wasn't just the king's trust he needed. He wanted his position to be without question. Especially with Sir Darrick. It was clear the surly knight despised him.

Drem had to succeed. The threat of repercussions against his family remained.

By midafternoon, he drew Aeron to a halt just outside Dunstable. The church was easy enough to locate. It rose above the villagers' cottages. The southwest gateway led to the smaller priory. That was where the author of the note had instructed him to go.

Drem stepped through the arched gateway and followed the path leading to the chapel. Warily, with one hand close to his sword, he pushed open the door and slipped inside. The chapel was empty of inhabitants. He strode toward the table holding the great Bible. The leather tome was closed, the clasp locked against unworthy eyes.

"May I help you, my son?"

Drem whirled around, his sword halfway unsheathed. The man who spoke so softly wore a long woolen robe without adornment. He was tall and thin. A halo of snowy white hair covered his head. His only bit of jewelry, a wooden cross that hung from a leather thong around his neck.

"God's bones!" Heat rushed to his cheeks when he realized the man of the cloth had heard his curse. When the man did not reprimand him, he began to wonder if he was an imposter. Drem refused, now, to believe what anyone said about who they were. His father's betrayal had taught him that much. To remain armed and untrusting had been his best lesson yet.

"Excuse me . . ."

"Call me Father Timothy, if you must. We're all brothers in God's eyes." His gray eyes twinkled with amusement as he motioned toward the grip Drem had on his sword. "Put your weapon away. 'Tis God's role to judge, not mine."

Still feeling the need to be ever vigilant, Drem nodded and let the sword slide into its sheath.

Father Timothy smiled at the sound of the hilt striking home. He pushed his hands into the voluminous sleeves of his robes. "Tell me, what brings you here? 'Tis too soon to celebrate the Assumption of the Blessed Virgin."

"I've a message . . ." Drem started.

"Ah, you wish to hear God's word."

"No." Drem glanced at the Bible on the altar. The note had directed him where to look. So far it hadn't sent him into a hornets' nest. "I wish to read of God's word."

"You wish to read it yourself?" The priest's pleasant countenance slipped for half a breath. "You know your letters?" He pursed his lips in doubt, taking in every detail.

The healing burns on Drem's head and hands began to sting with an uncomfortable awareness. He itched to be on his way. The sword at his side nearly sung with the temptation to be drawn out and used against the man. "Please," Drem said. "Turn to 1 Samuel, chapter 17."

"Ah." The priest's hesitant smile slipped back into place. He drew out a gold key from around his neck. "So you wish to read of the mighty David. You must be going off to France. 'Tis soon, aye?" He unlocked the clasp and carefully began to turn the parchment pages.

Drem caught the priest's wrist. "Might I have some time alone? To read?"

Seeing his hesitation, Drem pressed a coin into the priest's bent fingers. "If you would grant it, I would spend time with my Heavenly Father."

"Of course, of course, my son. When you are through with your meditations, you may find me in the gardens."

Drem released his hold and tried to feel remorse for the way the man rubbed the reddened skin. He watched him leave through the arched gateway before turning to the Bible. Aware of the treasure before him, with reverence, he turned the pages until he came to chapter 17. Tucked neatly between the parchment sheets was a small object, wrapped in linen, no bigger than his thumb. He looked for watching eyes, then gingerly picked up the barely legible note. It simply read, "Find its mate. Never stop."

Drem swore softly. Grinding his teeth, he set to unfolding the linen. A white and silver, swan-shaped brooch slid into his hand. Its emerald eye winked up at him. Swearing again under his breath, he placed the fabric on the opened Bible and smoothed it flat. The livery badge, fashioned into a dancing lion, was made of the highest order and quality. *I should leave it here. Let it molder and rot. Why should I place everything in jeopardy?*

Drem fisted the badge and brooch. His fingers disobeyed, would not release them. He glanced at the Bible. How convenient. The main character was David. The same name as his father's, though his father spelled it in the Welsh fashion, Dafydd. Had his father had the arrogance to draw him here only to thumb his nose at him? Rage began to bubble through his veins.

He had been tested and tricked. This was nothing but a fool's errand. And he no doubt was the fool who would soon feel his neck stretched on the block.

"Sir Darrick, I presume," he muttered.

Drem turned as a door whispered open. He saw no one. No movement. A sound, like the whisper of cloth, came before the pain to the back of his head. Then darkness swallowed him whole.

Drem peeled open an eyelid. Nathan's towering form stood over him. He grunted when the knight tried to roll him over.

"Arise. We mustn't tarry."

Drem sat up to gain his bearings and then tried to stand. He lurched forward. The pain exploded in his head. He clutched at his scalp and did his best to form words through clenched teeth. "Christ on the cross, who did this?" He cut his glance to Nathan. "Why...are...you... here?"

"Not here. Later." He grabbed Drem's elbow. "Can you ride?"

He shook free of Nathan's hold. "Aye."

Nathan's auburn brows rose. His mouth flattened in a tight line. "We must make haste. We'll be hard-pressed to arrive by morning."

Drem closed his eyes and soon realized his error when the spinning renewed its strength. "Aye."

Nathan put his arm around Drem's waist to support him. "You can explain on the ride back why you slipped out to Dunstable without letting anyone know."

It took everything Drem had in him to pull his back straight. "I had my reasons."

"It had better have been damn well worth it. There are some who'd rather see you in chains. They're sitting in judgment. Searching for your sins." Nathan left him and headed for the door. He paused at the threshold. "You just gave it to them."

Drem stumbled and caught himself on the table. The Bible was missing. Clarity returned with each burning breath. The livery badge and brooch were missing as well. He felt for his sword, his short blade, the small purse in his belt. They were all there. What thief attacks a man only to steal God's word and a torn bit of material? He wished he had more time to examine the swan brooch. Did it mean a message had been sent, asking for help from the Knights of the Swan? But who sent it? And why to him?

Still braced against the table, he slipped his hand inside his leather jerkin. He withdrew his trembling hand. Empty. His attacker had taken the note. Or had Nathan removed it when Drem lay unconscious?

"The priest?" Drem cleared his throat. "Where is Father Timothy?"

"Do you require help?" Frowning, Nathan folded his arms over his broad chest.

"I must speak with him. Thank him for his hospitality."

"'Tis my understanding he's gone."

"Gone?" Drem ran a shaking hand over his face. How was he to explain his absence and the reason for his ride to Dunstable Priory?

"One of the parishioners said he mentioned leaving in haste to see an ailing member of his flock. Weeks ago." Concern flowed from his gaze. "'Tis time we ride."

Drem forced his leaden legs to move toward the doorway. Thoughts of running from the knight raced through his head. He pushed them back. Running would only prove his enemies had won. He'd find a way to verify that his intentions were only to capture his father.

Nathan sat on his black stallion. He gave him a curt nod and held out the reins. "Mount up, young Drem. We set sail tomorrow morning."

Ignoring the pounding in his head, Drem plastered a smile on his face and strode to his mount. Soon enough, he would discover why Nathan had taken the note. And why the priest had disappeared.

Chapter 3

Drem gripped the ship's railing and watched the shores of Southampton slip out of view. He tore his gaze from the smoke that still lingered over the horizon. This had been his father's handiwork. Less than two weeks ago, Dafydd ap Hew and his cohorts had attempted to take King Henry's life by torching the ships. He could still feel the heat of the flames singe his skin as he'd helped put out the fires.

"How many men were injured in the attack on the king's fleet?" he asked the captain.

"Ack! I'd wager no more than two score. Outa that 'twas only one life that left us." The captain shot a glance and met Drem's eyes. "No doubt that poor soul has met the devil himself by now." His gaze slid to the bandages wrapped around Drem's head. "No doubt you've had your share of injury caused by that traitor. 'Twas a jackal in man's skin. Given half a chance, I would have strung him up from the yardarm."

Drem flinched at the disregard in the man's voice. Did the captain know just how closely they'd all been betrayed? He perhaps felt the cut the deepest. The only balm to his wounds would be to regain the king's trust. And that of the Knights of the Swan.

He turned to see Sir Darrick striding toward them. The invitation to join the Knights of the Swan was held captive by that knight's disbelief of his complete innocence. Drem supposed he should feel blessed that he still had the capability to breathe. It had taken every bit of fast talking to explain his disappearance. He would know soon enough if the note was a trap set by his father or by the knight charging up to stand by his side.

He sucked in the fresh air, tasted the salty tang on his tongue, and braced for Sir Darrick's barbed words.

"You'll keep no secrets from me, Drem. Of this, I warn you."

"Aye," he said. "I recall that conversation." He leaned his arms on the railing and looked out across the rolling waves. The brooch and torn badge were etched on his mind. The reason for his trip to Dunstable Priory weighed heavy on his conscience. But he would keep his own counsel until he understood their meaning.

Days later, Drem joined the king's soldiers and mounted up when Sir Darrick lifted his hand. There would be time for them to ride, a day or two to gain a foothold in the town of Harfleur. Once the town was captured, the stronghold would give them the defenses they needed. Then they would gain control of Paris or Calais. Then all of France.

After ensuring that his longbow remained wrapped, protected from the drizzling rain, Drem settled into the saddle. He glanced back at the wagons. The archery boys would march together until they made camp. They would have plenty of time to practice before the real battles with the French would commence. Each would continue to be tested. Ten accurate shots in a minute. No easy feat. But he would ensure all who were able would be ready.

Four days of riding, marching, and avoiding the French army. Four days to find their land legs. Four days to get over the seasickness that plagued so many of the men. The challenge had begun.

Brigitte did her best to change the way they looked and made short work of securing replacements for their own clothing. Piers had wanted to leave behind his old, threadbare shirt as payment, but she would not hear of it. They could not leave a trail for them to be followed.

"Quiet, *mon ami*." She wrapped her arms around his thin shoulders. They may have escaped Alexandre's Nest, but they were not out of his control.

They would have to bide their time before returning for the bag of coins she had hidden earlier.

Something had made Alexandre wary of her movements. Somehow, he knew she could not be trusted.

Weeks before, she had begun noticing one of Alexandre's fledglings follow her from one stop to the next. She had felt the little one's eyes on her, had even cut back a few extra times to try to trap him.

When he'd scurried back to report her activities, she knew it was time to make another attempt at escaping the Nest. Once she knew she was safe from prying eyes, she had taken out a few coins to pad her account and then filled the third bag with a few coins to appease Alexandre when he decided she'd cheated him. Her plan had not included the shower of coins raining over Alexandre's head, nor had it included Piers.

Improvisations.

Master Alexandre hated when she deviated from his plans. If he caught up with them, he would make her pay dearly. But trusting her instincts had kept her alive for this long. She thought she would continue listening to them until they failed her.

Brigitte drew up, pressing her back against the brick wall. The market was bustling with busy shoppers. The sweet smells from the patisserie made her stomach grind with hunger. The Assumption of the Blessed Virgin Mary was only a few days away. The women of the houses, their purses fat with money, were making their purchases for the holiday. Alexandre and his little fledglings would be very busy lifting all they could from the unsuspecting victims of chance.

"Piers, turn very carefully and tell me if you see them," Brigitte whispered.

He peeked out from the folds of the charwoman's apron Brigitte now wore. She had lifted it and the faded gray gown from the line of clothes hanging out to dry. It had been an extra blessing when Piers handed her a kerchief to cover her dark hair. She had thought to wear boy's clothing but nothing fit. People were more apt to distrust a poorly dressed boy.

Piers pushed the cap away from his face. The color was a striking match with his blue eyes.

"Lucie is over yonder, by the fat lady haggling with the poulterer. She's about to lift one of the eggs." He muffled a chuckle. "Hope she doesn't drop 'em this time." He chortled. "She made a mess of it before, didn't she?"

"Hush!" Brigitte warned. "We don't want anyone to notice us."

Shifting the basket they'd found on the tavern stoop, she gripped it close and struck out along the corridor of merchants selling their wares. They marched through the market square and headed for the outer wall. They could not leave the city until Brigitte returned for the cache of coins hidden right outside Master Alexandre's door.

The bells began tolling. Brigitte looked up at the sky, confused. Too early to call in the worshippers.

Claudette, the old woman who took in laundry, ran past. Her eyes were wide with fear. "English soldiers are marching this way." She grabbed at Brigitte's wrist. "Come quick. Hide while you can."

English ships blocked the harbor, cutting off Harfleur's port. Despite Raoul de Gaucourt's efforts to flood the land outside the walls, the English continued to pour over the fields and lay siege.

Brigitte walked with the masses of infirm, who had been ordered to go out through the gate. Master Alexandre must have had the mayor's ear again, advising him to send out the ailing for the enemy to deal with. The townspeople believed Gaucourt would be their defender against the horde of English curs. But there was a shiftiness in his eyes that made her skin prickle with apprehension. She would wager her last coin that he served only those who lined his own pockets and advanced his position.

She slipped off to the shadows, working her way past the sick and dying. The wagons that carried the English army's food supplies were not far. The foolish soldiers had thoughtlessly stopped them in the bog. Soon their wheels were mired up to their axles in mud. It would require a force of men to pry them from the sticky hold.

A pity for the soldiers. A prize for her.

The vision of Master Alexandre gnawing on an old chicken bone haunted her. If he found her again, it would be her bones he would devour.

All the more reason to snatch some supplies before everyone ran out of food. They would have their stomachs filled and she would have bargaining power. Power was everything. Master Alexandre had taught her that much. 'Twas why he made sure his fledglings were the ones doing the stealing for him. He did not know it yet, but he was about to discover that he was not the only one with power in Harfleur.

The driving rain kept the men huddled together like a pack of wolves on the cold, wet ground. The privileged, those born with title and power, had tents to keep their pretty arses warm and dry. She imagined those were the ones who would not notice anyone out in the rain. It was the miserable soldiers, those who knew how to fight for their food, who might give her trouble. She gave them all a wide berth until she reached one of the wagons.

The bog sucked and smacked with each step. She kicked free from the mud's grasping fingers and slipped under the canvas covering the wagon. On her hands and knees, she felt along the wooden planking.

Her heart sank. There were no treasures to be found. Piers would whimper another night in his sleep.

Only a few handfuls of grain left in their sacks. She stuffed the pockets in her skirt with the grain. Her hand bumped against something hard. She sniffed it. Sausage!

The bounty clutched to her chest, she slipped over the side of the wagon. The savory scent of the meat tempted her to keep the treasure to herself. Her stomach grumbled in protest. Fearing someone would recognize that sound of hunger, she inched her way to the hidden passage in the wall. It would be so easy to turn away. To run from the town of Harfleur. That monster, Alexandre. But Piers was too young to fend for himself outside the Nest. He needed her until she found a safe haven. Just until then. And until she had retrieved her things hidden in the Nest.

Her breath caught, her throat squeezing against the instinct to scream. A soldier walked toward her. In the driving rain? Did the lumbering ox have no sense to huddle with the other masses? Oh, why had he chosen this moment?

Calling on the street skills she had learned as one of Master Alexandre's fledglings, she blended into the thorny bushes. The folds of the cloak, wrapped tight against the wind and rain, made her undetectable. Rule One: blend in.

Reaching down, she plucked up a handful of mud and smeared it slowly across her face. The hood over her head, she pressed into the wall and closed her eyes. The sound of his footsteps were heavy. They became louder as he drew near. Her heart hammered against her ribs. When he paused in front of her, she was certain he would hear it.

She peeked out as he turned. He towered over her, making her stretch her neck to see his face. The rain had plastered his hair to his head. Dark auburn streaked across his cheeks. His lips were full and cut into a grim line. Green eyes, decorated with smile creases that belied his miserable countenance, searched where she stood.

Then he shook out his cloak from his broad shoulders. Water sprayed from his head and body. A deep sigh carried the weight and consequences of his life. He turned to carry on his patrol.

Brigitte shivered. The air in her lungs screamed to be released and she slowly let out her breath. Had he seen her? Had he set a trap for her?

She waited until the cold dripped through her hood. Rain seeped into her shoes. Muscles aching from inactivity, she hobbled to the crevice cut into the wall.

The dark tunnel held other dangers, but no more than what stood inside and outside Harfleur's gate. She prayed for guidance to avoid the spiderwebs and began the journey back to the boy.

How many days would they be forced to sit outside the walls of Harfleur? When Drem had decided to pick up his weapons and pace the confines of the camp he had thought it would clear his brain. Instead, it must have fogged his mind, making him see things moving in the shadows. Did the French have faeries hidden in their lands? Were they mystical like the lands of Wales? That must be it, for he was certain he had seen a faerie floating over the bog. That had to be the answer, for no one would be able to walk on the thick mud without being pulled under. Too much like the bogs of Wales he remembered. The damn stuff would be the death of the Welsh, of that he was certain.

He shook off the shiver that tickled its way up his spine. At one point he even thought someone had peered out at him, but when he'd blinked again it was gone. Perhaps his head was still jumbled from the attack in Southampton. The burning debris from King Henry's ship had given his skull a mighty large knot.

Drem felt for the blade hanging at his hip. He did not carry his broadsword. Damn thing was too heavy to wear on an evening stroll in a storm. The blade he wore tonight was half the size of his fighting sword. It gave him comfort knowing it was by his side.

He continued his prowl, letting the relentless rain pelt him in the face. The muscles around his eyes twitched until he drew in a breath and focused on removing the frown burrowing between his brows.

When the rain soaked into his leather jerkin and bore into his underclothing, he called pax and returned to camp. He sat beside the men to warm his hands over the fire.

Steam swirled from their shoulders, heads, and hands. No one was safe from the drenching rain. Even the men in the makeshift infirmary were damp from the leaking tents.

What reason did they have for staying here? Why not move on to Calais? Or Paris? This far from home, from England, they needed a base. Harfleur was that base. They had laid siege to the town as soon as they arrived. The parameter of the outer wall was squeezed until nothing could enter or leave. And they waited for the moment until the people began to give in to their demands. This, after they did not receive the welcome Henry had hoped. Henry looked at the claiming of France as his birthright. Isn't this what they had fought for over the last years? However, the people of Harfleur did not see it in the same light. They saw it as an invasion, not a deliverance from the useless, mad king of France.

"How much longer?" The soldier next to him poked the fire with a stick. "We'd do best to launch the trebuchets and burn them out."

Drem looked up from the fire. "You think you know more than those who command us? Have you information they do not?"

The soldier rose, tossing the stick into the flames. Embers scattered in the air. "I know we are dying off. Better to move on than die of dysentery."

"Aye," another groused. "I swear the fekkin' French are sending out the ones with the pox, stealing our food and infecting us before they go."

The soldier squatting next to him spat in the dirt and rose. "I'd rather die with a pike in my gut."

Silence stretched over the remaining men. Awareness of who sat with them at the fire made them increasingly uncomfortable. Isolation was not an uncommon event. Drem had known it the first day he was taken from his family. A Welsh boy in an English army found it difficult to make friends. But soon he was honored as a skilled bowman. An archer the young Prince of Wales admired. And now that Henry was King of England and soon to be of Normandy and then France, he appreciated his skill even more. But that was not all that kept Drem separate from the other men.

Although the burns on his head and hands were healing and the bandages were no longer needed, there was a strangeness about him that kept the men at arm's length. He'd heard the stories about his involvement in the attack on the king's ships in Southampton. The men whispered, unwilling to trust in his innocence, eyeing him warily.

Drem ap Dafydd, son of the traitor, Dafydd ap Hew. The man who plotted with Owain Glyndŵr and the French. All but the king's select knights regarding him with as much distrust as the person who brought the plague into a castle. Those men gave him a chance to prove his worth. Once. Now, they, too, even after delivering the king's offer of freedom, regarded him with an unreasonable dislike and distrust.

There was much to be said for moving on. Although his jerkin was barely dry, he took his own advice and searched out the few men who did know what the king planned. Drem had to make them aware of the restlessness.

He found the king's men ensconced in a tent. They fared little better than the rest. He had to admire that they did not demand special treatment, even though most were knighted or held a position as lord of a castle.

Drem knew his place. He'd been a boy from the Welsh countryside and barely admitted into their midst. Had he not saved those on the king's ship, he would be one of the archers laid out in the open, enduring the never-ending rains.

Sir Darrick looked up from the maps stretched out on the table and waved him close. "Drem. Come."

Drem hesitated, waiting to see if the rest of the men welcomed him. His belly was full of dread and he was wearily hungry for food. It made the decision for him, pushing him forward. The information he had to deliver would be unwelcome.

Nathan swept his hand through dark auburn waves of wet hair. "Best get in here before lightning strikes your arse."

Drem noted the sparkle of humor hidden beneath the comment. "Not the first time I get a jolt."

"Right. Must be what made you addlepated and think you could go off on your own," Nathan muttered.

The men bent over the map rose, cocking their heads to listen to Drem's response. His skin itched, warning him to tread lightly. "Aye. I don't wish to repeat that mistake." He stepped into the tent. The relief to be out of the rain was palpable. He caught the sigh before it embarrassed him. What he would give to stretch out like a cat in front of the brazier heating the tent. Instead, he warmed his hands and joined the men huddled over the map.

At Sir Darrick's nod, the map disappeared almost as quickly, rolled tightly into a tube and tucked away. Once again, an uncomfortable silence stretched inside the tent. Drem squashed the pain it caused him. There had to be a way to regain their trust.

"Sir Nathan." Drem bobbed his head, tilting his chin away from the group. "A word, if you please."

He stood in the corner of the tent, as far from the brooding men as it allowed, and waited for Nathan to join him. It might cause him more trouble, but he had to share the soldiers' concerns. It appeared Nathan was the only knight in their encampment who seemed to believe in his innocence. At least he hoped this was the truth.

Nathan's frown deepened. His brow furrowed. "What is it that you can't speak of among all of us?"

Drem swallowed. He should have left things as they were. But if they were to succeed, the commanders of the army had to know what really went on among the ranks.

"We have to make a move," Drem said.

"I know the men are restless."

"They are more than that. They're hungry."

"Then we'll bring in more food."

"There's sickness. It's spreading."

"We're aware. What would you have us do? We can't march a sick lot of men."

"Sir Nathan, I hear the talk."

Drem flinched when the knight grabbed his shoulder. "If we are to be brothers, you'll need to call me by my given name."

"Autumn is near upon us." Testing the waters, Drem added, "Nathan. Morale is failing. The men are missing their families. If we're to move, it should be soon."

Nathan folded his arms, glaring into his face. "The king decides."

"I know. 'Tis himself I have followed all these years." Drem gripped the hilt of his blade. "My honor should not be at stake here."

Nathan sighed. "It's not, lad. Not with me. But you need to fix it with the others."

"My father—"

"—is a man who doesn't deserve even the sweat off your arse."

"I can't condone what he's done. Nor can I ignore it. His actions have brought suffering on my family."

"Aye, and we all remember how you came to us. We wonder how we would feel toward Henry if we were abducted from our families. We carry that bit of doubt, wondering if we would be as strong as you. And therein lies the trouble. The doubt is where the fear resides. We would forever feel the need to retaliate. What better opportunity than when you are in the safety of those closest to the king?"

"Am I to always carry that burden? I gave my life. I could have chosen freedom, walked away from England. Washed my hands of it." He held out his palms. "But I chose the king."

"And we chose you."

"Then trust me to carry my portion. I deserve it."

Nathan nodded. "I can say for myself 'tis done. But I cannot speak for the others." His great hand rested on Drem's shoulder. "My thanks for the information. I'll carry it to the proper ears."

Nathan left him to stand alone. Much as he had always been. To his astonishment, his heart burned with the need to return to his family in Wales. It chewed on his nerves until he gripped the hilt of his sword, digging into his skin.

With each breath, a part of his soul bled into the loneliness. Fear erupted from the depths in which he had buried it long ago. Mam was long gone into the grave. He had missed the opportunity to see her one last time. But there was a baby brother yet to meet and sisters who needed their older brother to see they were properly wed. He needed to survive and care for his family. To what lengths would he be willing to go?

Nathan motioned for everyone to gather round. "You, too, young Drem." He unrolled the map for everyone to see. "I hear our men are in need of food and are anxious to claim France for Henry. We need to rebuild our stores before we move. What better motivation for our men than to gather what we need? I'll take one group of men into the forest. Sir Darrick shall stay here and ensure that the good people of Harfleur don't think they can escape."

"We've held them under siege for weeks. 'Tis certain a few have found a way in and out. How else could they have held out this long?"

"If you will," Drem said, "I've been studying the tunnels surrounding the walls. I would like to find their way in and out."

"Take some men with you," Sir Darrick ordered.

"No. 'Tis best if I go alone."

"Why you?" Sir Darrick demanded. "Why alone?"

"'Twould be too obvious otherwise. We'd make too much noise. You think no one would notice a band of haggard soldiers milling about?" He turned. "I want this done just as much as the next man. I came to take France for the crown. I did not come to sit on my haunches in Harfleur and wait for the fekkin' rain to stop."

Sir Darrick's stiffened shoulders, making his opinion clear.

Drem had had enough. If King Henry could trust him, the other men would have to accept him eventually. Mayhap today was the day. "If you don't want to trust me, 'tis your choice. But I don't intend to sit here on my thumbs, and I surely don't intend on wasting my life and the lives I take with me. And that is what I'll do if I bring others."

He swept up his leather gloves. "I'm going after dusk. Before the moon rises over the trees."

"Drem . . ." Nathan barked.

"Aye?" He paused at the entrance, hesitant to turn and see what the man intended.

"We'll expect a report upon your return."

Drem clipped a nod and strode out. They'd taken a chance on him. Now he had to prove they were right in doing so.

Chapter 4

Brigitte leaned against the brothel's red door and watched from the alleyway. Thanks to the siege, *L'Assumption de Marie* had come and gone without adding anything to their pockets or their stomachs. The pickings were slim. The market square was empty of all the wagons. The siege had depleted the fresh wares and everyone guarded their property with extra care.

"Piers, stay out of sight for a while."

"The Nest—"

"No! Master Alexandre must not see you."

His eyes welled up with tears. His thin face became blotched as he tried to keep from crying.

Brigitte held Piers's hand, consoling him with an awkward pat on the back. "It's all right. I did not mean to snap."

She worked her jaw. How had she become mother to this orphan? That had not been her intention.

"You'll keep us safe." His thumb caught the escaping tear. "Won't you, Bee?"

Brigitte's heart squeezed. She could not let them go back to the Nest. But how would they survive without coin or food? A tunnel led through the butcher's smokehouse. They brought the meat from slaughter through it so that the mayor did not have to smell it. He had complained the smell offended him. What did he think of the smells now that they had been under siege for weeks on end? Nothing came in to refill the storehouses, but things did not move out. The waste in the city of Harfleur was deep and decaying. There were whispers that sickness had arrived.

She feared if they were forced to stay much longer they all would succumb to either the English king's sword or the bloody flux. With food to fill their bellies, they would have the strength to fight both man and disease.

She looked down. Piers's trusting gaze penetrated the icy places that had become numb over the years of hiding and thieving. She smoothed the golden ringlets cascading naturally over his shoulders. "*Oui.* You are correct." She bumped his arm. "As usual."

He smothered his smile.

"If we are to survive I must forage outside the wall."

"You cannot leave us." Piers's voice rose in panic. "I shall go with you."

Brigitte looked up from the satchel she had made from an old shawl found hanging out to dry. "No. I'll have none of that. You will be safe with Claudette."

"She is only the laundress and washes the filth from stranger's clothing." He folded his arms across his chest, a frown furrowing his brows. "I wager she'll sell us to Master Alexandre for a few coins."

Brigitte bit her lip. The boy had a point. She took a chance entrusting him into Claudette's care. But she had to. The danger was worse if he came with her. "You're a clever lad. Keep a wary eye open until I return. If you get that itch, the one that catches you between the shoulder blades and scampers up your neck, rabbit off to a place where no one will find you."

She snatched a double hug. "When I return, I will bring back enough food that we shall feast while the others starve. Won't that be wonderful?"

He nodded, his little head bobbing in agreement.

"Piers," she warned, "I refuse to return to the Nest to fetch you. Do not do anything foolish while I am away." She held his gaze in a grip laced with unspoken warnings. "Swear it."

"I swear," he mumbled, hitching his shoulder to hide his face.

Praying she never had to act on those threats of punishment, she ignored the sheen of tears in his ice-blue eyes. "Listen to what Claudette tells you. Make certain to listen carefully."

The little boy sniffed and jerked his head.

"Go now. I'll watch until you find your way to her shop. She's expecting you." Brigitte bent down and tilted Piers's chin so she could meet his eyes. "I'll be back before the sun rises over the battlements. To this very spot."

"Be careful." His voice quivered as he squared his shoulders and slipped deep into the alley filled with drying laundry.

Brigitte followed until she could no longer see his form. She listened to the silence until the rats took up their foraging. How she would find Piers when she returned she did not know. But she would return. She had to, even though every fiber in her being told her to run as soon as she left the wall. And yet, something deep inside her knew she could not leave him behind. Besides, Alexandre had her money. She had worked too hard, taken too many chances to leave it behind. Mayhap she would barter with Alexandre for some of the food she brought back. That would require a plan too. She'd learned all too early in life that whatever she had, he would steal it from her. Her friend had become brutally ruthless. It was something that made her want to run even more.

Brigitte picked the lock on the butcher's store. She waited, listening. The shop was eerily quiet. The everyday *thwak-thwak* of the butcher's cleaver was silent. No reason to come to work if they were without meat to chop. No sausage to grind. No customers to buy.

Stale blood, soured from days gone by, filled the shop. The stench drew her to the door she was certain led to her escape.

Even though the place appeared vacant, she glided across the room, brushing out the trail of footprints. The door heading to the floor below was locked. She took out her bits of metal and ticked the lock open. The sour smell of blood leaked up the stairway. Her stomach roiled like a sailboat on a storm-tossed sea. The butcher should be punished for his abuse of their fresh water source. Sickness waited, ready to pounce.

Taking a deep breath, she slipped through the doorway.

After days of rain, the downpour trickled into an incessant drip-drip-drip through the tent. It was enough to drive Drem out of his mind. He waited for sunset and then dove out of cover. Once it was dark, he would explore Harfleur's walls without drawing attention.

Earlier, he had noted the narrow canal leading into the crevice. He walked closer. The bodies of dead animals polluted the water. He stumbled back. If this was considered normal, the people of Harfleur were a filthy lot. Was it any wonder the soldiers grew sicker by the day?

A shower of loose stones struck the ground. He dropped to a crouch and rolled to his side. Positioned behind a thorny bush, he waited to see who or what had caused the fall of rock. His muscles coiled in anticipation. It did not take long for the wavering shadow to appear.

A woman slipped through the crack. She bent to untie the knot keeping her skirt dry. Standing abruptly, like a hart by a brook, she scanned her surroundings, sensing the danger lurking nearby. He could not see her face, but her shape, silhouetted by the moon, gave him full view of her thin figure. She stood, like one of the statues presented at King Henry's court.

Drem tore his thoughts from what was hidden under her clothing and focused on the fact that she had begun to move toward the encampment. He surged forward, prepared to stop her.

The woman made a sharp left, veering away from the wagons holding supplies. He frowned. What did she intend if not to pilfer from the English? She paused. Her head tilted. The moon caught her fair complexion, her sharp cheekbones. Her dark hair, drawn into a long braid, glistened under the night sky.

He waited. What was she after? He inched forward, unable to stay back and watch her kill the men.

A plan to follow her return into Harfleur began to form. Once inside, he would blend in, gather information and deliver it to Sir Darrick. Surely that would force the knight to trust him fully. Drem warmed to the plan, even though it was not what they had discussed earlier.

The woman began to move again with stealth. She kept to the shadows, blending into the brush, her surroundings. Was this the faerie he'd thought he saw weeks earlier? Had he not seen her exit the crevice, he would never have believed she existed. Staying off the path, she worked her way back to the encampment and alongside the wagons. Fear and outrage gripped his insides when she turned, her arms empty. Did she think to poison the men?

Never stopping, she glided past the supplies and then entered the pear orchard. The fruit was inedible; this he knew because some of the soldiers had eaten it and become ill. Her hood dropped, revealing hair the color of midnight. It glistened under the winking stars that had begun to make their appearance. She bent, burrowing in the ground, moving the leaves until she found what she sought. Then, just as silently, she arranged her cloak and retraced her steps.

He stepped out to confront her. He blinked, adjusting his eyes.

How had he lost her? She must have slipped into the shadows. Catching a slip of movement in the moonlight, he found her before she escaped his watch. He stepped warily, following her to the entrance hidden in the wall.

He grinned. His pretty prey was trapped.

Brigitte tossed the canvas bag down the hole and scrambled after it. Darkness surrounded her. She held her breath and listened to the footfall. Her head buzzed with the need for air. Her hands trembled against her empty stomach. Lack of food had weakened her, making her vulnerable. Stars flashed behind her eyelids.

The movement outside stopped. She inhaled deeply, gasping for air. The earth and moss covering the tunnel filled her nose. The rustle of clothing, the thump of metal scraping the earth broke the silence. Pebbles slid down the face of the wall, rolling past her shoes.

Her blood pulsed in her ears as she slowly took in a breath. Standing with her back pressed against the damp stone, she willed the soldier to piss and move on. All the time she had been on the other side of the wall, she had felt the presence of another. Had she taken too much of a chance?

She curled her fingers, tightening her grasp on the satchel of food she had hidden under her skirt. Mushrooms and pears. The fruit would need time to ripen, but it would help tide them over until the foul English soldiers left them for another target. The mushrooms they could eat right away. It did not sound like a feast, but to those who had not eaten for days it would make the difference between starvation and life. The price of freedom from Alexandre was still being paid.

The sound of rocks crushed under a boot echoed through the tunnel. Her insides turned to liquid. Brigitte shielded her eyes to keep from being spotted by the lantern light. Very large boots stood so close to the entrance that she swore she could make out the soles. His feet shifted. As long as he stayed outside and did not discover her hidey-hole, she was safe. The people of Harfleur were safe from the English soldiers.

Had she sold the citizens of Harfleur for a handful of food?

A shower of dirt rained down on her upturned face. Her nose itched. Her eyes began to water.

Merde! She dared not sneeze.

Brigitte bent slowly. The bag gripped in one hand, she touched the dirt wall with the other and blindly worked her way through the tunnel. The pads of her fingers scraped against the rough stone, sharp edges biting the tender flesh. Her lungs burned, hungry for a full breath. She halted at the point where this tunnel intersected with another. Tonight she would take a different route. Her decision made, she turned and ran into a wall of human flesh.

The woman did not scream. Instead, her gasp was barely a whisper in the tunnel. This one knew of stealth, of keeping hidden from the enemy. Intrigued, Drem wrapped his arms around his prisoner, trapping her to his chest. After so many days confined with sweating men, he could not help noticing a pleasant floral scent when she moved. She must wear it on her skin. What else did she wear next to her delicate flesh?

He grunted when her foot connected with his shin. A lump of something dropped to the floor as she focused her attack on his body. He caught her wrists before her nails could do damage and spun her around. Mindful not to stomp on the bag, he kept his legs out of reach and pinned her arms, binding her wrists with a leather thong. "God's bones! Cease this fight you cannot win."

Fueled by his order, she renewed her struggle until he feared her arms would be dislodged from her shoulders.

"Do you want to bring the rest of the English army to us? Is that what you want?" He bent over her, using his weight to press her down to the earthen floor. "Stubborn wench, I don't mean to harm you."

Her knees buckled under his weight. Only the sound of their breath broke through the quiet in the tunnel. They stared at each other, panting, chests rising and falling, dragging in the damp air.

"Stay where you are," he warned. "Don't move." *Cache.* Assuming she wouldn't know Welsh, he searched for the French words he had been taught. "*Merde!*"

How had her nearness made everything escape his brain? Hands shaking, he turned to pick up the lantern he had placed safely out of reach. He held it out, swinging it from side to side.

Damn his bones. The wench had vanished without a sound. She moved like a wraith in the dark. Had he imagined her?

Drem wiped his mouth with the back of his hand, torn between giving chase to an imaginary woman or returning to the camp to report what he saw. But he had held her. Smelled her scent. Felt the heat of her body against his chest.

Oh, she was real, but also more talented in the art of deception and slipping away unnoticed. In truth, he had misjudged her. 'Twas his fault she had escaped him. But by Christ's blood, 'twould be the last time.

Chapter 5

Brigitte pressed her back against the wall and kept to the shadows. She twisted her arms to free them from the leather binding. The soldier had assumed it was tied tight. Alexandre's trick of positioning the wrists at the correct angle had worked. The leather had loosened, allowing her to slip from its grasp.

Breath hissed between her teeth as she took a step toward freedom from the tunnel. Vibrations from the attack upon the city shook the ground under her feet, nearly bringing her to her knees. Her heart skipped and skidded, racing like a colt in springtime.

Her arms burned where the soldier had touched her. She glanced at them, expecting to see her sleeves branded with his mark. It was him. The large one who had crossed her path when she stole from the wagon. She touched her lips. They had stood close, touching, chest to chest. Near enough to kiss.

Why had he hesitated and allowed her to slip away? *'Tis madness to think such things.*

Scrabbling over the stone, she searched for the crevice marking the butcher's doorway. Air fluttered in her lungs like trapped moths. There had to be a way out.

Not just out of the tunnel. Out of the Nest. The family. Harfleur. There might be danger outside the city walls, but the danger on the inside was just as great.

Who had betrayed the city's weaknesses? The many tunnels?

There were two who knew them. One who would do it for a hefty price. Her pockets were piteously light, so she had a good notion that dear Alexandre had sold his city and the people he claimed as family. Ever the one with an eye for the coin to be made, he would have ensured his pockets were plump and left the others to fend for themselves. Just as he had when he built the Nest. His power grew off the back of one scared soul at a time.

It was only a matter of time before Alexandre discovered how much she was truly worth. Anyone's soul to him meant only what he could steal from the highest bidder. He would play them like a child's flute, then toss them in the rubbish heap, only to play them again. It was a thief and cutpurse's way of the street. Although she had once thought of Alexandre's Nest as a safe haven, she now knew this was not the case.

Drem retraced his steps until he was back at the entrance of the tunnel. King Henry and his men needed to know of the passageway into Harfleur. Mayhap this was where the miners would begin their task of bringing the French to bend their knee to their new king.

"You there," the voice called out from the shadows.

Drem released the breath he had been holding. Nathan was not an enemy. Mayhap he even would support him when he made his report and gave his recommendation.

"Aye, Nathan." Drem lifted his hands to reveal they were free of the weapons hanging at his waist. Though why he had not utilized them against the woman in the tunnel he could not explain. Either the sword or the dagger should have been enough to bring her to heel. Confronting her barehanded should have kept her still, frozen by fear. Instead, she'd slipped away as easily as you please, bruising his pride.

Memories from the times the English army had visited his family's Welsh village returned to haunt him. His family hid, fearing retribution from the force of power that held their country in a stranglehold. The empty bellies of the elderly and children made one ignore the threat outside and find a way to provide for those who depended on you. His sister Terrwyn had been one who dared take that chance.

Drem shifted his shoulders as if picking up that burden. He would wait to tell Sir Nathan of the Frenchwoman. He had no proof she had done more than gather food for hungry mouths and empty bellies. However, being arrested as a spy for the enemy would aid no one.

No. He was indeed a hunter and he was the king's man. He would watch. He would wait. And then he would snare his prey. There had to be a way to succeed on both sides of his predicament.

Nathan stood, arms folded across his chest, his hand not far from the dagger tucked in his belt, and waited beside the boulder on the southwest side of the garrison. The frown deepened as wary eyes followed Drem as he crossed the distance between them.

"Where have you been, young Drem?"

"Doing a bit of searching for habits and weaknesses. 'Tis like hunting."

"And what did you find that no one else has discovered?"

"Another place for the miners to dig."

"Miners have had little success. Our one dig forward has been replaced with their two full wheelbarrows in return." The knight pushed off the stony ledge and motioned Drem to follow. Their long strides carried them toward the king's tent. "I suppose you'll want to report your find. Cannot blame you for that. But you may be too late. It appears there's an informant from the city who shared some additional knowledge about where best to strike and draw blood."

He motioned to the palisades and great guns. The pointed wooden stakes were burrowed into the ground, creating a deadly defensive line. The big guns, twelve in all, towered behind them. Three had been christened London, Messenger, and the King's Daughter.

The first shots rang out. The bombardment of incendiary balls of iron flew over the moat, crashing into the walls and towers.

They turned their guns, angling to strike at the center of town and into the hearts of the people of Harfleur. He prayed that soon they would accept the truth: King Henry would never accept defeat. France was his.

Drem spun to stare as the artillery struck the church steeple. Where was the woman? Had she found a place to hide until this nightmare had ended?

Brigitte's steps faltered at the sight of the butcher's door standing ajar. A tinny taste coated her tongue. She had been certain to close it securely before going into the tunnel.

With a puff of air, she scattered the moths beating against her lungs. Praying Piers had found a safe place to hide, she slipped into the shop. Outside, flames flickered through the shutters, casting monsters across the floor.

Crouching behind the counter, she waited. Shouts erupted. The building to the left whooshed into flame. Great stones hit the butcher's wall. The planks shuttering the windows clattered and fell to the floor. And still no one appeared from the shadows.

Brigitte stumbled toward the door as another shot bombarded the town square. Where was Piers? Still clutching the bundle of mushrooms and hard pears, she hurried to the alley where Claudette hung her laundry.

Hemp ropes hung in a dizzying, tangled web, empty of the everyday life the people of Harfleur had managed to hold on to while under siege. Remnants of the daily wash smoldered, filling the air with a pungent, earthy scent.

She covered her mouth with her cloak to soak up the moan crawling up her throat. "No! No! No!"

Claudette's home was blocked by a door torn off its hinges. It leaned against the frame like a drunken sailor. *What had happened?*

Brigitte stepped over the threshold. She let her hand graze over the split wood. Cool to the touch, it made her pause and examine it more closely. Ax marks.

Inside, the bar used to brace the door closed was broken. As if it had been kicked in. *Not by the blast of the English but by someone else.* A dirty boot heel tracked across the floor, scarring the dust powdered from the whitewashed ceiling.

Before leaving the safety of the doorway, she glanced at all four corners, searching, hoping to find someone still alive. To her relief, no bodies littered the floor. There was still the little side room where Claudette did most of her washing.

Brigitte braced for what she would find and cut a path across the room. Mindful to leave no sign that she had been there, she stepped carefully. Her hand hovered over the handle. Fingers tingled as she forced them to obey and open the door.

The room was dark, the tables and tubs turned over. Brigitte caught her foot on a chair leg. Steadying her palm on a bundle of forgotten wash, she heard a muffled moan. *Claudette!*

Her gaze shot around the little room. *Where was Piers?* She prayed he would signal he was safe. Her heart ached. The corners were silent and empty.

She knelt beside the woman she had thought strong enough to stand up to any threat. Lifting Claudette's shoulders, she gently rolled her onto her back.

"Claudette? 'Tis me. Bee."

A moan erupted. "Lord have mercy," she whispered in a gargle of pain. Her hand shook as she lifted her arm. It dropped weakly to her chest.

"Where are you injured?" Brigitte asked.

"My shoulder." She shifted as an explosion shook the room. White dust fell like snow. "What's that noise?"

Brigitte draped her body over Claudette to protect her when another blast sounded outside the door.

When she could hear again, Brigitte responded. "The English are using their trebuchet." Already knowing the answer, she asked anyway. "Was it that English king's devilish machine that brought down your door?"

"No!" Claudette tried to push up from the floor. Her arms shook from the effort. "The boy." Wide-eyed, she turned to Brigitte. "Not here?"

"No, please, that is what I need to know. Where is he?"

She dug her fingers into the woman's stout shoulders. Years of washing other's clothes had made them strong. She was not easily overcome. Or so Brigitte had thought. She felt desperate. Had the woman betrayed them to Alexandre? Her grasp tightened until Claudette gasped, pulling her from her fears. She released the woman, dropping her as if she were a hot coal from the hearth.

"What did you do?" she hissed.

Before the woman could come up with a bag of lies, Brigitte scrambled over the debris of the washroom until she came upon a carving knife. She rushed back, the weapon in her hand. Another blast from the siege machine whistled through the air, then struck the building. Pieces of the roof rained down, covering the washroom. A wave of shards slammed into the wall. A cloud of dust followed behind it.

Brigitte crawled toward Claudette. The woman lay on the floor, her mouth open. She turned, her face a mask of white, her eyes wide in pain. "I'm sorry, Brigitte. I didn't mean to lead them to him." She gasped at the effort.

Brigitte searched her face for the truth. "Please." She gripped the woman's hand. "Piers."

Claudette wagged her head slowly. "Don't know."

The tension in Brigitte's back loosened its hold. Perhaps he had hid himself, tucked himself away from danger.

Claudette's eyes shot up to hold Brigitte's attention. She squeezed her hand. "Harfleur is falling and yet Alexandre has become more powerful. How is this so?" Her hand dropped. "Brigitte, he stopped for a visit right after you left. Said to tell you . . . he knows about your secret."

"I don't—"

"It matters not to me. Find the little one. Escape before he makes good on his promise to bleed you dry."

Drem ducked from another volley of stone and questioned his decision to explore the tunnel on his own. The ground shook, nearly taking his feet out from under him. The stench of smoke and fear burned his nostrils. The cries of those in pain echoed over the alleyway until another volley from the trebuchet overcame everything in its path.

The building the woman had slipped into had taken a direct hit. His gut tightened, squeezing his innards until he thought they would burst. He wiped away the stinging smoke and dirt from his eyes.

Moments later, he blinked through the swirling haze and saw her.

She was joined in the doorway by a gray-haired woman who leaned into the frame for support. She hugged her arm close to keep from jarring a wounded limb.

"Be safe," she called out as his prey took leave. "Bring him back to me. I promise to keep him safe." When she did not receive a response, she called out again. "Do you hear me, Brigitte?"

Brigitte paused, then with a slight tip of her hand, she left.

The old lady kept her gaze on Brigitte until she could no longer be seen.

Brigitte. Drem smiled. Now he had a name to go with the pretty face. He patted his small sword and renewed his efforts. He would not lose her this time.

The woman moved with a grace that was mesmerizing. Tracking her proved difficult and required his full attention. Not an easy task with all the chaos. Entranced and curious as to her purpose, he followed her circuitous path, which kept her out of sight of everyone but him.

Once she paused, her head cocked, as if listening to the sounds within the sounds of the attack on Harfleur. She turned, searching. If she saw him, she did not flinch or run; she just kept on her way. The journey nearly made him dizzy.

The weight of his sword hung at his hip. It felt as comforting as a warm blanket during a snowstorm. However, because he had chosen to leave his bow and arrows at camp, his back and shoulder had a naked feel to it. He had no choice but to leave it. If he happened to disappear, those he called close would know something was amiss.

Drem shrugged his shoulders. A shiver trailed up his spine. It would be good to return to his tent and strap on a weapon that never failed him.

Wait! He paused, his foot raised in midstride. *Hell's hounds! Where did she go?*

Chapter 6

Drem could not believe his stupidity. The woman, Brigitte, was pressing something very pointy into the back of his neck. How in Christ's shattered bones had she gotten behind him without his knowing? He did not care whether it was a blade from the Orient or a sliver of wood from one of the buildings. It dug into his skin, and he did not like the feeling of it. Worse, though, was that she had known he had been following her. And now she was ready to let him know she was fully aware of his pursuit with that damned thing digging into the tender base of his skull.

He had followed her long enough to know she was a small sprite. No wonder he had thought she was a faerie that night. And he'd held her body long enough to recognize her womanly shape. He felt her strength and her weakness. She was a petite thing. Easy enough to overpower if necessary.

And she was slippery as an eel. He had lost her once before. This made the second time. Her pulling the knife on him from behind? That boiled his stones, plain and simple.

"Well," he groused, "what do you want to do about this situation in which we find ourselves?"

"You don't belong here." She pecked at him with her weapon. "You're making things more difficult." She pushed his back. "Go. He'll see you."

"Who?" Drem looked over his shoulder. Her head barely came up to his chest. "Don't you think whoever he is, he's hiding under his cot, waiting for the attack to end?"

"No." Her eyes, laced with a dose of fear, snapped with anger. "It doesn't matter to him. He will find a way to survive. His will is strong. Like one of the rats that litter Harfleur. He has his Nest and those who serve him. In truth, he knows where you are right now."

Drem spun, trapping the knife in his hands. Her gasp of surprise warmed the cockles of his manly pride. "No." Her breath brushed his skin. "Now we change tactics." With one hand, he yanked her to his chest and felt along her thighs. "What other weapons are you carrying?"

His balls tightened. 'Twas more than his pride that warmed at the feel of her pressed against his stomach. He shook free from the faerie's hold.

"*Merde!*" She struggled to free her wrists. "You must go. Now. Before I decide to bring you to him. To offer a bargain."

Drem could not help himself. Her full lips were too lush and intriguing. He had to taste her. Cupping the back of her head, he touched his mouth to hers. Ebony lashes lowered over flushed cheeks. Her mouth became pliable, tentative and cautious. He deepened the kiss, sinking into the luxury, tasting her until she responded with a hesitant lick of her tongue. A swell of passion washed over him. He let his eyes drift shut and he inhaled the flowery scent that swirled around his head.

An explosion shook the ground under his feet, sending shivers through his body. His blood heated until Drem thought he felt the flames licking at his clothes. King Henry may keep the soldiers busy through the night, but here, in the corner of town, was heaven.

"Forgive me," she whispered into his mouth.

Drem wrapped his arms around her waist. He leaned into her, wanting to envelop her, to shield them both from prying eyes. Somewhere another explosion rendered the night into submission. And then the explosion became personal as his head received a blow that knocked him to his knees.

Brigitte could not believe her misfortune. Nor how the English soldier had managed to follow her. His tenacious attention had cost her time she did not have to waste. She still had to get her things and escape from Harfleur.

Merde! Her first true kiss and it came from the enemy. The heat from his mouth, his tongue. It had turned her insides warm. It made her forget. The dangers. Everything.

The need to protect Piers floated into her thoughts like loose flower petals in a storm. She had to find him. Whether she should take him to Claudette or both take their chances outside Harfleur's walls she did not know. But they would not place their fate in the arms of this soldier.

Brigitte looked down at his unconscious form. The man was huge and heavy. Especially when he was unable to move his limbs. It took great effort to move him into the cache hole she had used when she worked for Alexandre.

Her shoulders twitched from fatigue. She should have left him on the street and let his own men kill him with their trebuchets and great guns.

She rubbed her lips with her knuckles. Damn him. He had cradled her as if she was an infant. Protected. No one had done that in years. But when he had touched his mouth to hers, gently, as if she mattered... *Merde!* She could not leave him to be pummeled by the English death machines. At least here, he wouldn't be hurt. He might have a pain in his head he would not like when he awoke, but he would be alive. And she would be long gone.

Brigitte leaned over his prone body. After adjusting his position, she brushed back his dark auburn hair and placed a kiss to the lump forming on the side of his head. She picked up the club she had used to strike him and put it in one of the many hidden pockets in her skirt. Patting the weapon like an old friend, she left the alcove.

Her only regret, before she left him, was that she did not know his name. It would have been nice to whisper to him when she dreamed of his kiss, for she knew she would the next time she lay down to sleep.

Drem awoke with a blistering ache behind his eyes. His tongue felt too big for his mouth. He must have bitten it on the way down to the unforgiving earth. The tinny taste of blood curdled his stomach in a wave of nausea.

His head pulsed in syncopation with his heart. He didn't need to feel around to know there was another goose egg left by one pain in the arse Frenchwoman. *Brigitte.* A name he would not soon forget.

Damn his head. It had taken another blow. Three times in several months. He'd only just been able to settle his helm on his head without wincing.

The pain was annoying. He was man enough to admit it hurt. But knowing she had fooled him so soon after he found her made his manhood shrivel. He had not even had time to gloat at his tracking skills.

Drem paused in his struggle to sit upright. His brows rose. If that did not surprise the rooster before sunrise, he did not know what would. Someone had folded his cloak to pillow his head. He patted his belt. The purse was gone, but a handful of coins were piled beside his cloak.

What kind of thief had he been following?

He rested his back against the crevice and listened to the quiet. The king must have decided to give the people of Harfleur time to reconsider their negotiation skills. Henry could be a patient man if he had a mind to be.

Drem had seen the man they had sent out from the safety of the wall to negotiate with King Henry and his men. They had laughed off his refusal to relinquish control of Harfleur.

Henry needed this town to garrison his army. He would not turn from it, defeated and ready to sail back to England. As if to prove that point, another English bombardment shot over the wall.

Drem crouched low. The missiles whistled through the air, slamming into buildings. Shards of stone needled toward whatever stood in the way.

It appeared King Henry's patience had ceased. Now if only Harfleur's defender, Raoul de Gaucourt, would concede defeat. Would the French admit they must surrender before the war machines destroyed the town?

While waiting in the crevice for the terror of the night to cease, Drem admired Brigitte's selection of hiding spots. It gave him a clear view of the activity in the streets below. Unfortunately, it also put him in danger from being struck by his king's weaponry. *At least no one with any sense would think to come up here.*

An ethereal silence followed after the series of bombardments. When it was over, a stream of townspeople poured out of doorways and corners of buildings. Then the cries of fear and heartache wove through the streets. Drem could feel their surprise, their disbelief at an actual attack behind the walls that always had offered a safe harbor from the enemy. Outrage began to boil over the cobblestones.

Drem watched it unfold, taking note of the numbers of wounded.

He reminded himself that they were his enemy. Preparing his report for the king, he counted the building casualties that would require repair.

Time dripped like honey while he waited for escape. His blade spun, catching the air as time flowed past the edge. His hands stilled.

That woman. He could not get her out of his mind.

Why hadn't she tied him up? Why not turn him in as the enemy he was? He could have been a bargaining piece.

Not that his king or the friends of the brotherhood would think him worth much. They would not be pleased by the distraction. But if he returned to them unscathed and brought back information for their cause, perhaps then the men would finally look beyond his father's treason.

A string of torches caught his attention as it wove past. An angry crowd filed through the streets toward the imposing building at the center of the square. Some carried the injured while others simply lit the way.

They stopped at the steps, shouting, "Gaucourt. Show yourself!"

Caught in the drama unfolding below, he nearly missed the person standing at the edge of the crowd. He recognized the cloak and the wench trying to hide behind the folds of the hood. She had been his prey for most of the night. Retaliation would be his by daylight. Of this, he was certain.

Brigitte kept to the fringes of the crowd, blending between the shadows, rubbing elbows with the wounded. She did not worry about being recognized. Faces were covered in plaster and dirt stirred up by the bombardment. It had an uncanny way of making everyone look like strangers. She slipped away from the terrified group when they stopped at the mayor's house and turned to go up the alley that led to the Nest.

At least that had worked for her.

So far, her plan to escape Harfleur and Alexandre had brought her in the opposite direction. She was now in the heart of the city. Once a safe haven, the Nest now felt like a trap, a toothy maw ready to devour her.

Voices behind her carried through the alleyway. Not because the men were shouting but because their anxious whispers cut through the battle-torn night. Recognizing the outraged male, she took a step back, working her way deeper into the shadows.

"I did not agree to this." Alexandre swirled his hand in the air, pointing to the smoking horizon. "'Tis your pride that sees us as we are. If you had done as you were told, we would be sitting down to a fine meal now. I gave you the information to feed to the English." He turned on the mayor. "Instead, we have to hide under the table until the English army decides to move on to a greater prize."

"The French army will come. The Count of Nevers. Burgundy . . ."

"No. You are a fool to think the nobles will stir themselves from their fires."

"But—"

"*Oui*, 'tis the truth. I have spoken to my . . . gatherers."

"Our people want a scapegoat for their pain. They want to retaliate." The mayor gripped Alexandre's arm. "You promised me the best plan was to hold out."

"You think to threaten me?" Despite the years of making others do his bidding, the master of the Nest was still capable of moving with the speed of a rat. The mayor's throat constricted under his fingers. "I will not be your scapegoat."

"Our reinforcements. Where are they? You promised they would arrive by now." His accomplice stumbled back.

Released as suddenly as he had been ensnared, Alexandre caught the stuttering man, purposefully straightening his sleeves. "Trust me." He leaned in, his lips precariously close. "I have a plan."

"You have the boy?"

"Our power will not be stolen from us."

Brigitte trembled at the hidden threat. Whatever he plotted, it was possible it involved the children of the Nest. She could not leave them behind to act out his play for power and control. She had endured his controlling authority long enough.

Despite the English siege, the ear-splitting bombardment that shook every bone in her body, she would hold to her original plan: retrieve her hidden cache and then snatch Piers before Master Alexandre dug his claws further into him.

After looping the shawl around her face and neck, she trailed after the two men. Her footsteps silent, just as she had been taught. A shiver scraped over her skin, warning her of the dangers lurking all around.

Chapter 7

B rigitte took the quickest route to the Nest. The flickering lantern in the window signaled that the master had yet to return. She waited, watching for his minions. The town may be under siege, but that would not change the schedule. Alexandre not only gathered coins from others, he also gathered secrets and used them to gain whatever he desired.

As she expected, the wraithlike shadows flittered over the alley walls as they poured out into the night. Even though he had yet to return, they left on a mission for their protector. Only the youngest would remain behind. This offered the best opportunity for her to slip in and out before anyone sounded the alarm.

Familiar smells of the place she once had thought of as home greeted her at the door. For a time she had found protection here. But now, something had shifted within Alexandre. She had seen it in his eyes. He had information he intended to use. Perhaps even against her.

Her mother's jewelry called to her from the secret spot. Anxious to gather her things, Brigitte kept to the shadows of the old building as she made her way to the cache of coins she had dared to keep from Alexandre.

Kneeling on the rough planks, she pried up the board. The wood bit under her nails. The loose board creaked before giving way. Unaided by a candle, she felt blindly inside the hole. She touched all the edges. Searching. It had to be there. Nothing. She blinked away the dawning dread. The hole was empty. *Alexandre! Bastard!*

Her empty stomach roiled, threatening to toss up bile. Tears burned her lids. It was worse than first she had thought. The coins she had planned on using to help her travel to Calais could be replaced, but her mother's brooch . . . that was irreplaceable.

She blinked, refusing to be beaten. The threat she had overheard earlier crept up her spine. She did not know how, but if he planned on making her the scapegoat for the villagers' wrath, she would take her pound of flesh first.

Excited voices flooded up the stairway. The door flew open. Children tumbled in like a pack of puppies. The bombardment of English missiles over the town of Harfleur must have garnered them heavy pockets. Not that Alexandre would allow them to keep any of it, but it might give them another night off the streets. They deposited their booty into the chest beside his great chair. Their chatter ceased the moment the master stalked through the doorway.

Brigitte slipped the boards over the empty cache. It behooved her to have an offering ready to give to the man who held firm control of the Nest. She hid her hands, wiping them under the folds of her skirt. Her future already wobbled as if she stood on scaffolding, awaiting the noose. Damp, guilt-ridden hands would tighten the rope. If Alexandre had the opportunity to test her pulse, feel her palms, he would be the first to kick out the block and watch her swing.

The room grew heavy. The children had scattered before his cane found their backs. Brigitte steeled her shoulders and released the fear that choked her throat.

"Alexandre." She rushed over to him. "Thank the saints you are safe."

He brushed by her and jerked off his cloak. Dropping into his chair, he swung a leg over the arm. His body, relaxed, showed no sign of agitation. But Brigitte knew the telling signs of his mood. There was a slight twitch near his left eye. One hand fisted, knuckles whitening until he forced his palm open. He watched her, reminding her of a snake, waiting to strike if she moved too quickly.

"Where have you been, Bee? The child you cosset was found with the washwoman. Why is that?"

"Piers?" She glanced at the children. Their nervous faces let her know they feared his mood. More so than the siege the English had lain upon them. "Where is he? I saw the building. Claudette." She swallowed the fear. "Is he safe?"

"Answer me, Brigitte." His glacier gaze nearly made her shiver.

Warning number two. Brigitte ignored the shiver sliding down her back. He had used her full name, not the one he had given her the night he had found her on the streets. She took little pleasure in knowing that the skills she had learned over the years had prepared her for this confrontation. If she got through this unscathed, it would be her best performance to date.

She moved closer to Alexandre, gliding near his knees but keeping out of reach.

"I was looking for ways to feed us. Obviously, gathering from the carts and wagons has become more difficult."

She held out the pouch she had lifted from the English soldier. She had thought to persuade her conscience that leaving him with a few coins was a benevolent act of goodness. Guilt bit at her conscience. She blinked at the unexpected pain. Unlike Alexandre's thin-lipped scowl, the stranger's mouth had been warm, compassionate. Shaking off the memory, she was surprised to care whether the soldier was safe and had found his way back to the other side of the wall. "But I did manage to find a bit of something to bring a smile to your handsome face," she offered.

The pouch of coins swung between them like a pendulum. The smile lifted the corners of his mouth, enhancing the frigidity of his glacial stare. He snatched it from her fingers, striking with the speed of the rats that infested the alleys of Harfleur. The leather pouch rested in his palm before he tucked it inside his surcoat.

"What else are you keeping from me, sweet Brigitte?"

She started to shake her head but caught herself. No fast movements. If she kept her balance, Harfleur would soon be out of sight, the Nest a bad memory. But first, she had to get back her mother's jewelry. It would require patience and some sleight of hand.

"What? I haven't kept secrets from you."

"Really?" He swung out his cane, catching her behind her knees. Brigitte fell to the floor, her face close to his foot. It tapped his impatience into the air. Should he choose it, his boot could kick out most of her teeth. The tick by his eye jumped once. She tensed as he grabbed her head.

"I think you lie," he said.

Bending forward, he pulled out a chain from under his jerkin. The silver filigree chain caught the glow of the firelight. The broken brooch, attached to the chain, swung out.

My mother's. Brigitte lunged. Her forehead collided with his face. The cool metal chain slid through her fingers as he jerked it out of reach.

"Bitch," he cried. "You will pay for this." Blood streamed from his nose and mouth. His hands fisted at his sides. "Greatly," he whispered.

Fury replaced the ice in his soulless eyes. The cries of the children mingled with the ringing in her ears. Shaking the stars from her vision, she scrambled to her feet and kicked his beloved cane to the corner of the room.

"Give it to me," Brigitte said. The building panic joined the pounding in her chest. "Hand over what is mine."

"You lie to me."

The chain still clutched in his fist caught the torchlight. She tore her focus from its call. The only thing left of Maman did Brigitte little good if he chose to beat her and leave her for dead.

She lunged again. A loop of chain slid farther out of his palm.

"You steal from me," he hissed.

He pushed her toward the great window. It faced the outer walls of the town. Brigitte glanced over her shoulder. Fire from the bombardment flickered outside. She stumbled over the threadbare rug. *Pay attention.*

"Eat. My. Food." He let the words drip between them.

She glanced down. The rubble-scattered street below was two stories down. *Keep calm. Stay on your feet. Something will come to you.*

A large shadow loomed across the street. It rushed to the building. The Englishman? She shook her head. Alexandre's punishing blow must have been worse than she'd thought.

The children moved closer, pushing and shoving, alight with gruesome anticipation. Alexandre had succeeded where she had not. He had their loyalty. All but one.

Bile rose in Brigitte's throat as she searched the chambers. Where was Piers? Why hadn't she seen him?

So focused on the execution of his "Dear Bee," Alexandre did not notice the advancing force coming through the doorway. ". . . take what I have offered. Thrown it back in my face."

One of Alexandre's minions shoved the shutters wide. Tobes. An evil grin stretched his mouth, reminding her of the gargoyle watching over the mayor's home. He handed the master his cane. Her heart ached at the loss of the boy's childhood. How had she thought anyone could escape this madman's Nest?

The door creaked open. One by one, the children began to scatter.

Brigitte schooled her expression to show no recognition of the man propelling his body and sword in their direction. *My soldier!*

"You want what is yours?" Alexandre swung his cane.

She ducked. Then arched backward as he came at her again. Maman's brooch shot out on the chain. Her concentration slipped. The heel of her shoe caught as she stumbled back. Tobes stood beside her. Close enough to grab. Pull her to safety. Shrugging, he stepped out of the way. Her fingers sliced through the air. The chorus of shouts and cries mingled with hers as she fell out the window.

Brigitte pinwheeled in the abyss as time seemed to hold its breath. The rope and pulley system used to haul up supplies swayed within reach. Her fingers caught the hemp as she flew past, then her grip tightened. A burning trail cut across her palm as she slid down the length of braided rope. Arms yanked from their moorings. Her feet caught the knots and slowed her descent long enough for her to take control. Her hands gave out and she dropped to the ground. Rocks and bits of wood, already chewed up by the English bombardments, cut into her body as the landing knocked the air from her lungs.

But she was alive. For now.

After following the woman who called herself Brigitte to the two-story building, Drem was certain he'd found the place she called the Nest. The throbbing in his head kept time to his footsteps. The crescendo came with each additional bombardment from the trebuchet. The king's beloved cannons. It would not be long until the people of Harfleur scattered and England claimed it as its own. He would be glad when he returned to the other side of the wall.

But first, he intended to retrieve his money from the wench.

Drem looked up as the shutters opened, illuminating a figure in the bay window. The wind caught a trail of smoke rising from the rubble below. A hood was thrown back, revealing a dark mane of hair. She turned, and firelight washed over her face.

His innards tightened. *Brigitte.*

He should gather his money and be gone. Back to the English army. Back to his brothers in arms. But he had to speak with her. That was his reason for following her in the first place.

Saints. Someone advanced toward her, threatening to strike her.

Head down, the hood of his cloak kept low, Drem ran across the street. He slipped through the door unheeded. Chaos erupted from the floor above. Dread inched up his spine as he climbed the rickety stairs.

Mindful of the danger in which he put himself with the enemy, he pushed through the doorway. A crowd of children, varying in age and size, pressed toward the tall man leading the charge against Brigitte. Some were alight with mischief. A few were wide-eyed, tears streaking their dirty faces.

Torches ensconced along the wall, wrapping the room in a yellow glow. The flames flickered and caught the azure highlights in Brigitte's hair. The tall man came after her, swinging his cane, striking and cursing.

To Drem's horror, she fell backward, crying out into the dark abyss. The children started to rush to the window until the man beat them back with the damn stick.

Drem charged, pushing and shoving his way to the man. The hilt of his sword slammed into the creature's face, knocking him from the window. He toppled over, hitting the floor like a felled tree. The whites of his eyes rolled back into his head.

"You've killed Master Alexandre," cried a lad too young to be a squire in training.

"He'll live," Drem muttered to the children. He had no concern for the monster, but the children didn't need to witness a murder. It was the woman he worried for.

Steeling himself, Drem looked down at the street. Brigitte was gone.

He spun on his heel and planted a foot into Alexandre's chest. The children, their faces sunken from hunger, no longer crowded around their leader. Instead, they hung back, pressed against the walls and into the corners. All but one looked at him with terror. Guilt nipped at him, reminding him that a siege damaged more than buildings.

The sobbing brave lad, with a mop of curls, ran toward his master and kicked him in the ribs. He grabbed the cane and tossed it out the window. Drem recognized the resignation in the boy's eyes. It was an emotion he knew all too well. The boy shuffled backward toward the door.

Before Drem could call out to the children, they disappeared down the stairs. Some were about the age he had been when Henry had conscribed him into his royal archers.

Memories shivered through him. The graves of loss were tossed open, demanding him to examine the pain. He shook it off. Always best to keep the past buried, where it belonged.

Drem gripped Alexandre's belt and recognized the leather pouch given to him by his sister, Terrwyn. There had been too many years between gifts. He was not about to lose this one. After stripping Alexandre of the coins, he felt for weapons. He did not need a dagger in the back.

A bit of silver glinted in the torchlight. Drem pried open Alexandre's fingers and slipped the necklace into his belt before he took off down the stairs. Hearing the shuffling of feet, he turned back, wary of what might come from behind. Instead of coming after him, the children turned their attention to their master.

Drem raced down the stairs. Prepared to find Brigitte's broken body, he dashed around the corner. The street was empty. He rubbed the back of his neck. How had she survived the fall? Where had she gone?

Why he cared he did not know. He had the leather purse, the coins returned. The weight of if felt familiar.

He looked up at the hazy sky. The smoke, stirred up by the bombardment and fires, covered the moon and stars. It might be nearing dawn. The time he had lost while lying unconscious left him unsure. How much longer until they started looking for him and questioning once again where his loyalties lay? *God be with me, what am I doing?*

The shutters overhead swung open, wooden planks clattering against stone. Rocks rained down, striking him on the back and shoulders. *Shite!* The little devils were intent on revenge.

Ducking for cover, he jumped over a short retaining wall that held back an untended garden. Once out of range of the children's missiles, he cut through the brambles and weeds strangling the path. The farther away from the lights, the darker it became. He stumbled over rocks and roots, going down on one knee.

He pushed up from the ground and stopped. His palm scraped over something soft, rounded. "Brigitte." He blinked in the darkness. Even to his ears, her name mingled with his breath sounded too much like a sigh.

The oddly warm feelings were immediately washed away by the cold blade, pressed to his throat.

"What are you about, Englishman?" she hissed.

Drem bent down, his face close to hers. He wrapped his hand over hers and nudged the blade away. She gave in much more easily than he'd anticipated. Her fingers, so much smaller than his, were encompassed by his large, ungainly hand. They trembled against his palm. He smoothed the ebony hair from her damp cheeks. Were those tears? That scared him more than he cared to admit.

"You're alive," he whispered. "I saw you go out the window. How did—"

She took a shuddering breath. "The rope slowed my fall."

He did not have to look at her hands to know there were wounds. Drem had sailed enough with the king to know the damage a rope could do to tender flesh. It took long days and nights until the calluses had formed and he had learned to stay out of the way of those wielding punishment. He would rather ride a stout horse for a fortnight than sail one day on the king's royal fleet.

"Here." Drem cut a strip from the linen shirt under his leather jerkin and wrapped it around her palms. "I know, 'tis more to be tended. We can't do it here." He cocked his head. "Do you think you can stand?"

"*Oui.*"

The shouts coming from the streets began to grow. A crowd was forming.

Her eyes widened. The lush mouth he had admired earlier pressed firmly into a narrow line.

"Any thoughts on why he would not be overjoyed that you live?"

"No," she spat out her response. "What are you about, Englishman? Why should you care what happens to me?"

"Call me Drem."

She scrunched her nose. "'Tis not a common English name."

"Aye. I'm Welsh through and through." He squared his shoulders. "And I serve my king unto death."

"Loyal unto death?" Her scowl deepened. "I had thought the same of Master Alexandre. But as you saw, he doesn't have the same affection for me. Now does he?"

He could not see her clearly in the deep blackness before early morning's light, but judging by her tone, she was already planning her revenge. If there was one thing Drem understood, women did not like to be mistreated. If it were his sister, bruised and lying on the ground, she would have had her arrows already nocked and prepared to impale Alexandre's stones.

"Then I think 'tis best we make our way to the wall. Appears your Alexandre has a plan to make you pay for disobeying his orders."

A veil dropped as she grew still. Then, as if drawing energy from the earth, she pushed herself upright. Drem rose with her. Afraid there were more injuries, he gently propped her against his hip. He steadied her by touching her arm.

"My cloak," she whispered. "They will know to look for it."

Drem had his doubts. With the mixture of dust and what he feared might be drying blood, the cloak was hardly what he considered recognizable. Still, he turned his cloak inside out and draped it over her shoulders.

They began the slow walk to the wall, retracing their steps, minus the crevice where they had shared a kiss. *And, do not forget, she stole from you. And she struck you.*

Details, Drem argued back with the warning angel at his ear.

"I will lead you to the cave," Brigitte said. "The townspeople: They won't know to look for you there."

Drem grunted in response. That might be her plan, but he had other thoughts. Mainly because he was not their prey. He glanced at his companion as she limped beside him.

Brigitte's face was pale under the dust and dirt smudging her cheeks. If it would not call more attention to them, he would have picked her up and carried her. That is, if she had allowed him. He had the begrudging feeling she would have pulled her blade on him again at such an offer.

Their pace was torturously slow. The skin of Drem's neck tingled with the feeling of being stalked. The promise of getting out of Harfleur relatively unscathed wavered as the wall came in sight.

And so did that uneasy sensation that they were not as safe as they told each other they were. As they drew near a row of shattered buildings, Brigitte's pace slowed. Like sap dripping out of a tree in winter. It took great restraint to keep from tossing her over his shoulder and running after all.

"What is it, Brigitte?"

The air shook. The ground rippled under their feet as English bombardment rained down from the sky.

Chapter 8

The force of the explosion knocked Brigitte to her knees. Clutching her ears to silence the roar that pulsed in her skull, she blinked away dust from her watering eyes and stared at the destruction.

"What is your English king thinking?" She spat out the grit coating her throat. "Soon there'll be nothing left of Harfleur."

Now that her ears no longer thumped out the beating of her heart, the sounds of moaning and weeping began to swell.

Drem took his cloak from her, wrapped his arm around her shoulders and lifting her to her feet. His frown cut creases into the mask of dust caking on his face. "My king is responding to your representative. You mayor was to meet with the king's men. We must assume that did not go well. If your people would agree and surrender, this would be over and done."

"You blame the citizens of Harfleur? We did not bid you lay siege to our town. Did we?"

His heavy sigh ruffled her hair. "This did not have to be. If King Charles had negotiated with honor, we would have arrived peaceably. King Henry did not want to bring war to a land and people that are his by birthright."

"No." She gripped his forearm and led him away from what used to be the butcher's doorway. "No, you cannot go this way. The tunnel will surely be destroyed. I'll take you to the cave. 'Tis on the other side, but we'll be careful to remain unseen."

Drem paused to look over his shoulder. His frown deepened. The air exploded with smoke, raining down on the carcasses of the dead and dying.

They huddled together, their bodies tensed, awaiting the next bombardment. Brigitte shivered in the autumn morning. Her breath caught as he shifted to offer her heat and protection.

"You must tell that monster we cannot take anymore."

"There is little I can do. Perhaps de Gaucourt's messenger will carry better news."

"There is no time," Brigitte urged. "Besides, I fear something is amiss with our mayor and his adviser."

Drem's silent frown deepened. The gold flecks in his moss green eyes reflected the light as the sun rose over the walled town.

What am I doing? He is the enemy! Brigitte compressed her lips, sealing off what she had overheard between Alexandre and the mayor. Who could she trust? No one. The boy Alexandre, the one to whom she had given her heart when he had taken her off the streets? That kindhearted person who had saved her from starvation, taught her to steal to provide for the fledglings, was gone. She had felt the change come over him. The angry moments now easily slipped into rage.

At first she had ignored it, made excuses for him until even those did not make sense. In the end, her plans to leave Alexandre and the safety of the Nest had been made too late. Where could she go? She recalled the time when she and Maman felt loved. Calais reached out to her, leading her to flee Harfleur. And then the English king and his army had sealed off her escape. Once again, she was trapped.

"What?" Drem shook her arm. "What did you overhear?"

Brigitte shrugged, plastering a mask of calm on her face. It was a replica of the one Maman wore when her paramour had abandoned them. "'Tis nothing." She waved off his attention. "'Tis babbling. Like a little brook. From the shock of the night."

Feeling the weight of his scrutiny, she added, "The fall. The bombardments from your army." The squeezing in her lungs came with as much surprise as the tears that threatened to blur her vision.

Drem leaned in, wiping her cheek with his thumb. "I recall there was also a kiss."

Brigitte ached to have him closer. To feel protected without being trussed up, snared by pretty strings. She must tread carefully. This, too, could be a trap. "And a club," she reminded him.

Drem grimaced and rubbed his head. "I'd rather remember the kiss." Desire smoldered in his gaze. His lips called for her to kiss him once again.

Heat stole up her neck. She cut off the guilt nipping at her heels before it could take hold. He was an English soldier. There was nothing he could do to help. He took orders from his master, King Henry V. Just as she took her orders from the master of the Nest. The punishment for rebellion against Alexandre would be harsh.

Aching for the comfort and protection she had known as a child, she closed her eyes and willed the memories to warm her.

"Brigitte," he whispered.

She let Drem pull her into his arms. *Just this once.*

He grazed over her skin, nibbling, tasting. The steady thumping of his heart gave her the luxury of resting with him. They stood together, each supporting the other in silence.

Brigitte felt his muscles tense. Then his pulse shifted its beat. She lifted her head to look out onto the streets. The townspeople were drawing near. She could not make out their faces but could hear the cadence of their raised voices. Who were they cursing? Did they think to fight the English soldier?

Movement to the side caught her attention. A tawny head of curls draped around a gaunt pale face popped up from a barrel lying on its side. Piers? What was he doing? Before she could warn Drem, the boy began crawling toward them.

"Piers." She waved him over with the flick of her fingers. "Hurry. Before you are seen."

Drem stepped over to allow them access to the shop. He eyed them. "I've seen you before. You were in the Nest."

Scowling, Piers nodded. *"Oui."* He tugged on her skirt and tilted his head. "I thought I lost you, Bee."

Brigitte folded over, bundling the boy into her arms. She held him, never wanting to let go for fear it would be their last time together.

Piers patted her shoulder. "I can't breathe."

Brigitte looked up. How had she ever thought she could escape?

"Do you know of a way out that hasn't been blocked or destroyed?" Drem asked.

She bit her lip. Was the stairway through the butcher's shop still intact? The ground rippled under her feet. The telling of a trebuchet being set up. She tensed. Another bombardment to rip apart their lives.

"Whore!"

"Traitors!" the townspeople screamed.

A rock struck the doorframe near Brigitte's head.

She turned. Alexandre led the angry crowd. Ropes swung in their hands as they marched closer. Drem nudged them out of view. His hand inched closer to his sword.

"That is the one," Alexandre shouted.

The children, whose scrapes and bruises Brigitte had tended, joined in, cursing the traitorous bitch. They picked up rocks and pelted them at her. Alexandre spread his arms, controlling the mob until he chose the right moment to set them loose. His chest rose. A tic jumped at the corner of his eye. The baritone voice, which he had practiced in his youth to use as a tool in his mastery of others, rose above the muttering behind him.

"Good people of Harfleur. Look at her. We took her into our bosom. And how does she show her gratitude? She cavorts with the devil's own. Treachery. She sells us to the enemy. Man. Woman. And . . ." He hesitated, letting the impact of his speech stir the townspeople even more. "And the children. She sacrifices your children, for what? To defeat us." Alexandre pointed at Drem. "To feed them to that English soldier."

A gasp washed over the crowd. Brigitte fought down the urge to roll her eyes. Alexandre was in rare form this morning.

"She is not one of us. She means to turn Harfleur over to the English mongrel." He shouted to be heard over their outrage. "What say you? What shall we do with her? With the English vermin?"

"Hang her! Hang him! Life for life!"

Brigitte blinked. The pain of betrayal cut her open, wounding her bruised heart. Piers tightened his hold on her skirt. Drem moved, closing in their flanks. His palm rested confidently on her shoulder. He moved the pad of his thumb, rubbing the tension in her muscles. She was not alone in her stand. She locked eyes with Alexandre.

"What proof has he against me?" she shouted to the crowd, letting her gaze burrow into the faces she knew. She spotted Claudette's pale face. Tears flowed down the laundress's cheeks. "Ask where our mayor has hidden himself. Where is Raoul de Gaucourt, our defender? And then ask yourself how Master Alexandre has survived all these years. Think you that he lives only off the backs of the small children of the Nest?" She locked eyes with Alexandre and curled her lip. "No. You who stand so close, you'll want to see to your pockets," she warned. "And then the mayor's. Who profits to sell you? As for me, I am leaving this infested town."

Brigitte took a deep breath. Either the bovine-minded people would take the time to question their actions or they would make plans to measure her neck against a length of rope. The ground trembled under her feet again.

"Don't let her make a fool of you. Grab her!"

Someone Alexandre had no doubt planted in the crowd shouted, "String them up, lads!"

Alexandre dropped his arms and the townspeople rushed toward the butcher's shop. The air vibrated with thundering feet and the whistle of the largest bombardment the English had yet to let loose. Roofs collapsed under the weight of the boulders falling from the sky. Screams ripped through the crowd.

Brigitte spun, throwing her body into her little group of supporters, pushing Drem and Piers deeper into the shop. The walls shook before toppling over like a pile of kindling.

The building fell into itself. Stone striking timber, shale tiles collapsing in an ear-splitting crescendo. And then there was silence.

Chapter 9

Drem braced his body over the child as the building collapsed. His shoulders ached from the impact of flying stone and mortar. The skin along his back stung. He must have been struck. The palms of his hands were scraped and bruised, but for the moment they held strong. Muscles trembling, he pushed to his knees. Splinters of wood shredded over his back in a waterfall. The ceiling offered barely enough room for them to crawl under.

He ran his hand down the lad's neck, where his pulse raced. He touched Piers's cheeks. His eyelids fluttered, as if he was afraid to see the worst, then snapped open. Wide-eyed, the boy gazed up at him. Drem finally felt as if he could take a breath. They were alive.

The boy's lip began to quiver. A tear leaked out, frightening Drem more than a score of bombardments.

"Brigitte," Drem called.

The townspeople's muffled voices broke through the rubble. Whether they had had a change of heart or were still intent on stringing them up as sacrificial goats, he could not take the chance of trusting them.

"Brigitte." He hissed out her name.

Had she been struck by one of the beams? She had rushed toward them, pushing and shoving them back. He doused the rising panic leaping in his chest. No, she was in the building. Hale and hearty.

She had to be. He needed to find her.

Piers wrapped his hand around Drem's wrist, keeping him from leaving his side. Blues eyes searched his. "Bee."

Drem nodded. "I'll find her." He ducked as a shower of rubble rained down. Keeping low, he shrugged out of his cloak and handed it to the boy. "Here, keep safe the best you can. I won't be far." He paused again, the need to give hope rising out of the rubble of their lives. "She'll be fine."

Crouched low, Drem crawled through the debris. Because of the destruction, everything looked out of focus, as if he stood in two different towns. They needed Brigitte to lead them out. Despite the siege, she had escaped the wall. She would know the way.

He reached out, carefully swiping his hand through the air. He bounced into what was left of shutters and roofing. The large stones that held the wall in place had tumbled to the floor. Shelves had toppled over.

A massive beam cut across the room. It had been used as a tie to hold the roof up. Throat dry, he swallowed the dread that filled his mouth. Had it fallen down onto the vibrant, fierce woman he had only recently met?

He slid his hand between the timber and the floor. Splinters nipped at his palm until he bumped into the soft folds of a skirt. It stretched over a motionless limb and rounded hip. Heat radiated through the fabric, pulsing, penetrating the fear that she no longer lived.

"Drem," she said. A moan dragged through his brain, carrying his name on her breath.

A flicker of light cut through the dust. Smoke curled and licked at the broken framework scattered around them. "Aye, 'tis I."

He scooted close, building a façade of calm so she would not see his rising concern. Smoothing back her hair, grayed by the dust, he fought back the urge to kiss her face, the arched brow, the smooth cheek. As if it would somehow make things right.

"Piers?"

"Safe." He cleared his throat. She searched his face for the truth. "For now," he amended.

The townspeople's threat continued to carry through the wall of rubble.

"We must not tarry," he whispered. "Are you able to move?"

"*Oui.*" Brigitte pushed up and stopped, her body wedged between frame and stone. Frantic, she tugged on her skirt, trying to pull it out from under the weight of the beam. She paused, drawing in a breath through clenched teeth. "I cannot."

He stilled her struggles with a finger to her lips and shook his head. Motioning for her to roll toward him, he braced his boots against the beam. Sweat popped out on his forehead. The wounds on his back screamed at him to let go. He dug in his heels, lifting until she was released from the beam's hold. He took in the way she favored her leg as she dragged closer.

Arms wrapped tight, they held on to each other, breathing in the strength to do what they must. He gently ran his hands over her body, searching for injury, thankful for no obvious signs of broken bones. Smoothing the hair from her face, he sought the lips he ached for when he had thought he would never have that opportunity again. She stiffened, as if caught by surprise, then leaned in, welcoming his embrace. He sighed at the sweetness, absent since he'd been taken from his home.

An air-sucking whoosh ripped them apart and brought reality to his blood-starved brain. Flames took hold and jumped like a wild animal.

"Shite. If we don't escape this place, it will soon be our funeral pyre," he muttered.

Offering his shoulder for support, they crawled toward Piers. Drem's injuries made the short distance feel like a long journey. He could only imagine how Brigitte managed it. By the time they reached the boy, smoke twisted its long talons into their lungs, squeezing the air from their bodies.

Brigitte held the hem of her skirt to her mouth to filter out the smoke and allow the rancid air in. A cough erupted from her lungs. Her vision began to blur. Eyes tearing, she moved as quickly as her aching body would allow. One thing she had learned while living on the streets and during her time at the Nest: one survives for oneself only. Yet here she was, alive for the moment, thanks to the man who should be her enemy.

With each lift of her good leg, she pressed on. The one that had been mashed by the beam lagged behind her. Again, if not for Drem, she would still be lying near the worst of the smoke, gasping for air. She allowed herself a glance in his direction. His mouth—that which had swept her away from her troubles more than once already—was firm and determined. Somehow, this man gave her strength.

A rasping cough tore her from her scattered thoughts.

"Here." Drem wrapped his arm around her waist and propelled her forward. "Almost there."

Piers lay still and quiet. Brigitte fell next to him.

"No. This cannot be." She had failed.

A familiar pat on her shoulder lifted her from roaring despair. Piers, his small hand that had brought comfort and connection, now brought hope.

Renewed by her fighting spirit, Brigitte lifted her head. Everything may be at strange angles and in total disarray, but she knew this place.

They were in the butcher's shop. If the bombardment had not closed off the tunnel, they should be able to escape both the fire and the townspeople. And she would be free from Alexandre's control. "Follow me," she said.

"Are you certain? Your injuries . . ." Drem said. The concern on his face clutched at her heart.

"*Oui.*" She motioned the others to follow. They mimicked her, holding garments to their mouth and nose, and keeping low, they crawled to the hidden doorway the butcher kept for deliveries.

Her pulse raced as the entrance loomed near. She struggled not to rush into the tunnel, but kept her choking breaths slow and regular. The door opened unhindered. An indescribable stench of rot and decay filled her nose and mouth.

Piers retched, gagging at the smell. He began moving backward.

"*Oui,* you must," Brigitte said. She motioned them through and slammed the door shut. The air began to clear of smoke. She closed her eyes, focusing on what lay past this obstacle. Provided the tunnel had not caved in, they would soon be outside Harfleur's walls.

Drem held out his hands, lifting her to her feet. She stood on wobbly legs.

"What do we do now?" He sent a cautious look toward the door. The fire they thought to escape began cutting through the thick panels.

He lifted her, cradling her in his arms. "Show us the way," he urged.

Brigitte pointed down the stairway cut into the stone. The slick mossy steps should lead to the underground spring, but with all the devastation, she could only hope it had not caved in.

Without question, he motioned Piers to join them as they began their descent. They left behind the threat of choking on smoke and being burned to death. For this, they took the step toward disease and the chance they would be buried under the rubble of Harfleur.

Chapter 10

Brigitte squinted up at the light cutting through the vast darkness that had been a part of their world for hours. Many fingers of the stony path had been cut off by debris and were now unpassable or treacherous underfoot. Their underground journey was twisted, turning them back on their route. She had almost given up; ready to sit down and cover her head with her cloak.

Indefatigable, Drem refused to release her. Paying no attention to her pleas, he carried her in the directions she thought she recognized. Instead, they found themselves in an unfathomable maze. Ironically, it was the ever-present stench that finally led them to the break in the wall of earth.

Brigitte lifted her head. The debris had begun to clear as they drew nearer.

"Stop." She smoothed her hand over the length of his sleeve.

His arm wrapped firm and strong around her waist as he set her on her feet. A wave of peace filled her, giving her the courage to look beyond the tunnel walls. She absorbed the heat of his body, letting his warmth seep into her muscles. His heart beat steadily under her palm. Solid. Sure.

Tilting her head, she breathed in the mixture of fetid water and fresh air. Just as she remembered, the fresh air seeped through the tunnel nearest the opening that led past the wall. Hope began to swell.

Squinting through tears that stung her eyelids, she searched past the pile of rubble.

"Drem, look."

A beam of light split the stone, exposing the crevice. A thin stream of air cut through the haze of smoke showing them the way.

Drem directed Piers to stand back. Brigitte braced her hands beside Drem's. Together, they strained to roll the boulder away. Sweat slid down her back. Her leg trembled. Bruises complained, pinching and biting at her flesh. Nearing the edge of exhaustion, she began to think again of giving up. So tired. Her lungs burned with every breath.

The stone shifted.

She looked down. Piers had joined them.

Drem counted. "One. Two. Three."

They pushed and shoved at his order. Again and again. The boulder tipped, then gave way.

They tumbled out, rolling onto the damp earth. Brigitte and Drem lay on the ground. Gasping, laughing. Piers lay giggling beside them.

Cool, fresh air slid over Brigitte's damp skin. Never in her life had she felt the relief of freedom she did at that moment.

The slide of metal, singing against leather sheaths sliced through their exhilaration. Brigitte's joy caught in her throat. Drem slid his hand over hers, pumping a warning of caution. Piers stilled beside them.

She looked up into the clear blue sky, then shuttered her eyes at the threat that swung over their heads like the Sword of Damocles.

Drem squeezed Brigitte's hand, willing her to remain calm. They may have escaped the Nest of Harfleur. Now they must survive the fires of King Henry's Knights of the Swan.

"Look who we have here," Nathan barked. He wore his battle helmet. The bridge covered most of his face. Narrow eye slits allowed him to see out and gave him a menacing look. Anger seethed from his cutting gaze and clenched jaw. His blade swung close to Drem's head. "You best speak fast."

"Nathan . . ." Drem began.

"'Tis Sir Nathan to the likes of you." The toe of his heavy boot made contact with Drem's ribs.

He sucked in a breath, fighting his instinct to jump up and beat the man to death. The rhythmic pump of Brigitte's hand, still clasped in his, pulled him from the cliff of stupidity. Nathan's broadsword could swiftly cleave their heads from their bodies before Drem had a chance to crawl to his knees.

A new taste, that of fear, mingled with the smoke still coating his tongue. He understood the threat to himself, but an unarmed woman and a defenseless child did not deserve this, even if they *were* French. They had become his responsibility and he would protect them.

He glanced at Brigitte and caught her attention. Silently, he willed her to understand. Her eyes widened.

Drem ignored the little shake of her head and flipped to his knees. To his surprise, the motion was still smooth. His muscles and tired flesh obeyed his commands as he blocked Nathan's sword with his body.

"You'll have to stab me in the back to get to them. You know that." He turned his head, locking eyes with the man who held his life in the steel of arm and blade. "But before you do, wouldn't you want to know what I've learned?"

A wave of relief washed over him, then pulled back like the tide when Nathan shifted his attention to Brigitte and the boy.

"And what of them?" Nathan snarled. "Would you have me believe they mean no harm? We've laid siege to their home." The sword dipped. "Ask yourself: Why would they? And there you have your answer. The bitch and her whelp would as soon tear out our throats."

"Ugly English cur," Brigitte hissed past Drem's shoulder. "If I wanted to do so, I would have done it in the night while you slept in that row of tents."

Drem gritted his teeth as she tried to push him off. There was no counting on common sense. Did he need to remind her that Nathan was the one with the sword?

"Hush," Drem said.

The swell of her breasts met his chest as she drew in a huff of air. He looked into her face. How many bruises lay hidden under the layers of dirt and sweat? Dried blood creased the arch of her brow. Her stubborn mouth set in a firm line that did not bode well. There had to be a way to get them safely to his tent.

He nipped the corner of her mouth, tasting and branding the woman as his. He looked over his shoulder. A seasoned warrior would understand one thing. "She's mine, Nathan. She's my hostage. My prisoner. Mine to plunder if I wish."

The knight grunted and let his sword drop. "Move on," he said, motioning for the men-at-arms who stood at his flank. He sheathed his weapon and crossed his arms over his chest. "What do you intend to do with the two of them?"

Drem tilted his head and gave Brigitte a slow wink. The fury leaping from her gaze gave him pause. *One step at a time, Drem, my boy.*

"If it suits you, Sir Nathan, I'm arising now." He lifted a hand, showing it empty of weaponry. "I would like to save my hide from any more abuse."

Nathan swept off his helm, tucking it under the crook of his arm. He shoved his fingers through his auburn mane, ruffling the matted strands sticking to his head. "You have my leave."

Drem pushed up, his aching bones arguing with the command. To his dismay, the stubborn knight did not move from where he stood. Nathan watched them, hawk-eyed, apparently holding his tongue until he could take a strip from his prey.

"Come, Brigitte." Drem bent to offer his hand.

She rose gracefully and stood with a regal posture. Her chin tilted up. She looked like an exotic cat, her claws barely sheathed.

He raised a brow, questioning her ability to keep peace until he sorted things out.

Nathan wandered over to the child. "And what is your name?"

The lad hesitated. He glanced at Brigitte for advice. With a tilt of her chin, she gave him permission. "I'm called Piers."

Bending at the waist, Nathan held out his gauntlet-covered forearms for Piers to grasp.

"Both hands," the knight whispered. "Hold tight."

He straightened, lifting Piers to hang on to him like an apple on the branch of a strong tree. The boy yelped as Nathan turned and set him down.

Nathan's smile faded as he turned his attention back to Drem and Brigitte. "This camp isn't a place for innocent children. The boy is too young for an archer apprentice. What madness makes you think he will better survive out here instead of inside Harfleur's wall?"

"He'd starve if left on his own," Brigitte said.

Piers walked up, putting his hand into hers. His eyes sparkled over pale cheeks as he watched the knight in awe. "Master Alexandre will beat me, 'tis certain."

Nathan shook his head. "The others will have more to say. But as for me, mayhap we can find some use for him."

Brigitte placed a protective hand on Piers's shoulder. "We will make our way. Alone."

Nathan grunted in an unhappy response. "Keep them close, Drem." He squinted over the camp. "The sickness has spread."

"Since I've been gone?" There had been dysentery in the days before he followed Brigitte. That had been one of the reasons he had taken it upon himself to track her down. If she had poisoned the men, it should have stopped the moment it left their bodies.

Brigitte stepped closer, her arms wrapped around Piers. Worry beetled her brow. "What kind of sickness?"

"Bellyaches. Fever." Drem glanced at her. "Bowel issues."

"'Tis the bloody flux?" Brigitte asked.

Nathan caught Drem's attention with one raised brow. He knew what he silently was reminding him. She was the enemy. They would not share the state of the men. Their weakness.

"*Oui*," she said. "'Tis what happens when the water is fouled. The food goes bad. Tell me, Sir Nathan, what have your soldiers been eating?"

"We shall deal with our men. On our own," Drem warned.

What could she do? Why would she help? He knew what it meant to be a prisoner. He had dreamed of finding ways to rid himself of his capturers. Every day he had plotted ways to kill them one by one.

Then, one day, he had awoken and realized that at some point he and Henry had learned to respect each other. Their youth, spent in battles, had forged a friendship.

"This is ridiculous! For years, I have nursed the children of the Nest. 'Tis certain I can help."

Nathan rubbed his chin. Coming to a decision, he pointed to the boy. "See that you keep him under your control. Drem, take them to your tent. Get them settled. Then meet us in the command tent." He began to stride away, then paused. "Bring the woman with you."

Brigitte watched the redheaded soldier walk away. The breath she did not realize she was holding exploded from her chest. She busied her hands to keep the trembling from showing and smoothed the folds of her skirt. The fabric had taken the brunt of her escape. Most of the holes would require needle and thread to mend. She stuck her fingers into the burned material and wiggled them.

'Twas unlikely the soldiers would have a spare dress for her. Mayhap the English had a miracle for repairs of something of this magnitude.

"Bee," Piers called. "Hurry."

Brigitte took a step to bring up the rear of their little group and winced. Her wounds needed tending before her clothing was repaired. As she limped along, she noticed Drem carried himself differently. He turned, his movements cautious and stiff.

She recalled the building falling in on itself. The crash of timber, stone, and plaster. He had protected them more than once, shielding them from danger. She squinted at his tunic. The thick leather was ripped and stained. Her stomach tightened. What lay beneath?

Alexandre had always commented on her light touch. It bode well in lifting a heavy purse or pinching a loaf of bread. The children called for her when they were ill or injured. Would her skills be enough to bargain with? She began making a list of the ingredients she would need to broker her usefulness.

The path took them deeper into the encampment. The stench filled her nostrils. 'Twas worse than when she had slipped through to gather the pears. How long ago was that? It felt like ages since she slept or had a decent meal.

Thoughts of Maman pushed the wretchedness away. The life Brigitte knew as a little girl, cossetted by the man her mother spoke of as Monsieur le Faire, was out of reach. It glimmered like the emerald in Maman's brooch. A worthless, broken memory. But for Brigitte, it was what kept her believing that somewhere beyond her present state of existence was a life worth having.

Ever since that first night out on the streets of Harfleur, that had been her vow. To find a better life. On her own terms. Better than the one she left behind.

Brigitte stared at Drem's broad shoulders and back. She had only to drift into the crowd of soldiers, move toward the edge where rows of souls clung to life. And not one of them would notice her. She could disappear. Slip away

Her steps faltered.

But how would escaping improve her life?

Chapter 11

Brigitte resisted the urge to run. Even though the soldiers had not advanced against them, their curious stares made the back of her neck itch. She had enough practice remaining unseen. Being the center of their attention broke all the rules Alexandre had demanded they learn or bear the brunt of his cane.

Drem lifted the flap of the tent and motioned for them to enter. Anxious to get out of sight, she pushed past him. Her brows rose.

More than one cot filled the cramped space. Barely enough room to walk. She stepped over a trunk, its contents spilling onto the dirt floor. Chain mail draped over the row of armor resting against the tent. Were they expected to sleep like a pack of mongrels? And with whom?

For the last several years she had managed to avoid the role of whore and she did not intend on making her debut performance with the Englishman.

A white jupon stretched out over a chest to dry. The red cross of St. George was stitched on the front like a blaze of blood. Broadswords hung on hooks beside the heads of the cots. Plates of leg armor were piled on the floor next to knee-high boots and spurs. Brigitte swallowed, realization pressing into the base of her skull.

A week ago she had watched thousands of English soldiers ride under the king's banner. But these were not just soldiers. They were knights. According to Alexandre, they took whatever they desired and destroyed the rest. They were not to be trusted.

Brigitte's throat closed. It became dryer than a creek bed during a drought. *Merde!* Sleeping under a bush would be better than this. She spun on her heels, colliding with Drem's thick chest. Her palms flattened against his leather jerkin. The beat of his heart matched her racing pulse.

Piers staggered in, eyes widened, accentuating the ridge of the cheekbones in his gaunt face. "Bee, did you see the knights and their armor?" He dodged Drem and Brigitte, making his way to kneel beside the metal plates. Scowling, he cocked his head. "Who's been caring for these? They're growing rust."

The grip on Brigitte's arms loosened but kept her in place. She did not dare look up at Drem. She was certain he sensed she meant to make an escape. His thumbs worked over her sleeve, traveling up to her shoulders.

He let out a breath. It ruffled her hair, tickling the sensitive nape of her neck. Piers prattled on. His words captured no one's attention until he leaped up from his position by the armor.

"My father taught me how to care for it. Said one day I'd need to know."

Brigitte brought her senses back to the tent. Had the lad a talent? 'Twas a good thing. The boy certainly had no skill in thievery.

"Where'd your father learn to care for armor?" Drem asked. "Was he a squire?"

The sparkle of excitement faded from Piers's eyes. He shook his head. "No. My papa fought for the House of Burgundy."

Brigitte gasped. She'd never asked how he came to be in the Nest, just accepted that Alexandre had offered him the same protection he gave all the other lost children.

"Papa fell at Soissons," Piers added.

"That battle was almost two years ago," Brigitte said. "What of your family?"

Piers walked to the entrance of the tent. The flap of canvas caught a gust of wind, making the covering tremble against its force. He gripped the supporting pole until his knuckles turned white. Time stretched as the boy fought to gather his wits. "I do not know."

His whisper slipped through Brigitte's defenses, reminding her how brave he was for one so young and alone. There were so many questions she should have asked him and had not.

"Why didn't you say anything?"

Piers pressed his lips together and shook his head.

"You were newly arrived in Harfleur when you came to the Nest. Where were you all that time?"

Drem caught her hand. Together, they surrounded Piers, offering him a wall to lean on.

"I know how it is to feel alone." Drem lowered himself beside him and said, "To wonder if your family is out there looking for you too." He knelt on one knee and offered his palm. Scars crisscrossed calluses and tender flesh. "If 'tis in my power, I shall find them for you."

Piers searched his face. Doubt washed over him before he dropped his lids to shield himself from more lies.

Drem tipped the lad's chin, holding him in his gaze. "I offer this in earnest. 'Tis my vow I make to you. One that I wish had been made to me when I was not much older than you."

Piers blinked, then nodded. "I'll hold you to it, sir."

Drem grinned. "Drem will do."

The simple action lighted his face, creating stars at the corners of his eyes. It reminded Brigitte of the night when she had watched the knight from the shadows. She had guessed correctly. The man liked to smile.

He looked up, catching her in the act of watching the exchange. And his expression changed. His smile vanished. There was a shuttering of his soul, a blocking of her perusal. 'Twas like planks of wood covering the windows at night. She could almost hear it slam shut. It left her feeling alone, separated from him and their budding friendship.

A knock thumped against the side of the canvas. A boy several inches taller than Piers stood at the entrance. Although not much older, his chest was broad, his arms already bulky.

"Hello, young John. How goes the archery training?" Drem asked.

"Good, Sir Drem. You've been missed. I'm told to give you the message that you are to come by yourself." He dropped a silver disc into Drem's palm. Eyes narrowed, he scanned the cramped tent. "The woman is commanded to stay here until she is called."

Drem nodded and rose. "Brigitte, there's a pitcher of water in the corner. Clean yourself as best you can."

"Piers . . ."

"May go with Young John." He glanced at the boys. "The lady needs her privacy."

"*Oui.*" The golden mop of curls bobbed in agreement.

"Young John, show Piers where he may wash off the soot. See that you keep out of trouble. There will be punishment if you don't."

"Punishment?" Piers squeaked. His feet took on the appearance of boat anchors, holding him to the spot. "What kind of punishment?"

A bloom of red spread over Young John's freckled cheeks. "Don't know about you, but I'll have to dig another row of trenches." He eyed the boy's smaller stature. "Imagine since your arms are puny, you'll be put to work gathering dead animals and such for the trebuchet."

Piers searched the bustling encampment, and then lifted his chin. " 'Tis all right, Bee?"

"*Oui.*" Brigitte kept watch over the boys as Young John led Piers away. She took in a breath and tasted the soot and smoke reeking from her person. It would take several scrubbings to get the skirt clean.

Drem bent to pick up a sword larger than the one he kept at his side. A muffled groan matched his stiff movements.

"Stop." She touched his shoulder. "The English king can wait. Your injuries need tending."

Drem shook off her hand. " 'Tis not the way of things."

The grimace that furrowed his brows made her insides ache. Instead of soothing him, she wanted to strike him and kiss the pain away. Somehow at the same time.

"So, is stupidity the way of things?" she snapped. "There is disease in this encampment. Do you want your wounds to fester?"

"What I want does not matter." He thrust the sword into the sheath. "There are several who would not care that I am wounded or that I meet my final end, toes up, in a bloody battlefield. That is the way of things."

Brigitte wet her lips. Although he stood in front of her, eyes snapping, hands on his narrow hips, she had to plead her concern. "Then offer me a vow as easily as you did Piers."

His slow groan let her know just how much it pained him saying more. "Go on."

"Promise that when you are finished, you will allow me to tend your wounds." She lifted her palm to silence his complaints. "In gratitude for helping me leave Harfleur."

Drem caught her hands. The reddened flesh looked as if it had been scorched in a fire instead of marred by the rope on which she had slid earlier.

"Care for yourself first." His voice thick and gravely, he cleared it before adding, "I promise to return as soon as I am allowed. Then we will talk more."

"And . . ." Brigitte pressed.

He wrapped an arm around her waist, pulling her to his chest. Her neck curved, baring the tender space by her collarbone. Unable to resist the liquid moan that poured out in a sigh, she shivered as he brushed his lips over her skin.

He lifted his head. The gold flecks in his eyes sparkled down at her before his stern soldier's countenance returned.

"And when I return, you'll have the grisly honor of seeing to my wounds," he said.

Brigitte stood at the flap in the tent and watched him march off, his back as erect as the wall he attempted to build between them.

She worked to slow her breath and the rapid beat of her heart. 'Twould serve her well to remember to fortify her own wall.

Drem strode across the camp. Brigitte's response to his attention aroused him like no other. He wanted to take his time, let their attraction unfurl, one kiss and one glorious touch at a time.

If not for the metal disc, formed into the shape of a swan no bigger than a coin, biting into his palm, he would have stayed. Even allowed her to see the many scars covering his body. But he had been summoned to a meeting of the brotherhood.

A warning rippled up his spine. Although new to the Knights of the Swan, he was a seasoned soldier of the king. Henry had not had the opportunity to give his blessing to his journey past the walls. There would be a price for his going off on his own. Not that Henry was vindictive toward his friends, nor did he use them bitterly. But he did like to be informed.

Were the rules different for him now than when he was an archer? As a Knight of the Swan, would he be allowed to venture off and follow the instincts groomed as a hunter? Serve the king in whatever way he desired. But above all protect the king. And that was what he intended to do.

Drem rapped on the tent. The flap whipped open. Air, thick with smoke from the tallow candles, crawled up his arms, filled his nostrils. The group of men standing around the table waved him entrance. Their narrow mouths were drawn into thin lines. An ominous foreboding whispered that he should run. Sweat trickled down his back, scoring his cuts and bruises.

Cheering came from the archers' camp. Drem jerked his head. Piers. Was he safe? Brigitte. Would she be there when he returned?

"Sir Drem." Darrick's voice cut through the fog that had manacled Drem's brain.

Drem shook himself free and dove farther into the cramped, dank tent. The man who he thought despised him the most held out his hand.

"Well?" Darrick asked. His eyes cut to his outstretched palm.

Drem allowed the knight to pull him into a back-slapping welcome. Salty liquid burned the corners of his lids as the men came up to him to offer brotherly punches to his bruised body. He made the turn in the tent until he came upon his friend and king. Although shorter than most, Henry carried his royalty and pride in his stance. The white scar near the bridge of his nose glistened under the candlelight.

"Welcome back, Sir Drem. 'Tis good to know the last bombardment from my great beauties did not drive you from this world."

"Aye, Sire, though they nearly had me a time or two."

"That would have been a shame. Would you not agree?" He rocked on his heels, mischief twinkling in his eyes. "I've decided. Given this is a time of war. That you have shown your loyalty for years. And . . ." He held up his hand. "Despite your father's treachery, the rites of the Knights of the Swan will be performed tonight."

He turned, casting his gaze over the knights who had marched with him against France. "I'm aware of some misgivings among a few of you, but this is God's cause and we will fight side by side, not among ourselves.

"Sir Darrick, you may proceed."

Drem knelt in front of his friend, his king, and winced. The wounds stuck to his linen shirt ripped open. Punishment had indeed come. Just not as he had anticipated.

Chapter 12

D rem walked beside Nathan and Darrick. He shook his head. The rite welcoming him into the brotherhood was brief. Vows and promises to keep the king safe were repeated. 'Twas nothing new. He had been fighting by the king's side since he was the young Prince of Wales. How many years had he proven he could be trusted? For what? The inclusion into a family. A brotherhood. No land came with the honor. He was still a soldier who took his orders like the rest of them. But now he had been given the task to serve, protect, and gather information. And he had been given the status of knight. Not just any knight; now he truly was a Knight of the Swan. He could now be called Sir Drem ap Dafydd.

They had been pleased with his report on the conditions of Harfleur. Their interest in Brigitte was unnerving. They wanted more from her than just the number of dead or the state of the storehouses. He had given his promise to Brigitte to watch over her. He prayed it would not keep him from serving his king.

"Go back to the woman," Nathan repeated. "Find out what you can from her. She knows more. 'Tis certain."

They paused outside the tent as Piers and Young John strode up. Blood streamed from their noses.

Several boys followed behind them. Their faces lit with outrage. They stuttered to a halt when they realized three knights watched them. Guilt spread through the crowd and they began to disperse like a morning mist over the bogs.

"I see the woman's boy is quick to make friends," Nathan said. He clapped them on the shoulders and left them as quickly as he could. "Believe I have an appointment with a comely wench who found her way into camp." He wiggled his rust-colored brows. "I'll leave you to your tasks."

Drem shook his head. How did that man slip in and out so easily? If not for his strength and skill with weaponry, Nathan would be worthless. Though he suspected Darrick felt the same, he kept his opinions close to his chest. "Aye. Appears the boy has another talent."

Darrick turned his scowl on Drem. "Talents?"

"The boy comes from Soissons. His father taught him about armor." Their gazes fell on the two boys, whose pace had slowed to that of those who were condemned to the gallows. "Says—"

"Have the woman mend your wounds." Darrick's attention remained on Piers. "I'd like to speak with the boy."

He turned at Drem's speechless response. "You think no one noticed you are injured but don't use your brain to see the surgeon? Christ on the cross. Next time deal with the wounds at once, before they worsen." He wrinkled his nose. "And mayhap add bathwater before you meet with the king."

Brigitte jumped back from the tent entrance as she tugged her bodice over her breasts. A shuddering breath made the front laces sway away from her chest. She slapped a hand over the gaping material. Warmth crept up her neck, heating her ears. They would soon burst into flames; she was sure of it.

Drem ducked to enter the tent. His broad shoulders consumed the knights' quarters. He let his gaze sweep over her, traveling from head to toe, then back to her breasts. "You're still here. I half-expected you to run." He stepped toward her. "I'm relieved you didn't."

Flames licked her skin. Trying to ignore the desire ignited in the tight space between their bodies, she plucked at the bodice. It loosened its hold on her pebbling nipples. Cool air blew over her skin, like a lover's kiss. *What has come over me?*

She tested her forehead for fever. 'Twas not as if men had never looked her way. But after a few days on the streets, she had learned to become invisible. Aided by Master Alexandre's tutelage, she could slip in and out, unnoticed. Why did Drem seem to know what she was thinking? How did he see past the walls she had built years ago?

Turning, she picked up the refolded jupon, clutching it to her stomach like a shield. The slash of a red cross reminded her of the sick and wounded they had walked past to reach his tent.

"Here." She shoved the jupon into his chest.

His fingers, long and strong, covered her hand, trapping her. The beating of his heart pierced through his leather jerkin and into her palm. He looked down at the wad of clothing. "You found the bar of soap and water."

Brigitte released the jupon. She took a step back, slipping her hand out of his grasp. Callused fingertips released her, caressing her skin. A tingle started at the base of her spine. She shivered.

His nose wrinkled. "The pungent smell of a meat house lingers on your person."

An ice flow slammed into the rush of gentle pleasure. Stars twirled in front of her face, flashing a warning to hold her tongue. She had just begun to consider her limited options when he had approached the tent. How could she undress with all the English soldiers milling outside? Their shadows and voices penetrated the canvas walls.

To no avail, she sputtered, "Where did you think I would find enough time to bathe properly? Besides, the pitiful amount of water provided barely allowed me to wash my face and hands. Why must you use a pot when there is a place where water is so sweet it must come from heaven?"

"My apologies." He stepped back, allowing the distance between them to grow. "I didn't have time to think about such things." He shoved his fingers through his unruly mane, raking through the chestnut waves coated with soot and sweat.

Brigitte busied her hands, smoothing her palm down the tattered skirt. "Your meeting with the king took less time than I anticipated. Mayhap later you will stand guard so that I might finish?"

His hazel eyes flashed, darkening to the color of the rolling seas along the shore. "You heard me tell the men you are under my protection."

There was nothing she could do to remove the smoky residue from her clothes. Except finish the job and burn them. Walking about like the day Maman gave birth to her would surely quiet his complaints. Being naked together caught her imagination and that irksome heat traveled through her middle. She tightened her thighs. A spasm of contracting muscles coursed through, building, flowing into her mons.

She forced her gaze to remain strong and firm. To glance away would show weakness. 'Twas what Alexandre had demanded in his training of fledglings. Timing. When to show strength and when to show weakness. She could not let Drem know her fear. "*Oui.* I also heard you say I was your woman. Your spoils of . . ." She twirled her hand in the air. "War."

"Had to be said." A jaw muscle jumped. "To keep you safe. We'll see what can be found to replace your dress. There are women in the camp who may have something to lend you."

"You wish me to wear a leman's garments?" Maman's elegant brocade and silk dresses flashed in Brigitte's mind. As a little girl, Brigitte never understood the covert whispers and laughter behind locked doors. Now she did. She'd sworn never to be like her mother. And here she stood, staring at the man who had the power to take care of her or give her to his friends.

"Until we break down Harfleur's defenses," he added. "Then you may have your pick from the nobles' wardrobes."

"Why would you do that?" she whispered.

He drew back. Raising her chin so she might read the truth written in his eyes. "Because I think you deserve better than you received at Master Alexandre's fist. And, oddly enough, I trust your word."

Stunned, Brigitte blinked. This knight trusted her? A thief?

A lost piece of who she was before arriving in Harfleur settled into place. Not a perfect fit. She was no longer that abandoned and heartbroken girl. She was determined to retrieve what was hers and then make her way to Calais. The city Maman had spoken of so lovingly, with hope. It was where they were to build their future together.

He lifted her soot-covered hair that she had frantically tried to tame. "'Tis certain you know of a place where we can bathe in private."

"*Oui.*" She licked her lips and glanced toward the flap in the tent. Her fingers curled, fighting the urge to stroke his whiskered jaw. She forced down the urge to rub against him like a love-starved cat. "Where is Piers?"

"He's been taken under Sir Darrick's wing." He plucked the jupon from her hands, catching her wrist before she could chase after them. "He is under his protection."

"Protection. Why?" Her hands folded into fists. "Because he is French?"

"Yes." He winced as she jerked to free her arms. "And because he

is from Soissons. Let Darrick discover what this is about. He is safe.
I promise."

"You promise. How many promises have you made and kept?"

"Too many. And all of them." He hesitated, chewing on his lower
lip. "I've been given an order by the king to have my wounds
cleaned." He began to lift the hem of his leather jerkin and groaned.
"I beseech you. Point me to the nearest fresh watering hole."

Brigitte shook her head and let the fear slip from her shoulders.
"Here. Let me." She pressed him onto the stool. His large body filled
her view. He ducked as she drew the leather jerkin over his head. A
hiss of air exploded.

The linen shirt, ruined beyond repair, stuck to the bloody parts of
his skin. The threads of the material, whether torn or singed, broke
apart in her hands.

But the broken body, hidden underneath, tore at her heart.

Fresh cuts and purple bruises competed with those that had come
before them. Old scars, white with age, slashed across his back and
shoulders. A fresh long scar, pink and angry, angled from his rib cage
to the curve of his hip.

Brigitte bent to peer closely at the work that lay before her.

Drem squirmed under her scrutiny. A puff of air blew across his
bare skin. His nipples drew up. He waited, holding his breath, aching
for her to touch him. Anywhere. Of its own accord, his body leaned
toward her. Hungry, searching for contact.

He prodded at the unusual sensation. This slip of a woman un-
manned him. She looked guilty of something. As if she had been
caught listening to conversations she should leave alone. For an instant, he felt the warning flare into his blood. But then she had turned
and his brain stopped working. The damp bodice clung to her body,
wrapping around her figure like a lover's embrace. Had she heard
what was said between Darrick and Nathan? 'Twas that what had
brought the wary look into her eyes? And then her mood shifted.
Like the faerie he thought her to be that first night. Angry at his stupid remark about her body odor, Drem groaned. He was a stupid, stupid man.

He twisted, ready to offer another apology.

"Stay still," she warned. Her cool hands pressed into his shoulders. "I must see the damage you've done."

A rustling behind him warned of the coming of the smelly unguents kept in the chest by his cot. He searched the room, listening for the click of the lid. He tensed, preparing for the stench. 'Twas usually strong enough to keep him from using the stuff.

"What is this?" She sniffed at the jar.

"Boar's grease and . . ."

" 'Tis rancid?"

"If you like, I can see the surgeon."

"No." She sighed. " 'Tis unnecessary."

She rifled through the chest, her silence leaving Drem to wonder what she intended to do to his scarred hide. Her small hand popped over his shoulder. A chunk of deep red resin lay in her palm.

"Dragon's blood?" she whispered.

"Aye. Purchased in London." That was the time he'd almost lost his life. He'd miscalculated the distance between his body and the tip of a lance. The barber had sworn it was the dragon's blood that had saved his soul from death.

" 'Tis costly." She snatched her hand back before he could grasp it. "You pay for this, but let this . . ." The jar of grease shoved under his nose, stealing his breath. ". . . rot."

Drem gripped the stool with both hands. "Just use the damn stuff and be done."

"No."

A warm rag stroked over his skin. It stroked over his back, his shoulders. The hair on his thighs lifted as her breath caressed his rib cage. The water cooled his skin.

"You have many scars." She slid her hand over the one that ran down his torso. " 'Twas a dangerous angle."

Drem hissed as she expanded her exploration. She left a trail of contradiction. Heat, rising, wave after wave, wherever she touched. Then cold emptiness came crashing down in the wake of her hand moving on.

"There is swelling here." Her fingers probed the bruise at the base of his spine. "Do you have stiffness?"

He looked down. His hands trembled against his thigh. As if they were spent from wielding a sword all day. He spun on the stool and grabbed her wrist. "You ask too much."

"I do only what is ordered." She scrunched her nose. "But I'll not use that ointment you carry around with you. Like adding a putrid dead body to your skin." She patted his chest, as if testing the coils of hair, tickling the already sensitive nipples. By all that was holy, when had his nipples become sensitive? They were used to the weight of a linen shirt, a padded gambeson, chain mail, and plates of steel. Instead, all he could think of was what the weight of her lips would be like as she suckled.

"Any more and I'll have you bent over the cot." He rose and regretted it immediately. Her lush mouth came perilously close to his crotch. His stones tightened, aching for release. He growled under his breath. He was a fool, trying to convince himself she meant nothing. He wanted her.

She rose with him. Fluid and graceful. "Your friends . . ." she said.

The muscles in her neck danced up and down as she swallowed. The tip of her pink tongue flashed between perfectly formed teeth.

He watched her mouth. Would it be wrong of him to claim her?

"Piers . . ." The wary shadows flowed back into her eyes. "They . . . they shall return any moment."

Drem shook free of the hunger that drove him toward madness. He had done many things while in the service of his king. Terrorizing a woman, prisoner or not, was not one of them. Until today. Guilt nipped at him like a rabid wolf. She was not his to claim. Was she? Is this what his sister had felt while in the hands of the English? If she heard of Brigitte's ill treatment, his sister would have his balls on a stick and roasted over the campfire by nightfall. Relief washed over Drem. The mere thought of his sister dampened the raging desire thrumming through his veins.

His brain began to work again. Although no one would pay a ransom for her, she was his prize from the siege of Harfleur. And his responsibility until they left on their march.

"Piers will be fine. I imagine he is learning the wonders of battle preparation." He watched her. "You did say he is not yours."

"'Tis correct. Alexandre brought him to the Nest a few months ago." She paused. Her restless hands stilled against his chest. "Alexandre had been excited that day. He kept speaking of windfalls. Coming to him like spring showers."

Drem filed away that information to share with the brotherhood. She winced when he caught her fingers. He turned her hands over. A crash of guilt bit at him again. "I need to tend to your palms."

"I should wait for Piers." She stepped back.

"No." Picking up his sword, he added, "We shall look for him while you lead me to this heaven you spoke of earlier."

The men littered the ground, lying on their cots, leaning against tent poles, all of them turning to stare at Brigitte. Drem gripped the hilt of the broadsword hanging from his waist. He glared at the men, willing them to stay away from Brigitte. From his woman. *She is mine!*

Her skirts swayed, stroking his legs. He swore he could feel the heat penetrating through his chausses and leather boots.

"I shall make you a salve that is better for your wounds," she said, "You'll see." Her frown deepened. She wiggled her arm. "First, you must release me."

"Aye." Drem sighed as he thrust his fingers through his snarled hair. His gallant promise of protection kept him from holding her as if he would never let go. "Come. We need to find a place to clean both our wounds and free us of the smoke."

"'Tis this way." She glided past the tents where pallets lay on the ground. The wounded groaned out their pain and suffering. Her hand slid up his arm. "Do they not have the medicine they need?"

Drem looked past her. How much should he reveal? She had been on the other side of Harfleur's wall just that morning.

He shrugged, allowing her to think he did not care. "'Tis not my concern."

Brigitte's shoes dug into the soft grass. "You think I do not see what is written on your face?" She shook her head. "I know you are a man who cares." Her lithe finger tapped the corner of her eye. "I'm taught to notice many things." She twirled it in the air. "To hear many things."

Drem blinked. The leather purse tied to his belt now spun between her fingers.

"And to acquire many things of value." She patted his chest before dropping the purse into his palm. "You have a good heart." She grinned up at him and winked. "I think I shall keep you. But first, I shall help you heal. Come with me. I shall tell you what we must gather."

Drem's steps faltered as she led him by the hand. She meant to keep him? Shite. What did she mean by that? She was his prize, not the other way around.

She urged him on as she ticked off the supplies. "I must gather thyme and sage. Lavender. Mint. We will also need garlic." Her face scrunched in thought and she added, "I'll need you to procure vinegar. Do your surgeons use it to cleanse wounds?

Drem snapped his mouth closed. "This is all for me?"

"Of course not." She waved her hand toward the camp. "'Tis payment for my safe passage away from this place."

Brigitte hid the smile that kept creeping up on her like a thief. *Merde.* What reason did she have to be giddy? No home. That foul Alexandre had Maman's broken necklace, her only connection to what was left of the memory of her mother. And he had her stash of coins. She would find a way to make him pay, to beg for mercy.

"Bee," Piers called out. His sweet voice turned her from her dark thoughts. They paused to let Darrick and the boy catch up with them.

Drem's fingers twitched under her palm. "I should have my hands free," he muttered.

Darrick cocked a brow in their direction. "Where are you headed?"

"Been suggested a bath would do a person good," Drem said. He slung his arm around Brigitte's shoulders, drawing her tight to his side. Her ribs reverberated from the steady thumping of his heart.

"The pool?" Piers piped up.

He bounced on the balls of his feet with more energy than she could muster. Her aching leg reminded her that she, too, needed a rest. The cold, clean water beckoned her from just over the knoll.

"*Oui*, Piers." She held out a hand. "'Tis certain you are in need as well."

"Lad, 'tis best you stay with me." Sir Darrick placed a restraining hand on the boy's slim shoulder. "Drem, there are signs of riders."

"French?" The rhythm shifted inside his chest.

"*Oui*," Piers said. He glanced down at the toes of his boots. "But they are not from Burgundy." He thumbed his chest. "This I would know."

"How many?" Drem scanned the hillside. He drew Brigitte closer, repositioning his body to shield her.

"No more than forty," Darrick said. "Keep an eye out for them.

"Seeking out information?"

"Or intimidation. Riders were already sent out to protect the archers. They ran the cowards off."

"Time for them to return to their nursemaids and have their nappies changed," Drem scoffed.

"But one must be aware."

"This I know," Drem murmured.

Brigitte flinched, caught by the surprise of his lips pressed to the top of her head. She pushed against the captivity of his arm. "Should we return to the camp?"

"No." He slid his thumb down her cheek. "As you said, I am in need of mending." The pad of his thumb, no doubt callused from time spent wielding a sword. "As are you."

Darrick clapped his hand on Drem's forearm. His stern countenance, a frown etched in place from too many years of scowling, made Brigitte's skin prickle. "We will watch for you. Be sure to return before the sun lowers."

"Aye," Drem said, accepting his counsel. He looked up at the sky. "Rain is coming. Best be on our way."

Grabbing Brigitte, he began to trudge up the hill. On impulse, she planted her feet long enough to look up at Harfleur's outer wall. Men stood along the buttress. Did she know them? Wishing she did not, she brought her hands up to her eyes. Squinting through curled fingers, she peered at the blond cap of hair that stood out like a shiny coin amid the dust. Her breath caught. "Master Alexandre." His head jerked in her direction. As if sensing her observation of his actions. Her back stiffened. "What is he doing on the parapet?"

She scanned the rest of the men. *Le Défenseur*, Raoul de Gaucourt, stood by his side. Did they have information that they would soon be delivered from the English army?

Chapter 13

Brigitte hastened her pace to the pool. Hidden by the grove of trees, it would provide privacy. More important to her, it would hide them from Master Alexandre's probing eyes.

"Don't be afraid," Drem called. "If I can protect our king, you should trust that I am well able to protect us from a small band of French nobles and their men-at-arms." His hand slipped over the hilt of his sword. "See, 'tis near and at the ready."

She ignored his reassurances and tugged on his hand. The soles of her shoes slid over moss and gravel, carrying her faster than she had anticipated. The air slammed out of her lungs when she hit the ground. Drem followed, sliding behind her and into the ravine.

They came to a stop, resting in a thick overgrowth of wild vines. The gentle sound of water gurgling over stones blended with their ragged breaths.

Unfamiliar laughter bubbled into her throat. She turned to see Drem's flushed face. Their eyes met. So many flecks of gold. They were like faerie lights in a forest.

Laugh lines crinkled as his chestnut brows arched. His lips, full and lush, lifted. In one swift movement, light as a pickpocket's touch, he leaned over to place a kiss near her mouth. He smelled of sweets, almond and honey. Like a warm pastry.

Brigitte caught the back of his neck and drew him closer. Their lips sunk deeper. Tongues touched, dancing and sipping. She tasted in return. Mint and ale.

Closing her eyes, she reveled in the pleasure cascading through her limbs. She wrapped her arms around him, holding on to the unfamiliar swell of desire crashing into her core. The herbal scent of crushed vines and fresh water, mixed with the intoxicating sound of the waterfall nearby. The crack of a dry branch caused them to freeze, their lips pressed together.

She snapped her lids open. The look Drem gave her silently told her to remain still and quiet. Not one to scream, she tipped her head.

He slid over, slowly rolling onto his stomach. He touched a finger to her lips. Still under the power of seduction, she allowed a small nip into the pad. The green in his eyes flared. A breeze blew across her damp skin. She took a shallow breath and dug her nails into the earth. She nearly had lost her head with this man while the enemy stood nearby. Enemy? She didn't know who the enemy was anymore. Even her mind and body betrayed her with this man.

Restless, she tired of waiting and rolled to slide down the rest of the way to the stream. She gasped when she felt a tug on her ankle. Drem lay below her; hand over-hand, he drew her down until she lay beside him.

His mouth returned where it had left off. Nipping and nibbling.

She pushed her palm between them. "Was anyone there?"

He cupped her hand, weaving their fingers together until they touched the core between her legs.

"Please." Her body betrayed her once again with little tremors. "I mean . . ."

"Shh. Trust that we are safe. 'Twas a wee rabbit. Nothing more." He nuzzled her neck and then, in one fluid motion, he rose and carried her to the pool. The crash of water over the stones brought the sensation of their flooding passion. It threatened to overtake Brigitte and wash her over the edge. Sanity slowly returned when he set her on a rock by the waterfall.

Drem used his toes to remove his boots one by one. "Sweeting, cast off your shoes."

Brigitte wrinkled her nose. "Someone should stand watch."

He moved closer and knelt beside her. Lifting her foot, he peeled off her shoe and hose. Long, graceful fingers caressed her feet and calves. Something akin to a kitten's mewling escaped her firmly pressed lips.

"Join me." Picking her up as if she weighed no more than an empty purse, he waded into the water. "'Twould feel so good." He cradled her in his arms and sank until the water touched their chins. When she tried to drift away, he clamped a hand on her thigh to keep her settled on his lap. "To be clean again," he whispered.

Brigitte shivered despite her efforts to remain aloof. There was so much man touching . . . everywhere. "Drem, I . . ."

His lips came down, slow, like rain in the last days of autumn. A steady drizzle. Then a downpour rushed over her.

He let go of her leg to reposition his hand on her waist. She floated up, skirts swelling, sailing like a cloud over a cerulean blue sky.

"Sweeting." He cupped her jaw and pressed his forehead to hers.

The laces holding the front of her bodice drooped, slipping from their moorings. He caught the lace with his teeth and drew it down until it let loose her treasures. Her breasts bobbed in the water near his mouth.

"My sweet *caru*." He leaned forward and caught the nipple. Suckling, he swirled his tongue over the succulent flesh.

Moaning, she grabbed the back of his head, raking her fingers through his hair. "Oh, *oui*."

With one hand, he untied his leggings. Stripping them off, he lay bare his pride and brought her down. Her skirt swelled, lifting over his legs. Dipping his hand, he palmed her mons. Its luscious folds unfurled like an exotic flower. Swirling his fingers over her nub, he felt the tip begin to grow.

He tested her opening with his finger. The eager walls contracted. His shaft nodded, throbbing with need. Mindful of their bruised bodies, he balanced her on his thighs. The water lifted her slight weight and allowed him to settle her on his cock. The tip nudged the opening. She wrapped her arms around his neck bringing her breasts to his mouth. He sought one and then the other nipple, lapping, nuzzling. "Please," she moaned.

Gripping her bottom, he lifted and then brought her cheeks home to meet his stones. Her walls sheathed him, tight. Like a new sword going into a scabbard. Unyielding. *Virginal.*

Brigitte gasped and froze. Her mewling quieted. Her passionate embrace around his shoulders loosened.

Shite!

He slid a strand of jet hair from her slender neck. His scarred hand trembled next to her perfect flesh. "My *caru*. Tell me you are not a virgin."

Her dark mane hid her face as she shook her head. Her fingers kneaded his shoulders. "I can't." She took a shuddering breath. "'Twould be a lie."

He swallowed the dry patch that formed on his tongue. A virginal thief? Did they exist? "Then I shall stop." He cleared his throat. "I shall do your bidding, my lady. My *caru*."

He shifted. The movement made her bob over his sword, still alert and ready. His bollocks screamed against his arse. They wanted release as badly as he did. More so, he wanted her. This Robin Hood in skirts drove him to distraction. A floral scent lifted from the misting water. It was as if he could taste her in every droplet.

"What does that mean? *Caru*?" She slid her hands over his chest. "I like the sound when you say it."

His nipples pebbled. He swirled his fingers over her hips, the roundness of her bottom. *He said that?* He searched his fuzzy brain. "'Tis Welsh." Rattled, he swallowed. "For *love*."

"Love," she mouthed against his lips.

Her hands slipped under the water. She began her exploration at his belly, running her palm over his ribs, smoothing over his hip, down his thighs and back again. Soothing and exciting. He throbbed, bouncing, nudging her palm until she complied, like a quick learner, and wrapped her fingers around him. He found her nub again, swirling until she let out a breathy, "*Oui*."

He gritted his teeth, praying to the Almighty that he would not spill his seed before seeing to her pleasure. Her newly found passion matched his, surpassing all he could imagine. A wave of desire swept over him, tumbling him in the seas, dragging him down until he could no longer breathe. He held on to the last threads of control, waiting for her release. And then she crashed with him, rising up out of the pool she called heaven.

They sucked air into their lungs like drowning souls cast from the sea. Aye, sweet *caru*, she was right. He had found heaven.

"Mine," he claimed into her neck. "Mine."

The first drops of rain splashed the tops of their heads, shaking them from the dream spun from the threads of passion. They had taken a chance, betting against discovery. 'Twas only a matter of time before someone came looking for them.

"We must hasten before our absence is noted." Drem sighed, reluctantly releasing her from his embrace. He assisted with the bodice, helping her put it back together. His hands shook, fumbling with the ties until she stilled his efforts and took over. Water glistened on her breasts. Like morning dew on a rose.

"I still have to see to the burns." Waves lapped at the edge of the pool as she waded to shore. She shook her skirt, wringing out the water. Her unplaited hair clung to her shoulders. The jet strands grazed her hips as she bent over.

"They are of no consequence." Drem took in a breath, already feeling the loss of her touch. "In truth, you have a healing way about you. 'Tis a worthy talent to have."

Gasping, Brigitte turned away. Her stiffened back walled him off, keeping him from reading her emotions. Her eyes on the ground, she searched behind the heavy foliage. "*Merde*," she muttered. "Think you that it means so little?

She paused in her muttering to cast a glance over her shoulder. Drem was certain she hoped it would shrivel his bullocks.

"*Fils de chien!*" Spinning around, eyes snapping, hands on her hips, she shouted at him as if to help him translate. "Son of a dog."

"What did I say?" He lifted the wet leggings from the boulder. Hopping on one foot, he thrust his legs in and gave chase. "What did I do?"

Her dark eyes glittered over rosy cheeks. Never had he felt so outmatched with an opponent as he did in that very moment. He searched her hands for weapons.

"Brigitte. I . . ." Would that he could repair what was damaged in moments of passion. Thoughts tumbled through his mind. *I took her virginity.* His loins tightened. *Aye, I still want her.* But what did he have to give her for something that could never be replaced?

"How dare you?" She wiped sweat and tears from her cheeks. "I'm not like Maman. I'll never be a *putain*." She shook her fist. "Not for Master Alexandre. Not for you!"

Drem dodged her fists and grabbed her arms, trapping them by her sides. "*Putain?*" Understanding began to seep into his passion-sated brain. "A whore?"

She hissed another curse. Her fingers flexed like a cat preparing to strike.

"No, *caru*. I meant no such a thing. Never."

Taking his life and those of his future children in his hands, he drew her in, wrapping his arms around her tense shoulders. Soothing her the best way he knew, he pressed his lips to her neck. He traveled to the sensitive spot he had found earlier behind her ear. Threading his fingers through her hair, he stroked her scalp until she sighed against his lips. The tension left her shoulders and back.

She tilted her chin. The depths of her eyes were bottomless and filled with heartache. Her mouth trembled as she searched for words. "*Merci*. I . . . forgive me. I thought . . ."

Drem kissed the back of her hand. He wished for more but restrained himself. There would be time for more, he promised himself. For now, he would be content to relieve her mind of any confusion. "You're mine because I care for you, Brigitte. I vow to protect you and never intend to harm you." His thumb slid over her lower lip. Before they returned to the madness of the siege camp, he had to sip at her sweetness once more. His mouth hovered over hers, waiting for her leave to steal another kiss. "Do you believe me?"

Grabbing the back of his head, she drew him to her waiting, parted lips.

Brigitte leaned over Drem's bare back. Their time in the cool water had taken some of the swelling out of his burns. She ached to place a kiss next to the scars. Lick the salt from his skin. Would he let her?

The words he had whispered still rang in her ears. *Mine*. What did he mean? She was not the same as her *maman*. She would not fall in love and be hurt when he abandoned her. But in the meantime . . .

She traced the white scars. The wedge of muscle, steely hard from so many hours of training. Even though chausses now covered his body like a second skin, she recalled the shape of his buttocks. They fit so well in her hands. She felt her core twitch deep inside her mons.

He flinched as she licked the drops of water from his shoulder. "You must be still," she ordered.

He took her hands, prying open her fingers. "What is this?"

"'Tis a snail." The creature's slime oozed over her palm. "For your burns." The look of horror turned this strong man into a frightened little boy. She could not contain a giggle. "Now, let me tend you." Her laughter ripped through the grotto as he pulled her into his lap. "As your king ordered."

Sighing dramatically, he unclasped his arms and set her free. Picking up his sword, he braced it across his thighs. The planes of his shoulders bunched and flexed as he cleaned the blade. "As you insist," he grumbled. "I assure you, my king would not order snails."

She kissed his ear, rimming the pink shell with her tongue as she spread the natural salve over his wounds. "And what of the other part of our day?"

"Aye," the male voice shouted from the trees. "What would your king say about that?"

Chapter 14

Brigitte recognized that voice. She almost did not believe it was him. His fashionable attire was gone. In its place was a padded gambeson and helmet. When she saw the cane, she knew it was the master of the Nest. Outrage beat a drum against her chest. She rose, emptying her palm of the snails.

"Alexandre, what are you doing on this side of Harfleur's walls? Have you betrayed the townspeople the same way you did me?"

Drem shoved her behind him. "Stay back," he hissed.

He stood, one palm braced against his well-formed hip, the other settled where his scabbard hung. "My lady Brigitte asked you a question. What do you want?"

"Bee," Alexandre said, "you cut me deep. I never meant you harm."

"*Oui.* You did and you will again." She pushed past the wall created by Drem's body. "Because that is who you are." She started up the hill, only to be stopped by a tug on her arm. "Where is Maman's necklace?"

"You speak nonsense. I don't know what you're talking about." Alexandre's knuckles whitened against his cane. His beloved weapon twirled in his hands. He came to stand beside an elder tree. "Is this how you repay my kindness?"

Drem drew his sword. The steel sang. It reflected the sun, catching the master of The Nest by surprise.

A destrier charged over the wall of bushes protecting the grotto. Its powerful chest drove into Alexandre, making him stumble. He pushed himself up from the ground, the limp more pronounced than usual. The piercing glare quickly shuttered behind a beguiling smile.

The cane twirled. Brigitte tensed. She knew what followed would bring pain.

Sir Nathan sat astride the chestnut war horse. The unsheathed broadsword rested over the pommel of the saddle. He shook his head. "Don't think you want to make that choice. Now do you?" He shifted the horse's head in Drem and Brigitte's direction. "Feel well enough to handle this one? Or shall I do it for you?"

The twirling slowed. "You can't harm me. I'm here for a parley with the king."

Leather creaked as Nathan leaned his forearm on his thigh. "'Tis so?" He scratched his jaw. "Then 'tis odd that you're here and those you wish to bargain with are down there." The sword whipped down, stopping at the jugular. "How many are with you?"

"A handful." Alexandre waved in the direction of the camp. "No doubt everyone is waiting for my return. I came for the wench." He drew himself up, back straight with forced outrage. "That soldier kidnapped her. No doubt used her." He snapped the cuffs of his jupon. "She is my fledgling and even if she is damaged, I want her back."

"Is that so?" Shock widened Nathan's eyes. A corner of his mouth ticked, jerking against a smile, until he smoothed it with a gloved hand.

"No," Drem said. He put his arm around Brigitte's waist.

"Good to see you're yourself again." Nathan motioned, and the hillside filled with foot soldiers. Archers moved out from the shadows of tree trunks and into position. "I believe we have an appointment with a siege party."

He shifted the reins. The foot soldiers moved closer, their swords drawn.

Drem pricked Alexandre's neck with his blade. "We're happy to grant you an escort."

"You expect me to walk all the way?"

"Aye, I do," Drem said.

Sir Nathan grinned. Leaning over, he held out his palm for Brigitte. "My lady?"

Brigitte looked at the great horse towering over her. To be up so high? She glanced at Drem.

"Save your feet. Go with Sir Nathan." He waved over a soldier to keep Alexandre in place. His long fingers wrapped around her waist and lifted her up. "Step on his boot. 'Tis why they are so large."

"That and other things," Nathan said.

Terrified of the height, Brigitte clung to his broad back.

"Never ridden before?"

"*Oui*, just not one so monstrous."

"Aye." Nathan chuckled. He smoothed a palm over the horse's mane. "She's a beauty, isn't she?"

"Move," Drem growled from the formation of soldiers. He kept his prisoner in the center, guarded at all flanks.

Alexandre sputtered at the prodding of Drem's sword. Brigitte squinted, trying to see the boy she once trusted. 'Twas impossible. That boy had been replaced by a heartless thief. Master Alexandre was up to something. His plans served no one but himself and his pockets. She would make certain that this time he did not succeed. And she would take what was hers.

Sir Nathan directed the horse to gallop ahead of the small army of men. Brigitte gripped with her thighs and prayed to the saints that she would not fall to her death. Her prayers were answered when he slowed their pace to a walk. She let loose the breath she hadn't realized she held and began to melt into the steed's gait.

"What does Master Alexandre want with you?"

"I . . . I don't know." Brigitte uncurled her cramped fingers from Sir Nathan's gambeson. "All I have ever been to him is someone who had a way with stealing."

"Ah, so you do not come from Harfleur?"

"No."

He ran a soothing palm over the mare's shoulders. "You wish to return to him?"

"No." Brigitte did not like the direction of his questions. She searched the horizon. Did he think she still worked with Alexandre?

"And how is it you came to this little harbor town?"

Did he test the strength of her allegiance? The towering knight would be surprised to learn she did not know the answer to that question either. She cared for the townspeople. The children of the Nest. But Master Alexandre? She now saw the darkness of his soul. No matter his plans, he would not take her down so easily.

"I was brought here by three men. After Maman died. I was to go to Calais, but they said Harfleur was a better place for me. They laughed at their little joke as their fancy carriage rolled through the gates." Brigitte dug her nails into the saddle. "Master Alexandre found me on the street the second night. I had thought him my friend, but that is no more."

She shifted to tap on his shoulder. "Sir Knight, do not trust anything he says."

"'Tis sound advice." He narrowed his eyes and nodded. "I'll keep that in mind."

Drem watched Nathan ride off with his woman. *She is mine!*

He marched toward camp. Their guest for the parley hobbled in front of him. Sweat dripped down his spine. Drem tested his back, twisting and turning. No amount of stretching made the burns scream with irritation. He would never admit it to Brigitte, but the treatment of snail slime had worked.

Master Alexandre complained the whole way down the hill. Drem knew the man was capable of base acts. Twice he'd witnessed Alexandre's attempts on Brigitte's life. Drem was ready to run the bastard through with his sword.

He found it interesting that as they neared the encampment, his need for his cane increased. The man was also a charlatan.

A group of archers headed up the hill. They carried axes along with their bows and arrows. Armed soldiers marched beside them, escorting the men to the wooded glen. Sir Darrick brought his mount up and waited.

"Don't take your eyes off him," Drem said to the soldiers. "I'll catch up with you shortly."

Sir Darrick nudged the animal forward. "Have you seen signs of the French?"

"Only the man they call Master Alexandre."

"Odd that he should go in the opposite direction, don't you think?" He shifted in the saddle, bracing a gauntlet-clad forearm on the pommel. "The archers are ordered to find timber to make posts for the trenches. I'll be on my way as soon as they are settled."

Drem nodded. "Remind them to make haste. There is bound to be trouble soon enough. The few skirmishes we've had have been too small. They are patient and will outwait us."

The hair on his neck prickled. Had it been only a rabbit? Or had the enemy directed Alexandre to the grotto? Parley or not, Drem intended on having a private meeting with the man.

"Henry is impatient," Darrick said. "I fear this parley will not go well for any of us."

"Aye. We are all ready for this siege to end."

A cold breeze swept over the hillside, pushing the meadow grass, bending it to its will.

"'Twould be well that we are on the march before fall sets in."

The crisp air bit into Drem's skin. His stomach twisted. A bitter autumn would be here before anyone was prepared. "Will the one they call the Defender attend the meeting with our king? Or are we to waste our time with the master?"

"De Gaucourt refused and sent out his emissary." Darrick snorted. "Mayhap he hopes we will do him the favor of killing Alexandre."

"'Twould not be that difficult." He shrugged. "Brigitte might even do it for us." Her fury flashed in his mind, warning him that he had best clear the air regarding the broken bit of necklace he had taken from the master.

Darrick lifted the reins, tugging the beast's head toward the archers. "Best catch up with them before Piers gets to him first." He paused. "The boy tells an interesting tale of how he arrived at Harfleur. If I didn't know better, I'd fear he's been kept hidden."

Drem scratched day-old whiskers. "To be ransomed? Who would pay it?"

"That is for us to discover." Darrick waved a salute in Drem's direction. "For now, know that the woman and boy are under our protection."

Drem hastened after the small group of men and caught up with them in no time at all. Their pace hampered by Alexandre's limp, they barely made it to the edge of the encampment.

His thoughts tumbling, he searched the people sitting outside the wall. Soldiers, women, those who were ill, afflicted with belly pain. He walked past those who had succumbed to the ravages of the sickness. Their tortured bodies were placed in a pit while the French waited for the rest of the English army to fall. He held his breath to keep from breathing in the stench and disease.

Where was she?

"Sir Drem," Piers called out as he ran to meet him. He came to a sudden halt. Eyes rounded, he looked like a scared rabbit about to bolt for the brush.

Drem knew fear when he saw it. He jerked his head in the direction of the boy's stare.

'Twas toward Alexandre. What was it he had kept exclaiming all the way down the hill? That he was not about to let a bitch steal one of his fledglings.

Drem tightened his grip on the sword's hilt. He waved Piers close and draped his arm protectively over his shoulder. "You're in good health. Have you seen our Brigitte?"

Alexandre's color went from pale as gruel to a flushed red. The cane stayed in his hand, clutched in a death grip. Drem's next step was to have that thing taken away, and he did not give a fig if the man toppled over like a stool with a broken leg without it.

"Aye. I saw her last talking to Sir Nathan. I'll fetch her now."

"Good lad. Have her meet me in our tent."

Piers scampered off in search of his Bee. Drem smiled. Darrick's watchful attention agreed with Piers.

Drem glanced at the glowering master of the Nest. He could roast a wild boar over the hatred flaring from Alexandre's black looks.

The master flicked his fingers and flashed a coin, then made it disappear.

Drem scrubbed his jaw. The reflexive need to find Brigitte itched, like an unreachable rash.

Alexandre supplied a smile, full of bared teeth that never reached his cold eyes. Tilting his head in a nod, he shrugged and dusted his hands of invisible dirt.

Movement over the ridge caught Drem's eye. A flash of sunlight. And then another, reflecting suits of armor, showing off a string of steel.

They thundered down the hill toward the group of archers.

"Sir Darrick," Drem shouted. "To arms, men! To arms."

His muscles flexed. It was too far to run to help them. He would never reach them in time. His broadsword was in the tent. No time to go for it now.

Drem spun on his heels. One of the wagon horses stood tethered to a cart. He grabbed the harness and leaped on the beast's back. He bent low and slapped its rear. It jumped forward, nearly unseating him. Memories of his childhood in Wales flooded his racing heart. No need for a saddle. He and the horse would do it together.

In the time it took him to locate a mount, several of the other soldiers were riding alongside him, shouting at the French curs. He cut his glance to the grim-faced knight, matching his pace. Nathan leaned forward, his broadsword swinging from his hip. They drew their swords in unison. Light bounced off the metal, reflecting the sun.

The images of the men he had trained with, fought with, flashed in his mind as some of them went down. The fighting quarters were too close for the archers to get off shots. The French knights swarmed Darrick's destrier. Their swords slashed and hacked at the men. As Drem drew closer, he saw that a few of the men carried cudgels and heavy maces. Some used the posts they had already cut from the elder trees.

"For England and King Henry," he shouted, uniting his force with those around him.

His mount shied from the deafening clash of metal, the cries of pain. Drem took off, propelling his way into the melee.

All too soon, the skirmish was over. The French retreated, their damage done. Three archers had fallen from the cut of well-placed swords. Another had had his skull caved in from the blow of a mace.

"Darrick!"

The wounded knight leaned across his destrier. The horse bled from cuts, a gash running over his rump. Both bloodied, but they were still standing. Darrick ran a hand over the animal, cooing softly in its ear.

"Drem. 'Tis good to see you." Nathan joined them and clasped their shoulders. "My thanks for leaving a few of them for me to send off."

Drem shook his head. "I feared we would not arrive in time."

Darrick grimaced. "Henry?"

"In his tent." Nathan grinned. "Pax. He has his sword and knows how to wield it should the need arise."

Drem watched over the men as they began the task of helping the injured and the dead or dying. They looked up as a cart rattled up the hill. Brigitte sat on the bench. Her mouth was set in grim determination as she pulled on the reins.

* * *

Brigitte gritted her teeth and fought the horses that would rather stay in the camp. They could smell death spread over the valley. So much destruction.

Piers had told her Drem's orders were to meet him at the tent. But how did he expect her to sit and wait? She had tried, but the sounds of the battle ate at her stomach. Bile reached her throat. She had to do something. She knew ways to help heal the injured and could haul the men back to camp in the cart. It made sense for her to do more than hide inside a tent and wait for news. That last brought her to make the decision to steal the cart and go out to the battlefield. What if Drem needed her?

She searched the meadow. Silence bore down on the small band of men. Only the sound of sweet grasses as the breezes caught their bobbing heads and rubbed them together.

One man separated from the group and headed toward her. Broad shoulders swayed as he ate up the distance between them. Relief turned her legs to liquid. She tightened her fingers over the reins.

"Stop," he shouted, motioning for her to stay.

The firm line of his mouth cut across his flushed face. His rigid back and marching pace urged Brigitte to obey his order. The cart horses bounced their great bodies into each other. Their ears twitching, they blew out nervous breaths and stamped their hooves.

Dark stains slashed across his chest. Sweat glistened on his forehead. Brigitte made an inventory of his strong limbs. He did not limp. Nor did he brace his arms.

Her legs shook as she disembarked from the cart. Licking her lips, she untangled her skirts and tried to regain control of the tremor that threatened to shake her to her core. She ran to him, her arms outstretched, aching to hold this man she barely knew yet cared so much for. "Drem, I . . ."

"Brigitte, you shouldn't be here." He started to touch her and withdrew his red-stained hand. "Stay where you are."

"I came to help." Her arms dropped to her sides. "If you don't need me, mayhap those who are injured do."

Grimacing, he glanced over his shoulder. "Aye, but I would spare you the gore from the skirmish."

"I've tended all matter of injuries at the Nest." She touched the spot above his heart. The padded gambeson had a tear in it that ran from neck to breastbone. Her pulse fluttered. She examined the hole. A blade had come close to ending his life. No blood. She took a deep breath to clear her muddled brain and press her point. "I've seen enough to know that I won't lose my nerve." Turning back to the cart, she picked up the reins and led the beasts toward the men.

He caught up with her and matched his paces with hers. "I'll take the reins."

Brigitte stared at his outstretched hands. Small nicks marred his tanned skin. He had gone to the aid of the other men without thinking of his own safety. "I'm well able."

At her resistance, he added, "These horses aren't battle ready. They'll balk when they smell blood."

"Here." The burn of blisters from the reins pulsed over her fingers.

Adjusting her gaze, she knelt beside an English soldier. She rubbed damp palms over her thighs and began accessing his injuries. Men who could walk on their own had started the trek to camp. The fallen who would never return home to their families were being tended by their brothers in arms or being loaded in the cart.

A French soldier called out to her. She turned to the man. His lower limbs were bent.

"Brigitte," Drem said softly. "Our men come first." He gave her arm a gentle squeeze. "I'll see to him."

"*Oui*," she said, glancing over at the injured man. The standard on his soiled jupon was a dancing lion. Like the one that had been emblazoned on the side of the carriage that had brought her to Harfleur and then abandoned her. She turned her back and wondered at the cold heart that would do such a thing to a child.

"Please." A boy, not much older than Piers, trembled on the ground. His shallow breaths shuddered as he fought the pain. Blood spread down his arm. "Please," he hissed through clenched teeth. "I need me arm."

"Young John, is it?" Her heart ached for him.

His brows beetled. "An archer, you see."

She soothed him, her palm on his forehead. "Let's get you to camp."

Drem knelt beside him. "Young John, 'twas an honor to fight beside you. You fought like a bear."

Sweat glistened on the boy's pale cheeks. "Please, Sir Drem, don't let them cut it off."

Brigitte ripped off a strip of material from her skirt to staunch the flow of blood. Young John caught her fingers. "Promise me?"

Not wanting him to see anything but hope, she kept her gaze on his face. "I promise." She swallowed, praying she could fulfill his request.

"As do I," Drem said.

Tears scorching the back of her throat, Brigitte rose and wiped her bloodied hands on her skirts. "Let's get back to camp."

She flinched as they walked past the fallen banner. Her heart thundering against her ribs, she stared at the dancing lion and recalled a childhood memory of an outing with Maman and Monsieur le Faire.

Chapter 15

Drem held Young John's hand until they reached the surgeon's tent. Fury boiled under his skin. The time to negotiate with Harfleur had passed.

He ducked his head. It would take a miracle for them to survive unscathed. He clenched his fingers. The swan coin the French soldier had slipped into his hand as Drem bent over him now bit into his palm and his conscience. How did the swan fit with the one he had hidden from Brigitte and the other he'd hidden from his brothers? Torn at whom to trust and whom to turn to, he decided to keep his own council until he knew more.

"Remember your promise," the boy said. He gave Drem a watery smile.

"Aye, lad. I'll have a word with the surgeon." He ruffled Young John's hair. "You're one of my finest archers. King Henry needs you to heal quickly."

Without a word, the surgeon, Flanners, had the boy carried into the tent. Drem kept silent, biting his tongue. The surgeon would know what to do. Wouldn't he?

"Brigitte." He plunged a cup into a barrel of water. "Hold out your hands so we might wash."

"*Oui.*" She shuddered from the chilled water as layers of dirt and God knew what else slid off.

'Twas always a relief to remove the remnants of a battle. He looked over her shoulder. Nathan and another soldier had braced their arms together and carried Darrick from the surgeon's tent. In a foul mood, his leg bandaged, Darrick nodded his head, motioning for Drem to follow.

Drem tossed away the drying rag, stained by the use of others.

"I apologize. I must . . ." He needed to follow orders, but to stand with Brigitte a moment longer, just until he knew she would be all right . . .

"Go," she said, shaking off drops of water from her hands.

He hesitated, fearing she might fall over in exhaustion. Her fair skin, a stark contrast to her dark hair, was closer to the color of porridge. Shock registered in her wide eyes.

"I'll stay with the young archer." She waved off his assistance and squared her shoulders.

"A moment." Drem cupped her jaw. Tilting her head, he placed a tender kiss on her mouth. Despite the horrors of the last hour, she responded to his touch. Her lips softened, trembling against his.

She slipped her hand over his. "Come for me as soon as you are able," she whispered.

He withdrew and suddenly ached from her absence. "Stay alert."

"And stay safe," Brigitte said as she scrubbed her hands against her arms. "Drem . . ."

"Aye?" Guilt washed over him. He could swear her mother's damned brooch with the ugly swan was pecking at him.

She narrowed her eyes, her hand cupped over her brow, searching the grounds. "Where's Alexandre?"

"Perhaps he is still trying to negotiate with my king."

"I don't like it." She stood, rooted to the entrance of the tent. "'Tis unlike him to be so visible."

"Trust that all is well, *caru*," he reassured her. As soon as he said the words, he felt the gnawing beast of doubt.

Brigitte nodded. Taking a deep breath, she lifted the flap. A haunted shadow passed over her gaze. The stench of sweat, blood, and the refuse from sickened men wafted through the air.

"I'll come for you. I promise."

The corner of her mouth tugged into a crooked smile and she waved him on.

Drem tramped toward the tent where he would meet his brothers. He prayed they would speak quickly and that there would be no prying questions. *Shite. Am I expecting miracles?*

He ducked his head to gain entrance. Shadows danced across the canvas walls. Men he had never noticed before were in attendance. He scanned the tent. Darrick lay on a cot, his leg bandaged from thigh to below the knee. A red stain bloomed on the bandage. His exertion to join the others must have jarred the wound.

The men crowded around the cot as they gave their report.

"Three injured."

"Four dead."

"Pits and trenches are dug."

"Posts cut and sharpened."

"Welsh miners are digging as fast as they can."

"Sabotage."

"Sit down," Darrick said.

They gathered stools or benches wherever they found them.

"Sir Drem, where's that shite-spreading Master Alexandre?"

"Left him with the soldiers when I ran to your aid, Sir Darrick." Drem cringed under the heavy silence. "They had their orders to bring him to camp. To stand guard over him until told otherwise."

Sir Nathan folded his arms over his chest. Dark stains marred his leather gambeson. "The fart-licking weasel must have known the skirmish didn't go his way. He gave the men the slip." His nostrils flared. "What does the woman and boy have to do with this?"

"Let it go, Nathan," Darrick said. "That boy, Piers, is a good lad who should never have been brought here. Says he comes from Burgundy."

"You've said enough." Nathan rose and waved a few of the men out of the tent. As soon as they were gone, he brought out his Knights of the Swan talisman. One by one, the others added their rings. The emblazoned swan was a reminder that some things were better left unsaid.

Drem let his roll out into his palm. He watched the swan wink back, mocking him for his stupidity. He should have said something about the messages someone was trying to get to him.

"We don't know what game the duke of Burgundy is playing," Nathan said. "There is infighting. His brothers . . ."

"The struggle between Armagnac and Burgundy continues."

Without taking his eyes off his brothers, Drem searched blindly for the leather pouch. His fingers came back empty. 'Twas gone. How could he explain what he had seen? What he had been given? Worse, he had lost the keepsake on which Brigitte had sworn vengeance on Alexandre.

"Too busy handling their illegitimate progeny." Darrick ran a shaking hand over his pale forehead. "The Duke of Burgundy was an ally at one time. I don't believe he will come to King Charles's aid this time. Orleans has too much control over the mad king."

"Where is Piers?" the outraged voice said from behind.

All but Darrick spun around to block the intruder.

Brigitte stood in the doorway. The short blade she carried gave everyone pause. Blood coated an old blanket she used as an apron to cover her damaged gown. Legs braced, hands on her hips, she looked like an avenging warrior priestess.

"Last I saw him, he was running to fetch you," Drem said softly. He reached out to soothe the fear from her brow. Realizing he had given the men something to note, he withdrew his hand.

"I thought . . . I thought to find him here. He likes you, Sir Darrick. 'Tis where they were to bring that wretched Alexandre. Is it not?"

Drem's mind began to spin. That little thief had lifted his leather purse when he ran up to him. He'd wager his last coin on it. "Would he run off with Alexandre?"

Brigitte's fingers curled tight around the blade they had yet to take from her fist. "Not willingly. No."

"The master could make him if the threats were against someone he cared for."

"Me?"

"Aye," Drem said.

She threw the blade on the table. "I've had enough of this siege."

Drem caught it before it fell over the edge. "And what would you have us do?"

"We've waited them out and given them time to seek reinforcements." Darrick lay on the cot, his leg propped. His flushed cheeks were like flares over his pasty skin. His hand never wavered from the hilt of his sword.

Brigitte took a tentative step closer. "Your men are digging in the wrong place."

A stocky man stepped out of the shadows. The familiar scar ran from nose to cheek. Drem recognized him at once. They had ridden together on many battles. King Henry would not take kindly to her criticism.

"Is that so? Seeing that you are an expert on this, tell us where you would have us dig. The man they call the master said to dig by the tunnels."

Brigitte narrowed her eyes, sizing him up. "Who are you?"

"No one of consequence, I assure you. But I do have the king's ear. What can you tell us about Harfleur that we have so grievously missed? We gave terms to de Gaucourt and still he refuses to surrender."

"Then tell your men to take the assault to the opposite side the master advised." She moved forward and knelt before him. "I beseech you. You have cut off the water and food. The bombardments continue to destroy the people. They can take no more."

She bent her neck, baring it to his possible wrath. "I have also seen the destruction of disease that ravages your men. There are things I can do to help them. Medicines, herbs that can alleviate their pain. Return their health. But I cannot do it here."

King Henry placed his hand on her head. "And if you are wrong?"

"Then I, too, am defeated."

Brigitte watched the English soldiers move their assault to the south side of Harfleur, as Alexandre had instructed. While they kept some of the soldiers in position to distract the citizens from their plans, a handful of men would sail their boats north, up the Lézarde.

And the English king would keep all Harfleur busy hiding from his guns and siege machines. All too soon, the bombardments began again. She flinched as another shot of stone struck the outer wall.

"You dare too much," Drem said.

She smothered a sigh as the heat of his body warmed her back. "I dare what I must. Alexandre is playing games with lives."

Turning from the sight of the men moving en masse, she searched the encampment for what felt like the hundredth time. "Have you seen Piers?

"No. I fear he has slipped away with Master Alexandre."

Brigitte frowned. "Why is Alexandre so determined to have him?"

"He spoke of financial gain."

"From whom?"

Drem placed his hand upon her shoulder and turned her attention away from the men. "We will find him. I promise." His thumb swirled in circles over her clenched jaw, her aching neck. "I will make it a priority to free him from Alexandre."

She leaned into him, wanting more. How did he manage to peel away the tension and worry and replace it with another need?

"Are you confident your plan will succeed?" he asked.

A shuddering breath came from somewhere deep inside her. "We can hope and pray. Or I can take steps to see that it will indeed break the siege."

His thumb slowed the dance over her skin and the trance began to fade. "What are you up to, my sweet *caru*?"

Brigitte shut her eyes. She did not want to see his censure when she explained the plan that had formed the moment the English soldiers began their move. Drem would not approve, but without it, the siege was bound to continue and more would surely die.

She caught his hand and pressed his palm to her cheek. Rolling it over, she placed a kiss in the center before folding his fingers over.

"A kiss to always keep beside you."

He wrapped his arms around her shoulders. His mouth moved over her scalp. "I am to help the men on the north side. I will return to you as soon as we have taken the wall." He pointed to a bundle on the cot. "'Tis for you."

Tears slid down her cheeks as she nodded in response. He hesitated long enough that she knew he questioned her behavior. After gathering his shield and sword, he ducked his head and left to do his duty for the king.

She ran her hands over a soft forest green woolen gown and gathered her cloak.

"The boy is ransomed!" Alexandre shouted. "I'm not about to let that fortune slip through my fingers."

"Now you have brought their attention to him. What do you think they'll do?" de Gaucourt asked, poking his finger into Alexandre's chest. "They'll wonder why you want him so badly." His nail dug into the gambeson. "And that woman, your precious Bee, will sniff him out like an angry mama bear."

"She is worth more to me hidden than found. There are those who never want her found." Alexandre pushed de Gaucourt's finger away. He hid his satisfaction when it bent back enough to cause the man to wince. "I gave the English king's men information that will keep them busy until reinforcements arrive. They are to struggle with the Leure Gate."

"Why would they believe you?"

"I told them you were weak. Your forces easily broken. They

think they have my allegiance. Not you. And they'll continue digging on the strong side of town." Alexandre noted the chink in Raoul's ego and quickly repaired it. "Of course 'tis a lie. That we both know."

"The south wall is well defended. But the people are beginning to voice concern. They need food and water. We have waited to hear word and yet nothing comes. Perhaps we should attempt to renegotiate. The English king's brother, the Duke of Clarence . . . would he be more sympathetic to our citizens?"

"No. I've seen the condition of their army. The soldiers are sick and weakened. They'll soon tire. Our reinforcements will annihilate them."

Le Défenseur was starting to show his weakness. 'Twas something Alexandre could not abide. Not when it put his life in jeopardy. De Gaucourt had assured him the town would never fall, but as a precaution, Alexandre had set into motion a plan to protect himself and leave Raoul de Gaucourt to deal with the avenging English.

"The boy. Piers." Raoul paced beside the window. "When Orleans hears he is in danger of being discovered . . ." He ran a palm over the back of his sweating neck. ". . . he will want to know how it happened." He looked up, his eyes glazed with panic. "I'll not be to blame this time."

Alexandre smelled his fear. Like rancid onions on the breath. "Nor will I." He twirled his hand, gesturing away the contagious anxiety. "Not to worry. It will never arise. That damned English king will never defeat us."

Chapter 16

Brigitte slipped through the tunnel that led into Harfleur. She rubbed her dampened palms over her soft woolen skirt. Piers's disappearance had caused her blood to chill. He would not leave without speaking to her first.

Guilt gnawed at her. She should have trusted Drem enough to tell him about the tunnel and her plans. She squashed the whispers from her conscience that he would never understand.

As a fledgling in the Nest, she had learned that timing was imperative for success. Once they learned there was a weaker entrance to attack, she became as invisible as a vapor of smoke. While the soldiers rushed to and fro like scurrying rats, she made use of that vaporous ability and left the tent unnoticed.

The relief in taking the necessary steps to find Piers and break the siege gave her the courage to go.

Thanks to Alexandre, the last time she had seen the citizens they had wanted her at the end of a swinging rope. Could she convince them to help breach the north wall and surrender to the English? 'Twas a gamble she was willing to take. Alexandre and de Gaucourt had to be stopped before all Harfleur was destroyed.

Resolute, Brigitte glanced to the shadows. She kept to the tumbled and shattered walls of toppled buildings. The town no longer resembled Harfleur as she had known it. It was a place of ruins.

The stench worked its way up through the alleyway. Covering her nose with her sleeve, she stumbled over the refuse. A hand, partially buried under debris, reached out in the struggle for life and lost the battle.

She hurried past the rubble. Dark pools stained the cobblestones. Fearing the next body she found would be someone she knew, she fought to keep from retching at the loss of life. Too much damage. Had anyone survived the bombardments?

What was left of an alleyway should have led to Claudette's laundry. The ground trembled. The buildings leaned to one side, threatening to collapse with the next explosion.

Her body slammed against the wall. No spirit flyer, but a warm and fleshly body wrapped around her waist. A tousled head of caramel pressed against her hip. *Piers!*

"What are you doing here?" he cried. His gaunt body dug into her hip.

Brigitte untangled his arms. Leaning over, she pressed her palms to her thighs. She drew in a ragged breath, proving to her racing mind that she was still alive.

"You were told to stay in the English camp. Why—"

"You're not supposed to be here. I promised—"

She caught his shirt before he could escape. "What?"

Tears welled in his sky blue eyes and a portion of her wrath began to melt under his gaze.

"Master Alexandre." Piers's lower lip began to quiver.

Her stomach clenched. "What has that monster done this time?"

"He saw me . . . lift something. Said the English would punish me. And when they did, you'd come after them." He gulped air like a landed trout. "I'd be responsible for your death if I didn't go with him."

Speechless, she hugged him tight. How could that man be so cruel?

"I don't want you to die too, Bee," he mumbled into her rib cage.

"Nor do I," she said. The fury-storm headed in their direction gave her pause. A mob of citizens marched toward them. Their buzz of rage boiled over. "We must hide before they decide to use a rope."

"Claudette will know what to do." Piers glanced over his shoulder before leading her into the alleyway.

Brigitte peered at the laundress's demolished building. "She lives?"

A beefy arm reached out of the shadows, grabbing Brigitte's sleeve. Before she could make her escape, she was wrapped in Claudette's embrace.

"Brigitte." One arm still in a dirty sling, Claudette gathered Piers to her ample bosom. "Hurry. Come this way." She directed them toward an angled doorway. Flicking her dress to remove the clinging dust and grime, she ushered them into the room. "'Tis temporary," she said.

Brigitte nodded. There was barely enough space to stand erect. Filth covered what was left of the laundry. But the air smelled only of smoke and was free of decay, a welcoming aspect from the death outside the doorway.

Colette stood with her arms braced over her ample chest. "So. What do you want?"

"To bring the siege to an end. To bring life back to Harfleur . . ." She gripped Claudette's fingers. "To surrender."

Claudette flinched under her hand. "To those English wolves?"

"I've seen what they can do. I know what they have. King Henry will not leave until Harfleur is released to him." Brigitte tightened her grasp. "Gather those who you trust. We'll bring this struggle for power to an end." She made one more assault. "*Le Défenseur* does not care for the citizens. Nor does our mad king."

"*Le Fou*." Claudette looked to see whether anyone had heard her and made the sign of the cross.

"'Tis all for their glory. Sacrifice the people." She squeezed her hand. "Let's stop this. Return to life. Mayhap a better life under the rule of a king who believes God has spoken and France must be returned to the rightful heir."

Claudette's eyes widened and then narrowed. "We will not be traitors?"

"No one must know."

Claudette shook free. "Then we do it together." She waved the air, clearing all possibilities but one. "No one else."

Brigitte nodded. The laundress had more than strong shoulders and arms. She had a sharp mind. They would make their way to the north side and find a way to let in the English. Once they controlled Harfleur, brought life back to normal, and rebuilt the town . . . the people would appreciate what had been done. Brigitte's neck itched, as if the heavy rope lay upon her shoulders like an anchor.

"Piers."

"*Oui*."

"Go. The same way I entered. Carry the message to Sir Drem. Hurry. Tell him. . . . tell him to make ready. We will open the tunnel near the Rouen Gate to the north." She gripped his wrists. "Do not let Master Alexandre or the fledglings see you."

His pale face flushed. "*Oui*."

* * *

"I'll strangle that woman," Drem muttered under his breath. "Then I'll kiss her back to life."

The news that Brigitte had disappeared reached him as they were about to breach the south wall. Unable to leave his post, Drem's only option was to dwell and stew on the fact that Brigitte had left him. Not an unusual state. Certainly not the first time someone he cared for had betrayed him. But this time . . . this time it ate at him like an old battle wound, a withering limb that ached to the core of his soul.

The bombardment hit the south side, echoing over the valley. The Defender's forces struck back. The blast rocked him on his heels. He braced his legs, ready for another.

Nathan rode up, his mount oblivious to the explosion of stone against stone. Smoke boiled over the wall and into the sky. He squinted into the setting sun. "Still believe your woman means no harm?"

Drem scanned the haze. He searched his soul. Did he trust her? Hadn't they spent time in the grotto? Knowing each other in ways only a man and woman could? "Aye," he said. "She'll tell us what she's up to in due time."

Nathan's horse snorted, as if to answer for his master. "'Tis a long path we chose. Bombardments are breaking through. Rather not stay here another day."

Drem bit the inside of his lip. Nathan's concern was more about the woman he had left on the north side than his desire to march to wherever their king led them. Drem shrugged. "No difference between here and the other side."

"Depends on the view." Nathan's grin, more feral than friendly, never reached his eyes. He shoved the scruff of hair from his face. "'Tis best you pray we confuse them. Our king grows impatient."

"I wager . . ."

A flurry of movement came forward. 'Twas like the spreading of the seas, parting for the messenger. *Piers? Where did he come from?*

"Let the boy pass," Drem shouted at the foot soldiers barring the way. He took a wide step forward. Then drew back and waited for Piers to meet him.

'Twas not the time to demand the return of his coin purse. There were more pressing needs. He would wait until they drew the information from the lad. But by God, he would teach the boy there were some who did not condone pilfering.

That morning Henry had decreed that Harfleur was not to be ransacked. 'Twas unwelcome news to the soldiers. Most had already planned how they would spend their deserved reward. But he was king of France, and Henry had pronounced that he would not allow stealing from his own people.

Piers dared not lift another item that was not his or there'd be worse than a verbal flogging coming his way. Drem feared the temptation for some would see him dangle at the end of a rope.

One of the foot soldiers clamped his hand over Piers's shoulder, guiding him through the troop of men. Nathan's destrier stamped, scaring off any would-be eavesdroppers. They made their way, pushing back until only the horse and rider remained to tower over everyone.

The boy panted as if he had run a race. His reddened cheeks flared under flashing eyes. He glanced away in the attempt to avoid Drem's gaze.

"None of that," Drem said. He motioned Piers over. "'Tis a surprise to see you."

"Bee," he puffed. "She sent me."

At the mention of her name, he searched the field. Hoping. "She comes?"

"No. I'm the only one small enough to get through the tunnel," Piers said. "'Tis partially collapsed, you see." His mouth, covered in dust, pinched into a frown. "She'll stay on the other side until we bring the wall down."

Dread filled Drem's stomach. It felt weighted, as if he'd eaten a load of the stone for the great guns. "Why did she send you?"

"Said to wait for the sun to set. There's a hidden gate to the north. Some of the shippers use it. 'Twas flooded by de Gaucourt's men. Watch for a light. Then you'll know 'tis clear to slip your men through." His message delivered, his knees buckled, dropping him to the ground.

Drem squatted next to him. "What of Alexandre? De Gaucourt?"

"They were gathering the citizens." He gnawed on his lip, catching a raw patch with his teeth. Worry marred his dirty face. "They followed me to her."

"Stay here." Drem rose. His hands clenched. He caught Nathan's eye. How was he to convince everyone else that they could not wait until sunset?

Brigitte clutched the stone to her chest and prayed no one would see her. Their plan was madness. Master Alexandre had his fledglings searching the town for Piers. And for her. He knew her too well and had been keeping watch for her return. Had he received word she had met with Claudette? Or had he purposefully allowed Piers to slip free?

She did not think it possible, but the fledglings were thinner now than they had been when she last tucked them into their pallets on the Nest's cold floor. Eyes sunken above sharp cheekbones. Pale skin stretched over thin bodies. Fear surrounded them, spurring them on.

Their relentless hunt kept her moving until she located the trader's tunnel.

Alexandre kept it secret for fear they would use it to escape the Nest's hold. Brigitte had followed him, using all the skills he had taught her. And then he had disappeared into the wall. Alexandre held no *magique* skills. There was an opening somewhere and she had vowed to find it.

The crevice, no bigger than a wedge cut into the stone, was usually underwater. With the flooding of the fields it now stood at eye level. If anyone happened to look up, she would be seen, a mouse hiding in its hole.

She watched the sun begin its slow, torturous decent. Time crawled. Like a creeping spider over her skin, it spun a web, trapping her with sticky threads of fear. Her bones ached from crouching in one position for so long. She eyed the shadows. They began to grow. Soon the joining of day into night would turn the evening sky purple.

If Piers had managed to get through the tunnel and reach Drem, he should have shared his message by now. The only way to know if he had succeeded was if they moved some of their army against the north wall and broke through the gates.

A chill seeped into the worn leather soles of her shoes. She moved back, her spine scraping the stone. The water level rose. The tide was coming in.

A light wavered against the wall overhead. Someone hovered over a broken parapet. The light winked off. Flashed on. Once. Twice. A third time. Claudette had fulfilled her mission.

'Tis now up to me. Courage swelled. *'Tis my time.*

Brigitte lowered herself until the water caressed her chin with fingers cold as ice. She took a shuddering breath and filled her lungs. Letting go of the ledge, she began to sink below the surface. The murky water swirled around her, blurring her vision. It weighted her skirts, dragging her in an iron fist. Too fast. Out of control. Her lungs burned, pressing, threatening to break her rib cage.

Pulling herself along the wall, she felt for the locked gate.

The descent took longer than she had expected. Her mind blurred. *What am I looking for?*

Sharp metal bit her fingers, bending them back. She cried out in pain. Precious air escaped, bringing the error crashing down. A flash of light stung the back of her eyelids.

The water churned as the muffled sound of bombardment struck again. Brigitte's mind cleared. 'Twas her only chance.

She gripped the iron handle and twisted. The gate swung open, dragging her out. Tumbling. Air ripped out of her lungs before she reached the surface.

Maman? Is that you?

Chapter 17

Drem knelt on the edge, marveling at the thick darkness of the water. He fisted his sword, preferring to do battle with a hundred men than wait for Brigitte to show herself. *Where can she be?*

"The parley has failed. The stubborn fools refuse us entrance. Harfleur must be taken by force." Nathan clasped his shoulder. "Come. We've waited long enough. The king's big gun is ready. We'll blow it open."

"Patience." Drem cringed. "She won't let us down."

"She's French. And a woman."

"Nay. She is fierce." His hand trembled as he wiped his mouth. He stared at the water's surface, willing her to come up for breath.

"That she may be. But there are many who are against her. You know that." He squeezed Drem's shoulder, making him wince. "Accept it."

"You saw the light. Just as Piers said. And this is where he told us to wait." He glared at Nathan and jerked out of his hold. "We stand firm. We wait. We gave her our vow. Just as she gave us hers."

"What is the plan after? Have you thought of that, young Drem?"

"She'll tell us when she arrives." Drem turned. "Please. Don't order the miners to retreat. Not yet. Give her a few moments longer . . ."

A wavering movement caught his eye. What would a fish be doing in this brackish water? Curious, he bent down on all fours. His heart thundered in his chest. Could it be?

His fingers cramped as he searched the frigid water.

"What do you see?" Nathan said from behind.

"Brigitte." Drem ignored the snort and reached out. Fabric slipped through his grasp. "'Tis her."

He jumped into the rushing stream and struck out toward the swirling material. He caught it. A skirt. Relief flooded him as, hand over hand, he reeled it in.

"Nay," he cried, his voice hoarse with emotion. He threw the empty skirt to the shore and clambered after it.

Panting, he lay on the rocky ledge.

"Sorry, Drem," Nathan whispered before abandoning their position.

The emptiness Drem felt matched only one other time. When he was a lad and a fortnight had passed since he had been taken from his family. He had felt all was lost.

And then, soon after, he had realized life had just begun.

Drem pushed up. His arms shook. His knees ground into the stone. "I'm here! Brigitte, I'm here!"

A shadow moved. It sent sheets of water raining over the tunnel floor.

The beauty rose up. Brigitte's gasp broke the silence like shattered ice. Then she sank.

"Brigitte." Drem dove in. He caught her, dragging her body to his chest. Stripped of all warmth, she was rigid and unyielding. Together they fell from the water.

He shoved her hair from her face. A ring of gray surrounded her purple lips. A bruise formed on her forehead as blood trickled into the arch of her brow

Drem knelt beside her and wept. Tears for her courage. Tears for her stupidity. Why hadn't she trusted him? They could have found another way.

He lay beside her. Too far away. He could not let her go so soon. Cradling her, he whispered, "*Caru*. Come back to me."

The tumbling had stopped. The burning lungs. The stinging eyes. Even her head no longer ached. She cursed the hunger for air that pushed her to rise too soon. She and the low ceiling of the underground tunnel had crashed into each other. Stars in a cold, moonless sky.

Brigitte floated after the light. *Maman?*

Do not let them win.

I'm so tired.

'Tis no time. Take off your skirt. Now.

Brigitte flinched at the order. She fumbled with the strings holding up the skirt. It drew away from her as easily as it had when she and Maman had servants to help them undress.

Free of the weight, she rose out of the water. Freedom slapped her awake long enough to gasp for breath. And then she sank deeper into the midnight depths.

'Tis right. 'Tis good. You are no longer alone.

Maman's tender croon rocked her as she floated across the sky. Up. Away from the struggle. Away from hunger. Away from the fight.

No! *You are not finished.*

"*Caru.*"

There was a handsome man who called her his love. She struggled to sit up, but the heaviness on her chest stilled her movement. Drem?

Her so-cold heart began to warm. It began to thump out a rhythm. Drem. Drem. Drem.

"*Cariad!* Beloved, come back to me!"

No longer wanted, the peace she had thought she craved felt like a trap. Brigitte swam through the murky darkness. Searching for the man who called out her name.

Heat beckoned her. A fire in the darkness. Having a target to aim toward, she pushed against the wavering veil and shot through.

Brigitte gasped. She filled her lungs with dank air and did not care.

The man clasping her close had his head buried in her neck. The warmth of his body drew her to his flame. A living light surrounded him.

She coughed, leaving her body weakened but completely free from the tunnel's grasp.

He drew away, taking the warmth with him.

Drem pressed his forehead to hers. "You're alive," he croaked.

Smoothing the hair from her face, he rained fiery kisses on her mouth, her cheeks. Her chin. And with each kiss, each touch, another part of Brigitte returned from Maman and the midnight sky.

Her hand floated up to his jaw. "*Oui.*" Her voice was deep, like a riverbed. Rough and gravelly. "We are not finished. Not yet." She pointed to the gate she had opened nearly at the cost of her life. "'Tis the way in. Tell them . . . to hurry. Before we are found out."

* * *

Drem kicked out, swimming deeper into the cold, murky water. He led the way to the gate Brigitte said she had unlocked. The portal would allow them to enter Harfleur.

The guide rope tied around his waist kept Nathan and a soldier-at-arms from swimming astray in the murky water. Another soldier fed them the rope, giving them a path should they need reinforcements.

The chill seeped into his bones. He had decided to replace his leather tunic with a linen one. His chausses offered little protection but the idea was stealth, not surprising the townspeople with his naked arse. The small sword he kept for close combat was strapped to his calf. He would have found comfort in having his broadsword, but Brigitte was adamant there was no room. She feared for his safety, that he would be caught by his beloved weapon, and had refused to be taken to the surgeon's tent until he promised to return unharmed.

His lungs began to burn as he searched for the gate. How had Brigitte managed through this liquid hell? An urgent need to breathe squeezed his heart, making it pulse in his ears.

How did she fare? Nearly losing her had shaken him deeply. He had been through many a battle, but the thought of her head injury made him queasy. Though he wanted to be by her side, he was avowed to serve his king. He took comfort in knowing that Darrick had promised to keep her in his care until Drem's return.

He made contact with the gate's iron bars. Relief rushed through him and he kicked forward.

A tug on the line yanked him backward, reminding him to slow down. The two behind him carried the weapons they would need once they breached the wall.

Drem's ears began to ring. He made it through the gate and waited for Nathan to pass. The soldier behind him began to sink under the weight of the swords. Drem grabbed the boy by the back of his tunic. He took the lead again, dragging the arms bearer with him.

They broke through the surface and clambered out. How long had they been underwater? A minute? And yet it felt like years since Drem had gazed upon Brigitte's face. The sky was still dark. They still had time before the townspeople awakened from this nightmare.

Drem snapped the rope twice, then one long tug. A faint response vibrated in return. Trusting that the message had been received, he tied off the line so that no one would see it.

Nathan nudged his shoulder and pointed.

Drem acknowledged that he saw the lights. "No time to waste."

Keeping low to the ground and against the wall, they hurried into position. Nathan and the soldier were to guard Drem as he raised the north portcullis. 'Twas a mad plan.

A bombardment from one of Henry's great cannons hit the north wall. Then another, the second striking the south wall. Then another to the north. The ground shook from the impact. Forcing the citizens to the south would reduce the casualties and give them time to regain their senses and convince Raoul de Gaucourt to surrender the town.

Drem and Nathan grinned at each other. The message had indeed gotten through to the king. The only step left to breaking the siege was to raise the portcullis; the soldiers would follow.

Brigitte awoke with a start. A gentle breeze caressed her cheek, lifting strands of hair to tickle her. She opened her eyes and blinked at the unfamiliar light. Sunbeams stretched across the floor. Tilting her head, she watched half-naked cherubs cavorting from cloud to cloud across the ornate ceiling. The mattress on which she lay eased with the slightest movement. It was worthy of nobility. How odd that it reminded her of home. Of Maman.

"Drem?" Her mouth was dry, her tongue thick. Had he succeeded? Was he safe? Tears slid down her face, trailing beside her ears. Her head throbbed from thinking.

A snuffling rustle caught her attention. Piers sat beside her, his legs curled beneath him. He rested his head on his arm, his fist pressed to his chest as if to ward off intruders.

"Piers," she said, her voice so raspy she hardly recognized it.

The heel of his boot hit the floor. He grunted as he straightened in the hard chair. "Bee!" he squealed, jumping to his feet. The bed shook under his weight as he bounced on the mattress. He peered at her, his grin stretched wide "You're back."

She swallowed past the raw patch in her throat. "Where's Drem?"

"Serving the king."

"The siege . . ." A cough rattled her chest.

"'Tis over." He ducked his head so that all she could see was the crown of his golden curls. She had seen this look before. One that foretold more to his story.

Brigitte pushed her body up on weakened arms. They shook under her weight. "And . . . ?" She plucked at his sleeve. "What aren't you telling me, lad?"

"Drink." He handed her a cup. "The surgeon Flanners said 'twould help with the pain."

Brigitte eyed the liquid and sniffed. "Watered wine would serve me better." Relief flooded her when he nodded and reached for the pitcher and a fresh cup. "*Merci.*" She watched the boy as she sipped the liquid, letting it trickle down her raw throat. "Have you seen Drem?"

Piers set the pitcher down. Shadows and sunlight played across his face, battling for control. His lip quivered before he caught it between his teeth. The bloom of his youth had faded while she slept. Determination now squared his shoulders. "He'll be along once he has dispatched the citizens who do not wish to bend their knee to their new king."

"Dispatched?" She saw something in the boy's eyes. A shadowed glance away before she could look deeper.

"The women and children?" A gnawing fear began to grow. Had she misplaced her trust in Drem to do what was right? She crushed the bed linen under her fingers. *What have I done?*

They turned at the sound of hobnailed boots striking the stairway. The door swung open. Light streamed in. The breeze rushed through the window and hall, as if to escape the room.

"Brigitte . . . my *caru*," Drem whispered from the doorway.

Damp waves of auburn clung to his collar. He rushed to her side and tenderly embraced her shoulders. His breath warmed her neck. He ran the pad of his thumb over her lower lip. The touch of his mouth to hers sent heat racing through her limbs. He smelled fresh, of soap and mint.

Her strength was renewed. The beat of her heart sped at the touch of his hand, the caress of his gaze.

Piers moved away from the bed. He picked up a porcelain statue, rolling it in his hands. "Aye. The fledglings have been forced to fly. To leave the Nest." He set the figurine down on the table. "Isn't that the right of it, Sir Drem?"

"Aye, lad," he said, clapping his hand over Piers's shoulder. "You know 'tis the way of it . . . for now."

Brigitte watched the looks they exchanged. Shadows filled their eyes.

"*Oui.*" Piers nodded, pulling away. "I'm to find Sir Darrick once you're awake." He squinted up at Drem, looking like an archer preparing for a shot. "You'll stay with her?"

"Nothing could move me from her side," Drem vowed.

Piers snorted and glanced toward Brigitte. There was something he wished to say, but he stopped short and snorted again before leaving them. The slow patter of his feet carried down the hall until it was nothing more than a whisper.

Brigitte lifted her face to Drem. He had secrets of his own. She would know what he guarded, what pained him. She ran her palm over the backs of his hands. Cuts and bruises marred his knuckles. Were there more, hidden beneath his tunic? She slid her hands over his rib cage, pausing when she felt the intake of his breath.

"Are you injured?"

"Your touch does but distract me." He lifted her hand and nibbled the pads of her fingers. Mischief glittered in his eyes. "'Tis a pleasant distraction. One that I never want to lose."

Brigitte could not let it go. "Then what darkens your eyes?"

He turned, glancing away to hide his secrets.

She tightened her fingers. "What does Piers mean? The children from the Nest?"

He frowned, his brow furrowing as he took a deep breath and started to turn away again.

"Where is Alexandre?" She searched the room, out the window, trying to recognize the location. She had been here before. Years ago. The night the men brought her to Harfleur.

"Drem, whose home are we in?" She arose from the bed, refusing to let him retreat. Her legs wobbled on unused muscles. Panic constricted her throat. "How long have I slept? Tell me."

"We feared for you." His voice was gravelly with pain. "You've been asleep for over a week. Your head..." His palm hovered over her forehead. "And then the fever. The cough." He snatched his hand away, smothering his mouth. Tears glittered from eyes as deep green as a forest.

She pressed her hands to his lips. "I'm awake now."

Nodding, he wrapped his arms around her shoulders. She rested her cheek against his chest. His heart drummed faster and faster. He drew her closer, providing protection.

"We've watched over you. Made sure no one but your friend

Claudette entered to care for you." He cleared the emotion from his throat and kissed the top of Brigitte's head. "Everything went as planned. You brought the siege to an end."

She lifted her head. "I did it to save the children from starvation. To stop the suffering."

"This I know." His arms flinched, as if he relived the scene. "The delay in opening the gates brought more fighting. There were casualties. From the siege or after." He shrugged. "Who can tell?"

She began to pull away from his arms. The thought of more deaths upon her soul made her ache to her bones. "They know who helped your king's cause."

"Our king," he corrected. "Henry has claimed Normandy. He must have promise of fealty. Those who do not bend the knee must leave the safety of the town."

He tried to draw her back, but she refused. This was too much to understand. She had betrayed the people.

"The women and children. They are caught in the battle of men. They should not have to pay anything more." Her muscles wavered in holding her up. She grasped the bedpost to steady her legs. A swarm of bees began to buzz inside her head.

"You're right." Drem picked her up, cradling her in his arms. Then he slowly lay her down on the soft bed. He smoothed her hair, tucking it behind her ears. "But there is little I can do until the soldiers leave on their march."

She looked up at his downturned face. "You're not marching alongside your king?"

"Soon. Harfleur is our garrison. Some of us are staying behind to rebuild. Darrick requires my help until he has healed enough to lead the men."

Brigitte's spirits lifted at the news.

"'Tis good to see your smile," Drem said. "Mayhap my delayed departure pleases you?"

"*Oui.*" Her smile deepened. There was still a way for her to make amends. And find her way to Calais. But there were several who could still stand in her way.

"Master Alexandre . . . Is he in your custody?"

Drem's eyes narrowed. His nostrils flared. "He slipped away. Left Raoul de Gaucourt to deal with the king's men."

Chapter 18

Drem paced the room he had been called to in the middle of the night. The few men who joined him sat at the table. Ale filled their cups to the brim.

Now that the ships could bring provisions into the harbor, everyone's living conditions had improved. But many of their men had died from sickness and exposure. Those who were too ill to make the march to Calais were being readied to board a ship to return to England.

Darrick's gray pallor had improved over the last days. Nathan was ever the hale and hearty knight. Drem thought the man was too stubborn to fall ill. And too fierce to let anyone injure him on the battlefield.

"Darrick, you can't mean to send the boy with the rest of the invalids."

"I do and I will." His fist landed on the table as he let the swan coin roll over his fingers, weaving in and out.

"He's a thief. Not as clever as some, but nonetheless a thief. One of Master Alexandre's fledglings."

"I'm sending Piers to your sister's holdings. Sir James needs to speak with him. You know his skill with drawing out what anyone has seen."

"Brigitte will fight this."

"We know." Nathan leaned forward on his arms and grinned. "'Tis for you to tell her."

"You knew of this?" Drem's stomach clenched. He had yet to retrieve his purse from the little pickpocket.

"'Tis not safe for the lad," Darrick said. "He doesn't belong here."

"Since when does Henry care whether a lad is under his command?" Drem bit back the bitterness he had thought long buried.

"We believe Master Alexandre has a considerable interest in Piers for a reason."

"Ransom?"

Darrick tipped his head forward. "The boy gave me this." The swan coin stilled. It rolled out of his hand and spun on the table before stopping.

Drem's stomach clenched again. He gnawed the inside of his cheek. 'Twas like the one he had found in the chapel, before it, too, had disappeared. Like the one the noble had given him after the skirmish. Was this one of the brotherhood's tricks to test his loyalty? He uncurled his fingers from the fist that had formed of its own volition.

Nathan sat back, his arms folded over his chest. "'Tis a call for our help. Is it not?"

"Did the boy tell you where he got it?" Drem asked.

"Said his father gave it to him before leaving for battle."

"You believe him?"

"I do." Nathan traced the moisture on the outside of his cup.

"Has de Gaucourt revealed what he knows?"

"Though in custody, he is now under the king's protection until a ransom is paid." Darrick shook his head. "He has sealed his lips and refuses to cooperate. Even now, we wait for him to deliver a message to King Charles."

"You're putting Piers on the same ship with the sick and dying?" Drem dreaded Brigitte's reaction when he delivered this next turd pile of information.

Darrick lifted his gray eyes to search Drem's face and then Nathan's. "As I said, Piers doesn't belong here. Have you not noticed how well his manners are for a street urchin? His respect for others' property? And he has an eye and ear for detail."

Drem could not help himself and snorted. "He is still a thief."

"And what have you done to rectify it?"

"What?" Drem smelled another trap. Had he waited too long to tell him about the chapel? Did it have something to do with the boy? Or with Brigitte?

Darrick leaned back to dig under his belt. His stare glittered like that of a wolf hiding in the bushes, waiting to pounce on his prey. He pulled out a leather purse and dropped it next to the swan coin. "Well, my brother, I suggest you start at the beginning of what you know."

* * *

Alexandre slipped out of the tunnel leading to the harbor gate. Now that the English were in control of the town they forgot to keep their eyes open. He wrapped his cloak around his chest and lifted it to cover his face as he walked past the reeking flesh of the dead and dying. Would that the bitch Brigitte was among the bodies. The woman Claudette had told him what he needed to know. Before she fell off the parapet. He shrugged. Just one more body on the piles of the dead.

Plans began to unfold, filling his mind like little birds made of parchment. Brigitte had cost him dearly. His Nest was gone. But soon he would have another.

He passed the Welsh ditchdiggers. Now that the task of burrowing under the walls was over, they had been set to digging more pits to bury the casualties of war. The siege had cost more than Alexandre expected. But it was a chance he had had to take. That stupid Raoul. *Le Défenseur.* "Bah." Alexandre spat on the ground, nearly striking one of the men wielding an ax. He cursed his inattention and picked up his pace before the man could set upon him. 'Twas Brigitte's fault he was preoccupied.

He found a stand of boulders on which to perch and watched the king's fleet filling the harbor. Their white sails bobbed in the water like a flock of gulls. Though he had been pushed from the Nest, he'd made sure some of his fledglings remained. Their latest news had put him into a rage he had never known before.

He had thought de Gaucourt would carry the blame for the lengthy siege. Instead, once he had surrendered the keys of the city to the king, they treated him like royalty. Feeding him comfits while he, Master Alexandre, had to settle for scraps.

A troop of riders came through the gate. Dust swirled in the air.

Alexandre sat up. English soldiers surrounded Raoul as that English prick, Sir Nathan, barked orders to his men. The large, red-headed knight's destrier pranced toward de Gaucourt. The toes of *Le Défenseur*'s boots scraped the ground as he straddled the wide-bellied beast. His cheeks heated at Sir Nathan's jest.

Alexandre concentrated, wishing he could hear what was being said. The news from his fledglings was correct. The king was allowing him to leave. Only the other day, he had stood in ridicule, a rope around his neck. But where would he go? Not to Burgundy. They had lost their pretty little packages. The duke would be furious.

"Better still," Alexandre muttered, "what have you told your new friends?"

The cane in his hands creaked from the pressure he put on the polished wood. Strangling his enemies had never been an option until now.

He shook his head to clear his vision. These spells were becoming thicker, more frequent, and harder to shake off.

A bird, cawing overhead, brought him back to the latest challenges to his plans for financial gain and power. The boy, their treasure, was set to board a ship and sail away. And it was that bitch who had surely made it happen. "Bee," he ground out.

He threw his beloved cane at the bird. Cursing the woman and all that stood in his way. "I will make you pay, my sweet."

Brigitte gripped the window ledge until her nails bent. "How could you?"

Drem drew her shoulders toward his chest. "'Tis for his safety."

"But you should have told me. Given me a chance to say good-bye."

"He'll make his home with my sister, Terrwyn, and her husband, James. You'll see him again." He paused. "When we return to England."

Brigitte took in a deep breath. Did she want to live in England with this man? No; her path was meant for Calais. She felt it deep in her soul. But the thought of not having him in her life, not seeing his smile light up a room ... it made her ache at the loss. How could she be in two places at once?

At the rise of dawn, one of the king's ships, loaded with the vast number of infirm and dying, left the harbor. It unfurled its canvas wings. The wind caught hold of the sails and carried them to England. Brigitte covered her mouth. *So far away.*

"You do want to return with me. Don't you, my *caru*?"

"*Oui.*" Harfleur's pennants no longer flew over the gates. Instead, the standards of St. George and the English king fluttered across the blue sky. The day had changed. And so had her life. Just as it had the day Maman died. Brigitte tilted her head and smiled up at Drem. "I would like some air. Would you walk with me?"

"Are you certain you are strong enough?"

"The cough is nearly gone." She lay her palm on his sleeve. "Please. I know you say Claudette took care of me, but I have not seen her since that night."

Drem frowned. A puzzled look drew his brows together. "She has not been to see you this week? Forgive me, I didn't know. I've been busy with the soldiers. The rebuilding. The prisoners."

Brigitte stroked his arm, soothing the tense muscles. "This I know."

"I would have had her stay in the Defender's house, but she insisted she had a comfortable room on the square." He smiled, but the gleam never reached his eyes. "Come. We'll look for her." He strapped on his sword and crooked his arm for her to hold. "You'll be pleased with the measures taken with the rebuilding."

"*Merci*," she whispered. Concern for her friend began to deepen, trickling down her spine.

Brigitte stepped over the mansion's threshold and into the square. The sun glittered, harsh against the cobblestones.

Townspeople watched as they passed. Each glaring face seemed to cut her skin. She drew her shoulders back and yearned for the days when she could move about like a wisp of smoke. "They despise me."

Drem lifted her hand, grazing her knuckles with his lips. His fingers tightened, drawing her attention. Flecks of scattered gold glittered in his stern countenance. "They should hold you in high regard. As a hero for saving them from more destruction."

"No." Her hand trembled as he led her to Claudette's. How much did they know? How could they have suspected she and Claudette of playing a role in placing the English in control?

Drem unsheathed his sword and pushed open an unlocked door. "Stay behind me."

Brigitte no longer heard him. She shoved past his braced arm and felt the room begin to spin. Claudette loved a clean home and had always polished the wood and windows until they shone. But the furniture had been tossed aside. Plates were tumbled to the floor. Bloody handprints stained the whitewashed wall.

Drem walked carefully around the room, then entered what had been her laundry. "She's not here."

"Then she might still be alive," Brigitte said, though with little hope. She pointed to dark, circular marks tapped out on the floor. "'Tis Master Alexandre's cane." A black wave of anger and sadness roared into her ears. She spun on her heels.

"You think the fledglings have returned?"

She slid a glance at him, fearing he would read her mind. "They come from the Nest. If they are here, I will find them."

"We will find them," he corrected. "And we will speak with them."

They made their way, climbing over toppled walls and crumbled buildings. "So much to do." She paused to shove damp tendrils from her forehead. "Where will the burgesses set up their wares? How is anyone to survive this?"

Drem leaped over a short wall and waited for Brigitte to gather her skirts. His brows rose at the sight of her calves. "Beauty and strength. What more can a man ask of God?"

His large hands encircled her waist as he lifted her over. Blushing at his approval, she cast her gaze over the garden. She wrinkled her nose. "Everything is no longer familiar."

In a fortnight, she had become a stranger in her own home.

"Aye. Henry is distraught over the damage required to gain Harfleur's surrender. But it is our garrison now. And we will rebuild." He pointed to the harbor. "Many of the burgesses did not wish to stay, so our good king has ordered two of his vessels to bring provisions. Merchants, fishermen, tradesmen, all are coming with their wares."

Brigitte turned at the sound of pebbles scattered over the alley. "Come." She motioned for him to follow as she led the way into the cellar. "The fledglings." She pressed a finger to her lips and pointed to the ceiling. "They'll speak with me."

"Sieges. Battles. They change people." He shook his head. "'Tis not the same world you once knew."

A trapdoor creaked shut, and the patter of feet ran across the floor overhead. Brigitte grabbed Drem's arm as he started to push past her. "You'll frighten them. Stay here until I call for you."

Although she received an annoyed grunt in response, she knew he understood her reasoning. Stretching up on tiptoe, she grazed his mouth with hers. Their kiss lingered. His mouth silently urged her to reconsider, to allow him to lead the way. His fingers rubbed the base of her back, caressing the curve of her hip.

He slid his hand over her jaw, his lips hovering over hers. "I bend to your will this once. I beg you, use caution."

"*Oui.*"

A thrill of excitement raced down her spine. Shadows stretched over the wall, bobbing as they scurried past. She stepped out and caught a fledgling. The emaciated child wriggled under her hand, thrashing for release.

"Tobes," she said. A bony knee struck her stomach. "'Tis me. Bee. I'm not here to hurt you."

In an instant, the struggle ceased. It was as she had told Drem. They knew they could trust her. She relaxed her hold. "There now," she crooned.

A scampering of feet came from behind. They surrounded her, swarming, pulling and pawing at her hair, her dress. Dirty nails scratched her face, raked her arms. Stunned, Brigitte cried out. She slapped at their grasping fingers. The orphans she had cared for, taught to lift purses and empty pockets, so as to please Master Alexandre, were no longer fledglings. They were like the rats that ran through the alleys.

"Varmints. Hold where you are." One by one, Drem pulled them from her. His sword drawn, he held them off.

Some scurried to the corners. One lad breathed in rushing gasps for air. He stood, facing them with enough rage to dim his wits.

Brigitte's arms shook as she pushed up from the floor. She untangled her skirt and walked to the children. Her skin stung from cuts, but 'twas the wary look in their eyes that sliced her heart. "Tobes. 'Tis I, Bee," she said again.

She limped beside Drem. They shared a silent understanding. They were the wall the children could not break.

The boy spat in her direction, but she was ready for him this time and avoided his aim.

"You betrayed us," he snarled. "Master Alexandre told us."

The day was stretching long and tiresome. Brigitte sighed, silently begging Drem to keep his silence. "I did what I had to. To save you." She waved at the others. "All of you. Food aplenty is arriving." She licked her lips, praying she did not overstep with the next. "King Henry wishes you to help rebuild. He'll pay you in kind by . . ." She glanced up at the sound of a sharp intake of breath. Drem kept his stern gaze focused on the children. She swallowed and charged on. ". . . by feeding you. Letting you stay in the Nest."

"You must first swear allegiance to your new king," Drem added. "Or leave."

"And I need to know where Claudette is hiding." She smiled, hoping to reassure the grumbling that had begun after Drem's pronounce-ment.

Tobes grunted, his hands on his hips. The others were silent. He had become the fledglings' leader and they awaited his direction. "Gone." He spat again and motioned with his hands. "Fly, fly away, little birdie. 'Tis what happens to traitors. Don't it?" He turned and ushered the fledglings back into the Nest.

Brigitte's thoughts raced as she worked to keep him talking. "Wait. Please. Let me get my things."

He stopped and looked over his shoulder. The cold gleam of his eyes chilled the room and made Brigitte's blood crackle with the icy threads of his hatred. "No need to come back here again. The bastard took everything with 'em when he ran. He'll return soon enough. Said to tell you that you can count on it."

Brigitte bristled. "You've seen him?"

"He moves about." Tobes shrugged his thin shoulders. "Like the rest of us." A leering eye scraped over her. "He doesn't sleep in a big fluffy bed, all cozying up to the enemy."

Brigitte grabbed Drem's sword hand. She clasped his wrist. "Come. We must go to the wall."

Thankful he had kept his weapon unsheathed, they marched across the square. Master Alexandre's threats were as real now as when the day turned into night. He blamed her for his losing the power that slipped through his fingers. Even now, she felt the fledg-lings watching as they passed collapsed buildings and closed shops. She feared if not Alexandre, it would be the citizens of Harfleur who would see her hang. Leaving the town was her only chance of sur-vival. She prayed Claudette had indeed left on her own two feet. Freely and willingly. And safely.

Much of the wall had sustained damage from the bombardment of the king's cannons.

"There is a space on the wall where he often took me. To show me. Warn me," Brigitte said.

Drem nodded and unsheathed his sword. They climbed the stair-way to the parapet.

"'Tis unsteady," he warned. "I will lead the way, let you know if it is clear enough to pass."

She found the location where she used to stand and remember her mother and the life they had before Monsieur le Faire disappeared from their lives. She looked out at the glittering harbor and the waves licking the shore, then to the valley below. The rolling meadow stretched out before her.

She stepped up to the wall. Her palms pressed into the stone as she leaned forward.

"Careful." Drem put his arm around her waist, keeping her from harm.

She looked down again. 'Twas as she feared. Tears filled her eyes, freeing her from the sight of the broken body. A white apron fluttered in the rancid breeze. "Poor Claudette."

She turned away, gritting her teeth until she thought her jaw would break.

"My love," Drem whispered as he pressed her head into his chest. "My *caru,* I will not let him harm you. 'Tis my promise."

Chapter 19

Brigitte trembled beside Drem. The visit to the Nest had brought them little information. But it had been enough to lead them to the outer wall. He worried the shock of finding her friend's body would send her into another sickness.

Darrick sat with his injured leg stretched out before him, his foot propped on a stool. He watched and listened as they poured out their findings to him.

"Claudette played a role in the surrender." Brigitte leaned forward, her hands splayed across the table. "You must find Master Alexandre. Make him pay for her murder."

"'Tis said he has fled." Darrick flicked a speck of mud from his hose. "'Tis nothing I can do about it."

"She didn't deserve to die," Brigitte whispered. Her shoulders hunched, she pressed her hands into the top of her thighs.

"And now you understand why young Piers had to leave," Drem said. "Before it was too late. He's safe now."

Darrick let his leg drop from the stool. "I'll see what I can discover. With the loss of so many soldiers . . ." He shrugged and rose to help Brigitte from her chair. Pain etched a line from his mouth as he held her hand. "We have soldiers and men-at-arms who will guard the garrison. And Sir Nathan escorts Raoul to King Charles and the dauphin for their surrender. My hands are busy with many things in preparation for their march. But we will know to watch for the fledglings and the master of the Nest. Drem," he added, "escort my lady Brigitte back to her chambers."

"Aye." Drem nodded. "We have much to discuss concerning the upcoming campaign."

"A word," Darrick said before they could escape. "With Drem," he clarified.

Brigitte rose, gathering her skirts to keep her hems from dragging the damp floor. Pausing, she turned. "I'll wait for you outside."

Drem watched the sway of her hips. She no longer moved to be purposely unnoticed. He suppressed a smile that threatened to reveal what he knew. Brigitte was discovering she had more assets than just a thief's light touch.

Darrick cleared his throat, drawing him from his appreciation of the curve in her lower back. "We've amassed all the provisions there are in Harfleur." He threw down his quill pen. "For the sake of Henry's desire to fulfill God's will and carry out the campaign. There'll be many more times the unhappy citizens will have to sacrifice."

"They're already an unhappy lot."

"I've received word that Mistress Claudette is not the only one whose life has been threatened."

"Brigitte?"

"There's a price on her head."

Brigitte watched Drem check each room of the house for intruders.

"Wouldn't you prefer to lie down and rest?" Drem asked.

Brigitte shuddered at the thought of being alone. She clasped her elbows and winced. The bruises from the fledglings had bloomed. For now, though, her heart ached more than her body. The Nest sought a new leader. Their mood bled hatred, forcing out all forms of humanity from the unfortunate. If they refused to comply, there would be more than a few bruises. The King of England and Normandy would not allow them to stay in Harfleur. He would have them cast out. The homeless French living outside the wall would pounce on them. Rip them apart like carrion. 'Twas best to stay under the protection of the English king.

"I should know this house if I am to reside here for a time, *oui*?" In truth, she had been here before. The first night she had been delivered to Harfleur, before she was released to the streets. Alexandre had arrived, the avenging angel, bringing food and warmth. A wolf offering safety to an innocent lamb.

"As you wish, my lady." He held out his hand. "But keep behind me." He motioned to the sheathed sword hanging from his belt. "I'll need my sword arm free."

Drem's eyes concealed the truth from her question. But she had seen that look before: when Alexandre wished to keep something from her.

Nodding, she had kept close to him but out of the way. She should have felt protected, but the hatred of the townspeople outweighed every other thought. The constant thump of construction drew her nerves tight. The bang of an ax made her jump.

Now, when she shut her eyes, she saw Claudette's body, splayed out like a broken doll, lying on a dung heap. Her fluttering apron stained with blood.

Brigitte picked up a porcelain shepherdess that sat on the fireplace mantel in the solar. She rolled it in her hands.

Drem stood behind her. When he drew her to his chest, heat seeped into her. Protection.

"There is one similar in the bedchamber. Piers found it fascinating." A tear slid down her cheek. "Mayhap it brought back memories."

He nuzzled her neck, his lips tickling her skin. "Mayhap it reminded him of his home."

She returned the figurine to the mantel. What would become of it when she left Harfleur? Who would take over the mayor's house? The final room to inspect was Brigitte's bedchamber. She shuddered, knowing that soon she would have to be alone.

Pounding erupted from the entrance. It echoed up the staircase. A runner stood below. He held out a missive clutched in his fist. "You are called, Sir Drem."

Thanking the man-at-arms, he unrolled the parchment. He tensed, then carefully folded it and placed it inside his surcoat.

"I must return to Darrick." He lifted her hair, his fingers digging into her scalp. "I fear there are no servants to see to your comfort."

"'Tis of no consequence," she said. "I know how to see to my own needs."

His brow furrowed. Was he questioning her?

"Stay and rest. Lock the chamber door behind me."

"'Tis safe," she said with all the courage she could gather. "No one will think to harm me here."

"All the same . . ." He kissed her forehead, his lips traveling to her temple. She leaned into the warmth of his caress. Tipping back her head, she allowed him to move lower. His teeth grazed her flesh, nipping her neck. A shiver raced down her spine. "Protect yourself, my *caru*."

Brigitte swayed on her feet as his fingers feathered over her collarbone. A groan slipped past her lips. She slid her hands through his auburn hair.

Just steps away, the soft mattress called to her. Lured by the desire to be swept away from all the pain, she tugged him closer. She wanted fiery waves to flow through her again, crashing over her mind and body. A few stolen moments in his arms. She took the first step, nudging to the place of heaven waiting for them to take their pleasure.

Flecks of gold in his green eyes sparkled back at her. His quick breaths matching her own. He caught her hand, lifting it to his lips. "I shall return as soon as I am able. I—"

"Promise," she finished for him. Turning her hand, she placed her palm on his chest. "Your heart pounds. As if you have run a race."

"I wish only to run to you, not leave you here." He trailed his finger over the curve of her hip. "Waiting."

"Wanting," she added. Boldly, she stroked the smooth tunic under his surcoat, dropping her hand lower. His breath hitched as she tested the bulging need growing under his chausses. It gave her pleasure to know his heart beat for her. Wanting.

"The next time we make love, I vow to do it properly."

Brigitte wrinkled her nose. "You are ashamed of what we did in the grotto? But I thought it . . . beautiful."

"Ashamed?" He groaned again. "Never. Next time will be slow and sweet, without fear of exposure. We will love the night away. Awaken to the new day, celebrating in each other's arms." Awareness registered. "Wedded as man and wife."

Brigitte gasped and shook her head. "I'm French," she said. "Your king will never allow it."

"He will. I will make certain he does."

"We barely know each other." Her hands shook as she smoothed damp palms over her skirt.

His glance moved to the bed. Amusement twinkled back at her. "I believe we know each other well enough." He stepped closer, wrapping his arms around her waist. "I want to know you even more."

His kiss made her head spin, stealing her thoughts and leaving her with desire for more. Tears slid past her lashes, trailing down her cheeks.

He sighed over her mouth. Brigitte prepared to feel the onslaught of loneliness whenever they were apart. Sir Darrick would wait only so long. They had tested his patience long enough.

Drem surprised her by lifting her off the floor. He cradled her in his arms and marched toward the bed.

Her breath caught. "Drem. What about . . ."

"Hush." He nipped the corner of her mouth. "We have much to celebrate."

Brigitte drew back to see if he was serious. "I have not agreed to wed you."

Drem grinned down at her as he lay her on the bed. "Then I shall have to persuade you."

Provisions were coming through the harbor and required Drem's attention. The people who had promised their allegiance complied with the orders, but there was so much to rebuild. A cold wind whipped through the room Darrick had claimed as his command post. The newly thatched roof rattled at the onslaught of the change in weather.

And sitting across from Darrick, knowing that he expected him to leave Brigitte behind, made his skin crawl with worry.

"I return to commanding the rebuilding of the garrison," Darrick said.

"You do not ride with Henry?"

"He has enough in the contingent to protect him. As he says, God is with him." Darrick cracked the skim of ice forming over the pitcher. He rinsed his hand in the frigid water and shook off the droplets.

"So we march despite the failing weather?"

"Fresh men-at-arms are sailing into the harbor today. They will be ready to fight for their king and country."

"We lost many good men. Archers, men-at-arms."

"Noblemen. Clergy," Darrick finished. "Death does not care a whit for station."

"What of provisions?"

"Take what we can as it comes in." Darrick dropped a ladle into a pot of stew that simmered over the hearth and limped back to the oaken table.

"The people . . ."

"Will find a way." He grimaced. "They have a hearth to huddle around. Whereas our men do not."

Drem thought of the archers. Most came from humble families. Farmers' sons who were forced by life's hand to learn to shoot an arrow or starve. Those who survived the skirmishes and the waiting time of the siege would know more suffering before this campaign was over.

"How long will it take to march to Calais?" Drem sniffed the aromatic flavors coming from the pot.

"If the weather holds? And the French do not wish to leave the warmth of their hearths?"

"Aye."

"Eight days."

"If all goes well."

Darrick nodded. He set another bowl of fish stew on the table. The savory scent of seafood and sage wafted into the room.

Drem's stomach rumbled. The sleeping dragon of hunger had awakened.

"If not?" he asked.

"Only God knows the answer to that."

The need to see Brigitte, to hold her and ensure her safety rushed into him. His quest to find the answers to the clues given to him at Dunstable Priory faded in importance. His duty to king warred with his love for the strong woman who had captured his heart when he was not looking.

"Brigitte . . ."

"Not to fear." Darrick waved him off. "You are to stay here. Continue with the rebuilding of the garrison."

Drem paused. The crust of bread used to sop up the juices in the trencher hovered near his mouth. "By whose order?"

Never had he been kept from the battlefield. His archers needed him. How had his life changed this much? A knighthood for the brotherhood was to give him more . . . reason for surviving battles and sieges. Being a Knight of the Swan should carry him into the battlefield. To fight by his king's side. *Damn it. My friend's side.* Not to stay back with the infirm.

"Henry desires it." Darrick held his gaze over the bowl of stew. It hovered near his mouth before he tilted it to slurp from the edge. He nudged the other bowl to Drem. "'Tis time we talk of your woman."

Drem's stomach soured. The stew no longer held the same appeal. "Aye?"

Darrick pulled out a pouch. He unfolded a piece of material and smoothed out the torn badge. His fingers pressed the embroidery onto the table. "The lad recognized this. Do you?"

"Aye," Drem said. He licked his cracked lips, wondering at the game Darrick played. "'Tis like the badge I saw when I visited Dunstable Priory."

"Nathan presented it to me before he left to escort de Gaucourt to deliver Henry's challenge to the mad King Charles. Said Raoul gave it to him." He circled the design. "Showed it to Piers." His gray eyes glittered with excitement. "The lad recognized it. Appears the boy's family will be willing to pay the ransom."

Drem examined the badge. "The House of Burgundy?"

"According to de Gaucourt, someone wanted to keep the boy hidden, secreted away until they needed him."

"Alexandre?"

Darrick shrugged. "What better way to hide the boy but in a nest of orphaned thieves and pickpockets?"

"Terrwyn will convince the boy to tell her what happened to him."

"And James will finish the rest by sketching the faces of whoever kidnapped Piers." Darrick looked up. "'Tis possible the Duke of Burgundy had a hand in this. If so . . ."

"We must tread cautiously when he offers his help."

Darrick dropped into a chair. "Go to Brigitte. Speak with her. Henry mentioned it again. He worries that she may lead you astray."

"She is but a pawn in this game of power."

"May I remind you of her background? 'Tis little we know of her except that she is French." He held up his hand for silence. "She taught the fledglings of that damn nest to steal. Who was she to Alexandre? There is word he seeks her. Is willing to pay any price for her."

Drem bristled. "Christ's bloody wounds."

"You still keep that ugly necklace from her. Why? Who are you protecting?" Darrick spread his hands over the wooden table. "What is your gut telling you? Mine says she hides a secret."

"I'm not my father." Drem clenched his fists.

"Never said you were like that treasonous bastard. If I thought you were, your head would be dancing on a pike."

"When will you trust that I know what I'm doing?"

"When you pull your head out of your arse and remember who you serve." Darrick winced as he pushed to stand. "Henry needs the information we gather. Our protection."

"He is my king and my friend." Drem fought to keep from lunging over the table.

"And she is a beautiful woman. How do you know what she plans? Who she puts first?"

"She helped us end the damn siege." Drem flared his nostrils, doing his best not to bloody Darrick's face.

"I'll give you that." Darrick pointedly stared at Drem's fists. "I must put the question to you. To her. Now. Why did she turn on the master of the Nest?"

"She could not stand for the injustice. The waste of life." Drem uncurled his fingers and paced the cramped room.

"'Tis a wise Knight of the Swan who questions the motives of everyone."

"'Tis a lonely existence," Drem muttered.

"And the reason why I have not let any woman lure me in, snare me with her charms." Darrick stepped closer. He clasped Drem's shoulder. "We are knights. And soon we'll ride into battle. Mayhap never to return. Leaving the woman with empty arms. Is that the end you want for your life? For hers?"

Drem shrugged him off. His heart ached with questions pressing into his soul. Did he want to end his moments with Brigitte? He did not know if he could. She had become a part of his heart the moment she slipped into his life. Like a faerie, casting her spell, she had captured his heart. Their stolen kiss. Her dark eyes, and the way they flared and sparkled with desire, filled his thoughts. Her sighs as she washed over passion's edge, carrying him with her. Had she been following Alexandre's orders, pursuing him for information? Drem shook free of the doubt. Their moments of passion in the grotto. They were real. Her courage, swimming to him, opening the gate . . . that was real. Aye, she might have secrets and sadness in her past, but together they would fight the shadows.

Darrick poured ale from the pitcher and held out the cup. "Henry trusts you with his life. What more can a king ask?"

"No more than any other man. Upon my honor as a Knight of the Swan, I won't disappoint him."

"'Tis why I'm placing my trust in you as well." He tossed back the ale, wiping his mouth with the back of his hand.

"I vow to tread carefully and not lose my head."

"Or your heart," Darrick added.

Too late for that. Drem gulped the last of his ale and set the cup on the table. "If Henry intends to ride upon the dawn, there is much to prepare. And the very people Brigitte stood against when she opened those gates to save them . . ."

". . . think us weak and ripe for the plucking once the king's army has moved out of the gates."

Drem took a deep breath. "Thus ring the notes of another late night."

Chapter 20

The king and England's army prepared to leave Harfleur early that morning. While the sun crept over the hills, Brigitte climbed the crumbling stairway to the parapet of the outer wall. She avoided the last place she had seen Claudette's broken body and searched the mass of men. They marched in waves. Foot soldiers, archers, mounted knights, and supply wagons. The king and nobles. Their traveling caravan created a trail of dust behind them. Their destination, Calais.

She bit her lips and fought back tears of frustration. Calais. The safe haven where Maman had directed her to travel was as out of reach as the moon.

The shopkeepers the king had brought to Harfleur were determined to make their new home prosperous and pushed out the French stragglers. Outside the gate was no better. Word came that the roads were dangerous with robbers and worse.

She pressed her hand to her throat. And somewhere out there, Alexandre waited to extract his vengeance. The nightmares grew in strength.

She rubbed her damp palms over the butter-soft woolen gown Drem had delivered to her that morning. It took her several attempts to ignore its beauty. Amber threads ran through the weave of the forest green material. The garment reminded her of his eyes. Golden chips sparkling when heated with passion.

Stroking the soft wool, she held off the questions as long as she could. But they came to her again. *Who had worn the dress before her? Why should she care? She was a thief. Once an instructor of the Nest.*

Her hand stilled. Drem knew the gown would fit her because his hands had roamed her body, measured her curves. Unlike a purse filled with shiny coins lifted from an unsuspecting knight, a dress was personal. Was she like Maman? Receiving gifts for favors of love?

Brigitte felt the pull, tugging her attention to the valley and the army's right flank. The king's banner fluttered as the standard bearer nudged his mount. A knight sat upon his destrier, his broad shoulders stretching his leather jerkin. The rising sun glittered on the polished surface as he turned to speak to the king. *'Tis Drem.* Her heart leaped in admiration and excitement. She pressed her stomach against the parapet and strained to hear what was being said. Fear swept through her. *Please. Please. Do not take him away from me.*

The powerfully built king clasped Drem's forearm, then he whipped his mount around. He galloped toward the knights and soldiers waiting for him to join in their march.

Drem's midnight steed, Aeron, did not move. He lifted his head, searching the wall until he found what he was looking for. Raising his gauntlet-covered hand, he saluted her. To her relief, he rode toward the gates instead of on the campaign.

His pale face was stern. Roses bloomed over skin stretched across high cheekbones. The wind tugged his auburn curls until he clapped his helmet on his head. Barking out orders as he walked past, his focus on those left behind.

Brigitte let go of the wall's ledge and moved away on watery legs. Drem had not gone with the soldiers and he was displeased. How long until he showed himself to her again?

Days later, the weather had shifted over Harfleur and Drem had yet to seek her out.

Storms drove in from the harbor. Rain pounded the streets, washing the town's destruction into the ditches. Mud coated the streets with a slick sheen, making footing unpredictable. A thin layer of ice shifted and crackled with her steps.

Wind whipped at Brigitte's clothes, plastering the damp folds against her legs. She clapped a hand over the hood of her cloak to keep the driving rain from soaking through. Lifting her skirts, she tested the surface before climbing the steps to the Nest. She cast a furtive glance toward the alley, then the garden.

'Twas madness to venture out of the house. And she feared doing nothing of import would indeed turn her into a babbling fool.

Drem would be infuriated when he learned she had come here

without him. The preparations for the archers had kept him away for several days. Even though he had placed a guard at the door, she felt the tension of the townspeople rising. When she had awoken that morning, she had found a note by her bedside table. No doubt a fledgling had slipped into the house while she slept. It left her little choice. She had to speak with them. Explain her reasons.

They held her responsible for their plight. They threatened rebellion against the English soldiers. Brigitte had no desire to find her neck stretched by either faction.

Now that some of the supplies were reaching the harbor, the routines of the garrison had resumed. The king had ensured that shopkeepers were brought in from England. Fresh soldiers had arrived to protect the garrison and with them, coins for the taking.

She rested her hand on the trapdoor's latch and listened. Morning had always been the quietest time in the Nest. Most of the older children slept off the previous night's escapades. Soon the younger ones would be awake, distracting the burgesses while others lifted their wares.

'Twas her one opportunity to search for the treasures Alexandre had stolen from her.

A handful of mud struck Brigitte in the back. She spun as the next one splatted next to her head. Squaring her shoulders, she thrust out her jaw, determined to confront the rabble. "Stop. I'm one of you."

"Traitor!" someone shouted. "Whore."

"I had no choice." She sought a tender face that would remember how she had cared for them. "Don't you see? 'Tis Master Alexandre that brought us to this—"

She cried out as the mud clods pelted her body. The soft missiles became more painful as displaced shopkeepers and other adults joined the mob of fledglings. Intent on returning fire, Brigitte ducked down to retrieve her own weapons of mud and stone. She hissed as a rock cut her cheek. Stars appeared in front of her eyes, filling her head with a buzzing roar.

She staggered through the door, slamming the bolt home, before crashing onto the floor. Voices carried through the wooden panels as they shoved at the barred access.

Scrambling to her hands and knees, she crawled to the trap door. She would return to her old ways, what she knew. Become invisible to those who did not want to see.

*   *   *

Drem rubbed a weary hand over his eyes. Sleep had evaded him for several days and nights. The new archers were put through their paces. Those who had been with him since the beginning of the siege were given an hour or two of rest, but they, too, had to be ready. Their numbers had been decimated by sickness and disease. They had underestimated the timing and the tenacity of the French. The weather had turned. The days were shorter, the nights colder. And now the king had taken their warfare to the French enemy.

Rain pelted the thatched roof. Drem looked up at the ceiling as the pitch of the storm changed. His hand froze over the parchment. Horror tightened his grip on the quill pen, smearing the words he recently had written.

The door opened. Wind ripped it from Darrick's hand, bouncing it against the wall.

"Christ's bones," Drem growled. He slapped his hands over the documents, trapping them before more damage was done. "Shut the damn thing."

Darrick grunted, slamming it behind him. He unwrapped his great cloak and shook it out. Ice pellets flew.

Tilting his head, Drem listened to the drumming on the roof. "'Tis a bitter day."

"Worse tonight."

Drem threw down his pen. "At least we have a fire."

Darrick curled his lip and tossed his cloak on a peg. His wound had healed, his limp less pronounced. The man was angry as a bear prowling a cave. Drem understood his mood. He, too, wanted to be riding in the storm, knowing the power of his destrier charging forward into battle. But orders were orders. Henry wanted them to keep the garrison under English rule.

"D' you intend to speak with your woman?" Darrick asked.

Drem leaned back in his chair. He wished the knight had taken to disobeying orders and rode out of the garrison. The horse's arse would not let go of what he thought needed to be done. Not that Drem didn't want to . . . but Christ on the cross . . . being ordered to wed a woman took the heat out of the moment. There was also that little bit of information he had to share with Brigitte. Her mother's brooch still weighed down his purse. Though why she wished to keep the broken bit of jewelry made no sense to him. He had kept it with him, hoping to learn the meaning of the piece from the priory and now this.

"Haven't had the opportunity, as you well know, brother."

"Best get on with it. I've heard reports of grumbling among the people." Darrick glanced up. "The joining of you and the French-woman might bring peace to the garrison."

"Or a rebellion."

Brigitte hid in the shadowed alley while the early autumn storm pelted her bruised body. She dared not step out until the crowd of angry citizens gave up the chase. Pressed against the stone wall, she watched the townspeople run past. They pushed and shoved until they were in the middle of the square.

Soldiers moved in to restore order. Men-at-arms made their presence known, grabbing at some of the fledglings. Muddy and wet, the children slipped through their gauntlet-covered fingers.

She shivered. Rain seeped through her cloak and trickled down her back. Weary and heartsick, she waited, watching for a moment to climb the steps in safety.

Covered in mud, the taller boy, Tobes, stalked the streets. He stopped and stared up at the mayor's house. He pointed at Brigitte's bedroom window and shouted, "You don't belong here no more."

The message delivered, they slowly began to disperse like the wraiths Alexandre and Brigitte had taught them to be.

She walked cautiously toward the building. Her legs trembled as if she had run through the city. Flashes of her past. The many times she had faced the chance of being caught and branded a thief. They burst through her thoughts. How had she allowed Alexandre to coerce her to thievery when he cared so little for anyone but himself?

The guard presented his pikestaff. It clicked against the stone. The sword at his hip caught the street lanterns' light.

"Bugger off, street trash," he growled.

One of the English boys, a squire she had seen with Sir Darrick, stepped up to her. "What do you want here?"

He seemed taller than the last time she had seen him running with Piers. His arm looked healed from the skirmish weeks before.

Her hand trembled over her mouth. "Please. 'Tis I, Brigitte."

Doubt pulled his brow into a scowl.

"I'm Piers's friend," she added before a shiver took over.

Recognition lit his face. "Let her pass, Godfred," he said.

Relieved, she lifted her sodden skirt and stumbled up the steps before they had a change of heart. She paused, her foot on the last step of the stairs. "*Merci*, Young John."

Blushing, he ducked his head and bent in an awkward bow. "I must away." He turned. "Godfred, don't let anyone pass through those doors."

The soldier grunted at the boy's audacity, giving him an order, and planted his staff over the door.

Brigitte took a shuddering deep breath, climbed the formidable stairs, and stepped into her bedchamber. Her steps faltered. When had she come to think of this house as hers? She shook her head at her madness. Indeed, she could no longer stay in Harfleur. Her heart broke at the thought of leaving Drem. Tears streamed until she could no longer control them. Her chest heaved with silent sobs as she slid her back down the closed door. It took too much effort to strip off her clothes or make a fire. Instead, she sat on the floor, still in her mud-coated cloak and dress, and wept.

Drem's chest constricted at the sight of mud streaked across the floor. He stormed up the stairs, taking two steps at a time in his wide stride. Fear struck him. He had promised to keep her safe. 'Twas a mace to his heart. She had been accosted while under his protection. Why had she returned to the Nest?

Young John followed close on his heels. The boy panted like a hunting dog after a fox. "Shite," he muttered. A horrified look made him glance toward the chamber door. "'Tis that her weeping?" He stopped with his knuckles white against the hilt of his small sword.

"Aye." Drem bit his lip. He willed the courage to take the next steps. To knock on the door. Feeling the boy's pain, he added, "Run along, lad. Tell Cook I order them to serve you an extra trencher tonight. And John?"

"Sir Drem?"

"Have someone bring up buckets of hot water for bathing."

Young John's eyes rounded, but he did not waste any time. He raced down the stairs as if a pack of wolves were on his tail.

Drem waited and listened to the tone of the wailing. It had shifted ¹d now came in starts and stops. He gripped the handle. No greater battle had he faced than the one that awaited him on the other side. He opened the door.

Brigitte lay on the floor. A puddle of mud and rainwater pooled around her feet. He knelt beside her and gently lifted her raven hair from her neck. Dirt streaked across her face.

"Ah, my *caru*," he crooned. "Hush." Sitting on the floor, he drew her into his lap.

A hiccup erupted and shook her body. She buried her face into his chest and wept harder. Confused at what to do, he patted her shoulder. "There now. You'll make yourself sick. We don't want that, do we?"

Her shoulders stiffened under his palm. At a loss as to whether she was injured or angry, he cast a glance around the room. Why had she disobeyed his order and left the chamber?

"Can you let me see you?"

"No," she said. Her mouth moved against his leather jerkin. "I never cry." She sniffed. "Never."

"I have," he said, adding, "a time or two. Although 'tis usually when a maiden tells me no."

The tears had eased. Relieved, Drem ran his fingers through the tangled mess of her hair. Bits of dried mud fell to the floor. "Let me help you," he whispered.

Brigitte gave a halfhearted nod, but it was enough to encourage him to press on. He rose with her cradled in his arms and carried her to the chair by the hearth and set her on her feet. She stood still, her head down, as he began to peel away her clothes.

"You'll let me?" he asked.

"*Oui*," she whispered.

His heart clenched. Where was his strong lady thief? Sweeping the fur from the bed, he spread it before the hearth. He tugged on the ribbons holding her cloak together. The ties slid apart. Removing the sodden, heavy cloak from her shoulders, he hung it on a peg by the fire. Lifting her mane, the color of a starless night, he let the dampened strands flow through his fingers.

Freed from the weight, she took a shuddering deep breath. But still she kept her face hidden from him.

He kissed the crown of her head. Wanting to have her gaze upon him, Drem knelt before her. He took one clenched fist and uncurled her fingers. And then the other. Dirt coated her skin, and under the dirt were cuts and scrapes. He held her as if he were holding a bird in his palm.

Tears slid down her cheeks and landed on their clasped hands. He thumbed the tear, lifting it away. Kissed the damp spot until it erased the sign of sorrow.

"Lift your foot. Place it on my knee."

She complied, steadying herself on his shoulder.

Progress. Drem hid his smile. First one and then the other, the shoes were removed. She stood in her woolen stockings and let him slide his hands under her skirt. He unrolled the damp wool, peeling it from her slender calves. Her toes curled into the fur he had placed to warm the floor.

"Your gown is drenched clear through?"

"*Oui*," she said.

Rising, he gently turned her so that she presented her back. Tugging on the ties, he freed her from the gown. She shivered. The gossamer chemise enhanced her charms instead of hiding them from view.

Yanking the blanket from the bed, he wrapped it around her until she was once again covered. Darrick was correct. He had many questions to ask her. But for now . . . Drem wanted to stare at her beauty forever. He wanted to hear laughter in her voice, her eyes alight with passion.

They jumped at the knock at the door.

Seeing Brigitte's distress, he pointed to the small alcove. She nodded silently.

He hesitated before letting in the servants. Two boys carried in a large oaken tub. A buxom woman followed behind with buckets of water. Steam curled from the rim. She bent low, smiling as she set the buckets down.

"Is there anything more you desire?" Hovering, waiting, she allowed him a view of her wares hidden under her bodice. "'Tis my desire to please you."

Drem glanced at the shadow hiding in the corner. When would his passionate lady return?

He waved off the eager servant. "Aye, bring in more water."

"My *caru*." After waiting until they were alone again, he closed the space between them, speaking low so as not to bring attention. "I must return to my duties. Linger in the tub. Wash away the pain of the day."

She nodded her head.

"There are many things we must speak of." A long pause hung between them until he stepped closer.

"I will wait for you," she whispered.

Chapter 21

Brigitte watched the servant continue to carry the buckets into the bedchamber. Where had they come from? She had asked days before for heated water for a bath and been informed she must make do with the pitcher that stood on the bedside table. Why had Drem felt the need to leave? If only he had stayed until they were finished with their task. Nothing was safe anymore.

She flinched when the woman stopped to stare. Brigitte recognized her face. She had given chase, cleaver in hand, after one of the children who had thought to steal scraps of meat.

The butcher's wife's eyes narrowed before turning away. "So 'tis true what they say. They harbor a thief and a whore while the rest of us sleep in the rubble they created." She kicked a bucket, spilling the water onto the floor.

Brigitte stepped out of the alcove. "Get out," she ordered through gritted teeth.

"Oh, I'll leave, don't you have a care about that."

Brigitte shoved her toward the door. "Out." The fur dropped from her shoulders, revealing the diaphanous chemise.

"I'll be sure to share the bit of news with the one who seeks you out," she said. Her eyes dropped to Brigitte's exposed shoulders. "That one'll pay me well indeed."

"Do not return," Brigitte said. She glanced around the room until she found what she sought. Running to the table, she picked up the short dagger she used for cutting her food. "You'll keep your silence or . . ." She pointed the tip of the blade in the woman's direction.

"You think to threaten me?" The butcher's wife thrust her chin in the air. "Look you. Already heard about the chilly reception you received earlier today. There are many who want you dead. Step outside. See who greets you next time. You'd do best to leave and never come back."

Brigitte stared until the woman shifted uncomfortably. "Go," she said, pointing her weapon at the door.

It slammed behind her. The flames in the fireplace flickered and then rose. Silence followed, drowning out the drumming in Brigitte's ears. She set the blade nearby and with shaking hands began the task of filling the tub.

She rubbed at the flecks of mud clinging to her temple. The wretched woman was right. She no longer belonged to the family of the Nest. If she was to survive, she had to find a way to leave Harfleur without anyone being the wiser.

She untied the ribbons that held the chemise in place and let it drop. It slid down her hips to pool at her feet. Firelight bounced off the crest of her breasts. She turned, letting the warmth penetrate her bare skin. What did Drem see when he looked at her? She tested the curve of her hip, her bottom and thigh. Did he see a thief?

She shivered as she touched the places where Drem liked to nibble. At times, he was like a boy with a sweet. She would hate to leave him. But what would become of them once the king became bored with his new conquest?

Steam swirled around her as she stepped into the tub. She hissed at the heat and lowered herself. Sighing, she used a scrap of linen to cleanse away the mud sticking to her limbs.

Wind rattled the shutters covering the windows. The tapestries used to keep out the cold were drawn and offered the illusion that this was where she belonged. The storm raged outside. It slipped down the chimney, attempting to steal the flames. A chill rushed over the room. The candles flickered. The sound of ice hitting the roof, the shutters, stole the last bit of peace from Brigitte's thoughts.

She rose. Her breath created clouds of fog as she hurried to keep the fire going. Donning the chemise and fur, she brushed off her dress and cloak. Peeking through the crack between the shutters, she searched the streets. Soldiers walked the night, braving the winter storm that had come upon them.

"Too soon," she muttered. The winter had come too soon for everyone.

Brigitte waited. The flames on the candlewick dimmed. The stack of firewood grew thin. And she waited for the man who gave her hope.

* * *

Dawn entered. Morning awakened, like the creaking of old joints. The water in the buckets had iced over. Brigitte stoked the fire and huddled in her bed. Afraid of asking for anything from anyone, she prayed Drem would remember she waited for him.

Two days later, the storm continued to battle the building, demanding entrance.

Restless, Brigitte finished polishing Drem's armor and then settled on organizing the many pouches hidden in his bags and satchels. The purse she had lifted from him before lay in the pile. Picking it up, she weighed it in her palm, deciding whether to give in to her curiosity.

Best to stay her hand at once. The habits of thievery came too easy to some. She tossed the purse on the table. A silver disc emblazoned with a swan cut into its surface rolled out onto the surface. She rocked in the chair and stared.

Memories filled Brigitte's head. She had seen one like it before. Maman's lover had placed it in her hand and told her to find him in Calais. 'Twas why, on her deathbed, her mother had sent her to the city by the sea.

Brigitte rubbed her temple as she rolled the coin between her fingers. Alexandre had had her practice this exercise hour after hour until she could let it play over her fingers while blindfolded.

There was another time she had seen the coin. She searched, recalling the events that had brought her to Harfleur. The men, passing something between them. And now Drem carried it. What did it mean?

Alexandre knew who had brought her here and purposefully kept her away from Calais. She intended to find out what he knew.

Something else was in the little leather purse. She shook it. Her breath caught in her throat as Maman's necklace slithered into her palm. The ugly swan, broken in half, stared up at her with its unblinking emerald eye.

The coin dropped through her fingers like a live eel diving for the comfortable shadows it knew best. The knight had a great deal to explain. What else had he kept from her?

Drem stumbled into the bedchamber. Icicles had formed over his dampened hair, crackled and fell from his shoulders. His neck muscles screamed. How many days had it been since he lay down his head and closed his eyes? He kicked the door shut with his heel and stumbled over discarded buckets. His boots slid over the frost-coated planked floor.

"Shite! What in God's creation . . ."

"I've been waiting for your return," Brigitte hissed. She grasped the small dining dagger as if it were a broadsword.

He pushed back his admiration. She would not understand, and judging by the gleam in her eye, she had no intention of listening to his weak excuses for keeping away from her. The tone warned him to tread cautiously. 'Twas like a banner, waving to announce the enemy preparing for an attack.

"Bastard," she said. Her voice hitched with fear and anger.

Drem edged close, feeling like a hunter of a brilliantly intelligent wolf. He had no chance of winning this battle.

Choosing not to confront her, he turned and shook out the icicles formed on his cloak. "Can I please have a place to lay my head in peace before I ride out to meet the king's army? Mayhap decent food that does not taste like dried death?" *And this woman. Could she not welcome him instead of threatening to cut off his stones?*

"*Caru* . . ." he said.

"Do not call me . . . that . . ."

Searching for what was amiss. Drem glanced around the room. Empty buckets lay cast aside. Embers from a fire struggled to remain alive. Brigitte stood in front of him, her chemise offering glimpses of the curves and secret places he desired and dared him to cross the line of denied admittance.

"Brigitte . . ."

"Don't talk to me of love . . . my sweet *caru*."

"What disturbs you?" He continued to search the chamber for signs to explain her disposition. "You've had to time to rest, have you not?"

She cocked her head to the storm brewing outside. "They say I'm your whore."

"Who says these things?"

"The butcher's wife." The knife in her hand cut through the air. "Everyone. They stand outside, yelling vile things."

Drem strode past and unlatched the shutter. The storm attacked, slamming into his weary body. Shadows slithered over the buildings. Was someone moving back into the alley?

"At least when I was in the Nest, I still had my honor," she said from behind him. "I've lost everything." Her voiced hitched, but she carried on with determination. "What more can I lose?"

Drem could not help himself. Pride leaped in his heart for the warrior who now stood beside him. He slammed the shutters closed. More guards were needed outside the entrance. But their number were already stretched.

"My love, hear me." He stepped cautiously, closing the gap between them. He dragged his fingers through her hair, tilting her chin. "I must ride to the king's army. They are in dire need of supplies."

"And I have had nothing to eat since you left." She struck the air with her hand. "I must leave for Calais. Now."

He glanced at the empty table. No one had thought of her needs, himself included. "I will rectify your hunger, but 'tis not safe to travel alone." Capturing her chin, he said, "We will eat and then ride together."

"It will take too long. Winter arrives early."

"'Tis too dangerous for you." Brigitte started to pull away, but Drem tightened his embrace. He would not lose this moment. "We are not to be separated."

"Why?" she cried. "You have many to choose from. They think me a traitor. A whore and a thief. Why would you care for someone such as I?"

"Because you steal my breath. You make me desire to be a better man." He kissed her forehead. "To believe there is more to my life than fighting by my king's side."

She turned to walk away. Doubt had shuttered and clouded her eyes.

He gathered her close, fearing if he let go he would lose her. "We can defeat those who are corrupt, those who wish you ill."

Her passion had dissipated, scaring him to his core. Her face was set in stone. He shook her, fighting against her desire to ignore what he said.

"You deserve better. You deserve to be treated with honor. Today. This very day. We ride to Calais." His heart broke, knowing something had happened to dampen her spirit. Where was his lady thief? "We ride to save the king." He pressed his lips against her cold, unresponsive form. "We ride to save us all."

The storm gave no sign of abating. A layer of frost already coated the backs of the horses. The cart, loaded with supplies, complained against the cold and the weight of its cargo. The wind bit and ice crystals formed over beards and eyelashes.

Brigitte tugged the cloak closer. She nodded her thanks when Drem tucked the fur around her legs. Exhilaration swept through her as they passed under Harfleur's gates. Freedom, the likes of which she had never known, beckoned her.

"The storm looms over our king and his soldiers," Drem said.

"'Tis why we travel at this godforsaken time," Brigitte grumbled, her arms shielding her chest. "Is it not?"

"The weather. The timing..." He offered an appealing smile. "People are dying."

Brigitte fought down her sympathy. He had lied to her and would continue to lie until he explained why he had her mother's brooch. Her hands fisted of their own volition. She forced them open. A chant to never be noticed echoed in her head. She would use this man and, broken heart or not, cut him loose and sail on to her new life. She forced an understanding smile. "You are the knight. I am but a maiden." Her eyelashes fluttered with determined precision. "We go where you will."

"And we ride to..."

"Calais." She announced loudly. And to seek out Alexandre. She cast a glance to the sides of the road. Who followed them, only time would tell.

Chapter 22

Brigitte glanced up at the roiling clouds. Black spirals sliced into the gray skies. The dark, acrid scent of smoke covered her tongue. "*Chevauchée,*" she whispered under her breath. The English army's trail was an easy one to follow. Her throat tightened. They had burned the fields, driving out everyone in their path.

The harassing Frenchmen drove the king's men deeper into the belly of France and farther away from Calais. The silence between Drem and Brigitte grew heavy and brittle with each passing village. The people stared after them, their eyes haunted by the atrocities that had befallen them.

They passed barren land, stripped of life. The French had also burned villages and fields before King Henry and his soldiers could replenish their provisions. And they had destroyed all manner of protection from the weather, forcing both French and English to sleep on the frozen ground and battle the elements.

Bitter air cut her throat. She coughed into the shawl wrapped around her neck and wished for a hearth to warm her fingers and toes.

Although snow had refused to fall, winter's stepdaughter had appeared in its place. The frigid autumn storm bent what was left of the brittle leaves, tearing them from the trees. She crushed life under her heel.

Brigitte shuddered as their cart rolled past bodies frozen on the ground. Ice cracked and strong men broke while waiting for Drem and Brigitte to save them.

Drem kept casting glances toward Brigitte. He knew. There was something amiss, but the foolish man did not understand they both had crossed the line of trust. Brigitte did not know how to rebuild that bridge. But reach Calais? She would find a way. Her mother's broken brooch cut into her palm, demanding that she loosen her grip.

Drem nudged her shoulder with his as he maneuvered the cart horses over the ravine. "And what shall you ask the king when we are through?"

"For truth. Justice." She shrugged. "'Tis certain it matters little."

Drem drew up the horses. "We spoke of talking freely. Do you recall?"

She flicked a clot of dirt clinging to her skirt. "*Oui,* but then you were but a soldier. Now I discover you are a knight. One who shares the king's private thoughts."

"I'm but his friend. Nothing more."

Brigitte turned. She dug into the pocket hidden in her traveling skirt. "Then perhaps if you do not have the answers, you'll ask him to explain why you've hidden the fact that you've had my mother's jewelry all this time."

The cart horses came to a halt. The reins hung loose between Drem's hands. Her heart sank as she noted the redness creeping up his neck. The tick in his jaw.

Brigitte let the chain slide through her fingers, dangling it between them. "I would have liked to know I could trust you with my life...." Her throat clenched as she wound the chain in her palm. "And with my heart."

Drem stared at the ugly little bird. Darrick had warned him time and time again to speak to her about the brooch. Return it before she learned of his duplicity. "I'm sorry, my *caru.*"

"Stop." She fisted her hands, whitening her knuckles around the necklace. "You may not call me that. Ever again."

"You can trust me." He swallowed the lump that pressed into his throat. His tongue felt thick and heavy. How would he repair this?

"*Merde.*" She shifted her seat until they no longer touched. The wind whipped, cutting through their clothes. She huddled deeper into the fur. "I think not."

One of the men-at-arms who rode ahead to scout out the enemy returned on his destrier. He cast a wary glance at Brigitte, then turned his attention to Drem. "A village not far from here."

"Aye?" Drem asked. He had had enough reports of destruction. "Pray 'tis fit to stay there and warm ourselves until daylight returns."

"Up until this point it has been untouched. There is an inn of sorts."

Drem shook out the reins. "Then we go." He glanced at the tight lines that angled away from Brigitte's mouth. "There will be time for us to settle this."

She folded her arms across her chest and glared in response. "We are headed away from Calais. At this rate, if we are not killed before, it will take weeks instead of days to reach the shore." She watched the sun begin its descent. "There are bound to be refugees who are headed to Calais. Mayhap this is where we part ways."

Drem gritted his teeth until his jaw ached. He took a deep breath. The woman was maddening. He kept his silence, searching for the words to keep her by his side. Or a rope to bind her and keep her out of their enemy's arms.

Their little caravan of wagons and soldiers stopped in the center of the village. The windows were shuttered. No one came out to greet them. Groaning, stiff from the achingly bitter cold, Drem climbed down and held out his hand for Brigitte to take.

With two words, the men-at-arms began to circle and set posts around the valuable provisions.

They waited while Drem pounded on the barred door. He would not give up and threatened to break the planks with his fist.

Brigitte turned. "Mayhap we should sleep in the barn with the wagons and horses."

"No. You are a lady of position. Are you not?" He watched the color leave her wind-rubbed cheeks and knew that she did indeed keep her own secrets. He plowed his shoulder into the door. It creaked as someone on the other side lifted the bar.

Clasping her hand in his, he led her into the warmth of the inn.

The short, rotund Frenchman rubbed his hands together. Behind him stood a haggard woman, strands of gray hanging loose from the twist of hair atop her head.

"You'll find nothing of value here," he said.

"We seek nothing but a place to warm ourselves. To hide from the storm until daylight. Then we are away."

"How do we know you mean no harm?"

Brigitte stepped forward. "Please, monsieur, madame." She dipped a slight curtsy. "We ask only for a respite." She sniffed the air with appreciation. "'Tis that the scent of fresh bread that fills the air?"

"*Oui.*" The woman's response gained her a reproving glare from the innkeeper.

"'Tis a heavenly aroma. A miracle." Brigitte breathed deeply again. "Oh, and sausages." She licked her lips.

Drem hungered for those lips to touch his with as much enthusiasm. Her eyes sparkled with amusement.

"Come. Come," the innkeeper said, waving them in.

"We haven't enough to sell," his wife said.

Ignoring her, he continued, "The sausage is my own recipe. Passed down through generations."

"Then how 'tis yours, husband?" his wife muttered.

Drem arched his brows in wonder as the innkeeper stepped closer. He feared the little man wanted more than coins for their stay.

"We, too, are but merchants who have been displaced." He caught Brigitte's eye. "My . . . wife and I seek but a place to rest." He ignored the tiny gasp and pressed on. "My men will guard not only our possessions but you as well."

Brigitte stepped forward and touched her palm to the little man's arm. "We have money to pay for our night's stay." She turned. "Don't we . . . husband?"

There had been a time when Drem had hoped to hear her call him by that name. But tonight, it sounded like a curse rather than an endearment.

"Aye." He did not care for the way the innkeeper's eyes lit up with greed. "But only enough for one night."

"Welsh, are you?" He tapped the side of his head. "I have an ear for the tongue of different lands." A frown creased the man's brow. "How is it a Frenchwoman and a Welshman are wed?" He grasped Drem's wrist and turned it over to feel the calluses on his fingers and palms. "A merchant with archer's hands?"

Drem curled his fingers. The weight of his broadsword gave him comfort should he need it. But close contact would make it difficult to wield. And there was Brigitte to consider. Did she recognize the danger they were in?

Brigitte stepped beside him, closing the distance. She touched the small of his back. The caress stirred his loins.

"My husband was once a great soldier. But sadly . . ." She ran her hand over his biceps. "He was grievously wounded while fighting at Soissons. I thank God he did not lose his fingers like so many." Tilting her head, she raised her chin, allowing the folds of her cloak to fall away. Her pert breasts lifted with each ragged breath. "Still, 'tis heartbreaking." She wiped at the water leaking from her darkened eyes. "I ask you, kind sir, not to speak of it. For the children we will never be able to birth."

Her feint appeared to work. The innkeeper's wife sniffed in sympathy.

"Husband. Stop bothering them with your questions. Can't you see they are weary?"

"Aye, that I am," Drem said. He made sure to take an exaggerated limp toward the trestle table.

"Sit here until the mistress airs your room." The innkeeper held out his hand. "Monsieur Bastion."

Drem nodded and led Brigitte to the bench. They sat together, shoulder to shoulder, his sword unhindered.

"Madame . . ."

Brigitte looked away from the warming fire. She had finally begun to feel her toes again. The woman watched her expectantly and waited for a response. "De Marneir," she said without thinking.

Drem's shoulder and thigh stiffened against her.

Monsieur Bastion rubbed his hands. "I knew someone by that name. Lovely, lovely woman."

Madame Bastion hissed. "And where is she now?" She snapped her fingers. "Gone. With that man . . ."

"You'll not speak of it," the innkeeper warned.

"Phtt!" she waved him off. "You spoke of it with the other one who came seeking information. How is this different?"

"Silence," he growled, drawing up his short stature.

Drem rose. "I thank you. My lady grows weary."

"*Oui*, I see that she does." Blanching, the woman recalled her station and curtsied. "Follow me, madame. The men will talk of nonsense while you are settled. I will send up a meal of fresh bread and my husband's famous sausages. Perhaps some wine as well?"

Brigitte cast a beseeching glance to Drem, asking him to hurry. He nodded and smiled. Lifting his fingers to his lips, he set sail a kiss into the air.

The stairs were surprisingly steep. She thought she might never reach the top.

The innkeeper's wife chattered as she led the way. "We get but a few travelers this way. 'Tis good to know the damn English king has not destroyed everything. If only our nobility would convince King Charles he is not made of glass. *Le Fou*." Her eyes widened, realizing what she had said could be construed as treason against the mad French king.

"You mentioned others asked about de Marneirs. Perhaps they are long-lost relatives."

"Phtt." She smoothed her palms over her apron. "His tongue and way with words would melt a frozen bank of snow." She shivered. "Angered my husband well enough when he left without paying his bill."

Brigitte's attention caught. Indeed, it sounded too familiar for comfort. "Did this man have a cane?"

"*Oui*, but 'twas all for show. He was . . ." she winked, ". . . robust and fit as they come."

"And did he give his name?" Brigitte turned to the bed and ran her hand over the blanket. She shrugged. "I ask only because I had an uncle who used a cane. I thought perhaps 'twas him."

"*Merde*." She fanned her flaming face, plucking the bodice from her chest. "If that be your uncle, I am the king of England. This one was hale and hearty. Sly as they come. Randy only when he wanted to talk."

"Mayhap he is a cousin? Did he give his name?"

"But of course. He called himself Monsieur Fledgling. Fitting really, the name. I heard word he's been seen from time to time. Dare not seek him out, though. My husband will put a branding iron to his arse if he sees him again."

Brigitte bit her lip. That she would like to see. Mayhap after she first extracted the information she needed.

She dug into her pocket. "If you should happen across him please let me know. I would dearly love to reunite with family."

Madame Bastion plucked the coin from Brigitte's palm. She ran her thumb over the smooth surface. "Only between us?"

"*Oui*." She nodded. "'Tis best our . . . husbands not know everything. Don't you agree?"

Chapter 23

Drem climbed the stairs to the bedchamber. The door loomed before him. How was he to share a room with Brigitte without making love to her? Guilt nipped at his heels like a pack of wolves. He needed to explain his actions without revealing all his reasons.

He touched the latch, testing to see if the door was locked against him. It gave him pause when it did not open. There was sense in barring the door behind the innkeeper's wife. But did Brigitte intend him to sleep in the barn? A freezing pile of straw did indeed seem more enticing than an angry woman.

"Horse's arse," he muttered under his breath. 'Twas time to brave the storm within.

He rapped on the door. "Brigitte, 'tis I. Let me in."

A mixture of relief and absolute terror swirled in his gut as she cracked open the door. Light streamed around her, creating a halo over her head. Dark brown eyes, filled with wariness, snapped at him. His avenging angel.

Taking a deep breath for courage, he walked in and wrapped his arms around her shoulders, trapping her against his chest. Her heart beat wildly against his. Hope welled. Mayhap she would listen, accept what he told her. "My *caru*."

"We cannot go on this way. I must leave you." An aching space spread between them as she stepped out of his arms. "I travel to Calais in the morning."

"You cannot travel alone. 'Tis unsafe." He folded his arms, blocking the doorway. "I won't allow it."

Her voice caught before she continued. "I hear a caravan travels that way. I will join them."

"Brigitte—"

"Madame will return with our meal." She went about the room, feeding the fire in the hearth, withdrawing the blanket from the bed. "When we have eaten, you may choose between the chair, the floor, or the bed."

"Where do you intend?"

"I sleep alone."

A relentless tapping came from the other side of the door. "Madame and Monsieur de Marneir," she called. "As requested, I bring all you desire. Guaranteed to make your mouths water."

Drem arched his brow. De Marneir? Why had Brigitte chosen that as their surname?

Brigitte brushed past him. The transformation from outraged woman to placid wife happened in a trice. Her fingers fluttered over the tray like a covey of quail. She cooed over the loaf of bread and sausages. A simple sip of wine—testing for her darling husband, not doubt—brought a sigh.

Envious of her attentions to every detail of the victuals that were set out on the table, he ached to have her peruse him with such care.

They ate in silence. Brigitte fidgeted under his watchful eye. The bit of parchment Madame Bastion had delivered now lay against her breast, branding her with its secret. She wished nothing more than to eat quickly and pretend to sleep.

"Shite, woman." The knife clattered against the table. "What game are you playing?"

She sniffed and slowly, carefully, placed her dining knife beside the trencher. It rolled under her fingertips. Constantly playing, keeping her fingers limber, was a habit Alexandre had enforced daily. Splaying her hand quietly over her thighs, she leaned into her chair. She plastered a serene smile on her face as she forced her body to relax. She was foolish to think he would readily agree to her plan. He was already angered by her announcement that she was going to Calais alone as he rode to the king's aide.

"I play at nothing."

She did not want to arouse his suspicions further. She had Maman's necklace. And she would soon know Alexandre's whereabouts. Soon she would travel as she had intended before the English had ruined her plans. What more did she need? His heart? The caresses he gave her when he watched from afar? His love? To hear him whisper *caru*?

"Brigitte," he said, pushing back from the table. "As you say, mayhap 'tis time we parted." He lifted her hands, brushing them against his lips. "I would ask, though, for your patience as I explain why I kept the jewelry." Flecks of gold winked through the forest of pain in his gaze. "To ask your forgiveness."

"No need," she said, pulling her hands from his. "'Tis nothing to forgive." Her skirts swished as she paced from the bed to the window. "What is left of Maman has been returned to me. That is all I ever wanted."

"All?"

She placed her hands on her hips. "*Oui*. All."

Drem grunted and shook out his cloak. "Take the bed. I'm off to the barn to see to the men and horses."

Brigitte bit her lip. "Where will you sleep?"

"Do not fear. I'll take the chair." He stood at the door, hesitating as if he needed to say more. Adjusting his sword, he added as he left, "If charity strikes you, I would accept a blanket." He shrugged. "If not, the warmth from the hearth will suffice. 'Tis more than the soldiers are enduring this wicked eve."

The swirl of his cloak shadowed the doorway and he was gone.

She let out a breath she hadn't realized she had kept locked in her lungs. Drained, she dropped onto the mattress. What had she expected? That he would stay? She had made it known as she pushed him away that there was no room in her plans for him. She feared it was too late to call him back.

Turning to the window, she opened the shutters slightly to allow the moonlight to filter in and read the scribbled note. Alexandre's hiding place had been found.

Brigitte stuffed the note under the mattress and leaped into bed as the door opened.

Drem felt his heart turn to ice without her by his side. How could he fix things if the woman would not listen? He shook the shards from his cloak and tossed it on a peg. The jug of wine the innkeeper had sold him for a hefty price offered a bit of comfort. He set it on the table beside him. Temporary solace.

Brigitte lay in the bed, her dark mane spread over the pillow. She breathed softly and rolled away. The slope of her back, the curve of her hip, her trim ankles. They all called to him, to trace each tender shape with his fingertips. Slide his tongue over her skin and watch her shiver as she tried to control her reactions.

He drew back his hand, so close now he nearly caressed her skin. The woman had made it clear she no longer desired his touch. Dropping into the chair, he braced his feet on the hearth and let the heat seep into his frozen toes. He wished his heart was as numb.

"I have to tell you," he muttered, hoping his confession penetrated her dreams. "I have to explain myself for I need your forgiveness." He rolled the cup of wine between his hands before pulling a long drink. "I can't go into battle wondering if you hate me with all your being. I need you to understand. To say a prayer for my soul now and then."

Silence greeted him. "Dafydd ap Hew is my father and he is wanted for treason. He plotted with Owain Glyndŵr and the French to overthrow the throne of England. Part of the Southampton plot." Emboldened by wine, he continued as he stared into the fire. Did he betray his brothers by telling her anything more? "Several nobles were beheaded. Not Dafydd ap Hew, mind you."

He quaffed the drink and poured himself another. Might as well numb the memories.

"No. He's too cunning for that. He'd rather sell his own son than pay for his crimes. Put his family in danger. But he's out there." Drem tapped his chest. "I can feel him here. Eating at me." He slumped deeper into the chair, his shoulders rounded. "And that brings me to the *why*."

After glancing to see if she still slept, he played with the pitcher and debated whether he was a fool or a coward. Perhaps both. "Your *maman*'s necklace. I saw one like it before. An ugly thing not easily forgotten. At Dunstable Priory. 'Twas a message. A warning or a cry for help. I didn't know. I thought my dah was teasing me, making me pay for foiling his plans. I feared others would look upon me as a traitor for keeping the knowledge secret. I had to keep it with me. Study it. Use it to draw my father out of his rabbit warren."

The fire brought life back to his feet. He wiggled his toes and imagined what it would be like to have a fire waiting upon his return home, his woman warming his bed.

"I'll take my chances with the man who tossed me away," he said. "Even though we'd just met and I didn't know how that ugly brooch tied you to my father, I wanted to keep you by my side."

He took a shuddering breath and set his cup on the table. The wine had reopened the wounds of the past. "I intended to return the necklace. Soon. But I failed you. Didn't I? I promised you safety, and instead, you took the punishment from your people. All for a bit of remembrance of your *maman*."

Leaning forward, he rested his elbows on his thighs and buried his head in his hands. He'd been a fool to think telling the sleeping woman would clear his mind. Now he would have to relive it all again when she woke. The thought of her disappointment and distrust in anything he said made his heart ache with loss.

Brigitte opened her eyes and stared at the wall. She watched the fire dance over the shadows and listened. His voice filled with loneliness and despair.

She tugged the fur off the bed and rose. Her chemise grazed her nipples and they pebbled. Memories of his mouth, drawing on them until they formed a bud, sent threads of desire through her blood. She padded across the room. Cold air fogged her breath until she drew closer to the hearth. And to Drem.

The man's chin had dropped to his chest. Strong legs splayed out. His fingers were lax against the chair. Long golden lashes dusted his cheeks. The fire caught the highlights in the waves of the auburn curls, licking his broad neck. Corded muscles, built strong over the years by the weight of his helm, stretched from shoulders to head.

Placing her palm on his shoulder, she lowered herself to kneel beside his chair. Warmed by the fire, protected by the fur, she leaned her cheek against his knee and closed her eyes. "You are forgiven," she murmured softly.

He touched her head, smoothing her hair, tracing the shell of her ear. She turned into his hand, her lips making contact with his palm. Rough calluses and ridges from years of archery creased his hands. They brushed up her neck. The pad of his thumbs made a whirling pattern over her skin, then nudged deeper, plunging into her hair.

Drem leaned closer, raising her so that their lips could meet. He hovered over her mouth, making her ache for what he had yet to give. Yearning, she pressed her hands into the tops of his thighs.

"I want you to—" She couldn't finish. Frustration warred with hunger. How did you tell someone what you wanted when you didn't know yourself?

"Shhh," he said as he layered fluttering kisses over her eyelids.

Wanting more. More of everything. She let the fur drop from her shoulders. Rising, she bent over him until he could see her desire revealed through the chemise. The mere thought of his tongue, his mouth suckling her breasts, made her nipples ache for his touch.

Drem's eyes darkened with appreciation. His hands stole around her waist. Strong fingers encircled her as he stood and carried her to the bed. He set her down, his eyes never leaving her face. "I want this with you. To share the night together." His hand hovered over her mons. "If you'll have me." He waited, caressing the ribbons that held the chemise together.

Heat from his hand carried through the air, warming her core, making her wet with desire. She closed the gap between them. To lie with him again, to feel him inside her, pulsing with life, would make the farewell so much harder. But she could not deny herself the pleasure. She forgave him.

"Oh, *oui*," she breathed. Brushing her hand over his burgeoning flesh, she thrilled at the knowledge that this would be her gift to him. A night of love and tender good-byes. 'Twould forever be etched in her memories as she hunted down the man who had given her mother the necklace.

Before dawn, Drem awoke to the unfamiliar comfort of the innkeeper's mattress. Thin but sturdy, it was heaven compared to sleeping on a cot or the cold, hard ground.

Waking up next to his woman made his day brighter. Though a quiet sleeper, she was indeed a vocal, passionate lover while in the throes of climax. His cock awoke refreshed from the night's love play. He grinned. There were ways to see the sunrise that did not require one to leave one's bed. Best to ensure her day started with pleasure before heading out into the cold. He rolled over to gather his Brigitte into his arms. *My caru.*

Chapter 24

Brigitte's limbs quaked under the woolen skirt. Their night of love had left her weary and sore. She trudged up the hill, stepping past bodies, frozen, abandoned by their comrades. Their empty eyes followed her on this fool's errand.

Frost covered the desolate fields and trees, their bark branded by the fires. The French and then the English army's *chevauchée* had left them wasted and barren.

Regret trailed beside her. Drem had given her all he had to offer. Much more than she could give in return. She had no family. No money. No maidenhead. And, apparently, she had no soul. How else could she manage to leave the man who had stolen her thief's heart?

Drem was a knight of the king. And she had nothing of value. She bit her lip and tasted blood where the cold had already wreaked its havoc. 'Twas best for Drem's future with King Henry.

One day her broken heart would mend. Until then, she must ignore the pain and press on to keep her vow to Maman.

Madame Bastion's note had said the caravan headed to Calais hid nearby in the village. She must make all speed if she planned to join them.

Wind caught the cloak, flapping it against her legs. Grasping it between her hands, she pressed it to her chest. Her knuckles, red with cold, cracked. Ice formed on her lashes, making it difficult to blink. Why did leaving a man who kept so many secrets make her feel as if she left behind a part of her soul?

She tried to warm her heart with the promise to provide Drem with information about the brooch. He was right; it was an ugly piece of jewelry. She had always questioned why Maman treasured it.

She crested the hill. Smoke spiraled from the chimney of a small thatched building. Cautiously, she kept to the edge of the trees and watched for movement coming from the little house.

Ice cracked under foot, scattering a covey of quail. "Hello, little bird," Alexandre said.

Brigitte turned, gasping, as the cane struck.

Alexandre paced the hut. This peasant's home was little more than a pigsty. He sniffed. The pomander did nothing to quell the odor. Tossing it to the table, he bent over his naughty little fledgling. He clenched his fists. She'd brought him to this . . . this hell.

He kicked her chair. "Wake up," he shouted. Pleasure welled when she jumped. Good little bird. Obedient little bird. "You've lost your touch, Bee. I knew you were coming." A wave of loss washed over him. "Have you forgotten everything I taught you?"

She blinked, eyes wide, and drew back until she noticed the ropes tied around her wrists. "What have you done?"

He dangled the necklace with the broken brooch. When he was through with her, he would sell it. The swan's emerald eye winked at him. He chuckled, enjoying the thought that the ugly beast shared a secret with him. "Happy to have it back where it belongs: in my purse," he snarled, his amusement vanishing. "But not enough to pay me back for my hospitality at the Nest." He dropped it into the pouch hanging from his waist. "Stand up." He threw her cloak to her. "Our journey is just beginning."

Brigitte caught it and struggled to put it on despite the binding around her wrists. "Let me go. You no longer have need of me."

"Ah, but that is where you are mistaken." He grabbed her by the back of her neck. 'Twas a mystery why God fashioned such frail bones to hold up one's head. The laundress, Claudette: hers had snapped with one good blow. It angered him to know he had been driven so low. If only others would do as they were told. "See that you obey my orders this time."

Brigitte stumbled as he shoved her over the threshold. The wind pushed them as if to warn them to turn back. Alexandre narrowed his eyes against the cold, peering into the storm. "Come, dear Bee, we are away to Calais. Just as you desired."

Drem sank down on the mattress. Brigitte's cloak was missing from the peg. It should have been hanging near the hearth, warming before they left to find the king's army. Had she gotten up to use the privy?

Heat flared up his neck as he thought of their passion throughout the night. Warmth filled his muscles. Their night of love had left him rested and relaxed. He smiled. Perhaps she needed a moment to collect herself.

The sun began to burrow through the cracks between the shutters. The time of waiting out the storm was over. The well-rested horses would need feeding and then they must be on their way. He had a duty to perform.

In haste, he drew on his leggings and shoved his feet into his boots. After donning his shirt, he added the padded gambeson for warmth and protection. Then the leather jerkin.

Bending to pick up his sword, he noted a bit of parchment between the mattress and ropes.

The scrawled message urged her to leave at once if she was to meet with the caravan.

Drem paused. He looked for signs of what he had missed before. The small knife she used for her meals no longer lay upon the table. The ugly broken swan brooch and swan coins were missing as well. He felt for his purse. Hounds of hell! His money was gone too.

How much distance had she already put between them? On horseback? On foot? The only way to know was to interrogate the innkeeper's wife.

He raced down the stairs. His hobnailed boots struck the steps rapidly. The main hall in the inn was bare of life. Drem checked the rooms. They were empty, abandoned. Apparently, his fine Welsh blood and French currency had not been enough to keep them there.

His chilled breath released puffs of fog into the air. The door stood open, letting in the cold. A skim of ice had formed over a bucket.

They had done their work well. The kitchen was empty. They had poured water into the hearth, dousing the fire and leaving it in ruins. It would seem they were several hours ahead of him. But which direction had they taken? And had Brigitte traveled with them of her own free will?

He ran out to the barn and kicked open the door. His men grumbled as the light streamed in. "Erick. Godwin. Why are you not about?"

Erick, newly arrived from England's farming country, sat up. Bits of straw clung to his dark brown hair. Looking confused, he scratched his head. "Don't remember much after Monsieur Bastion served us a meal. Said you sent over those fine sausages." He made a face. "Only ate half of mine. Had an odd taste, if you ask me." He turned to look at the man beside him. "But him . . ."

Godwin, the man-at-arms, had recently returned to duty after a bout with dysentery. His skin had turned a sickly green before he bent over and retched into the straw. Shaken, eyes wide, he wiped his mouth with a trembling hand. "Poison?"

"Aye." Drem could not look at them. They could have died while he made love to the thief in his bed.

"Fart-licking bastards," Godwin muttered as he tried to put his clothes to rights.

"Can you ride?"

"Well enough." Godwin paused. "We don't mean to make 'em pay?"

"Too late for that. They've flown for the hills like the black-hearted French crows they are."

"Sir Drem?" Erick pointed to one of the empty stalls. "They've stolen one of the mounts."

"Just one?" His heart sank. Did Brigitte think nothing of stealing the cart horse? "See what else is missing."

As daylight broke through the heavy gray clouds, a new spiral of smoke billowed on the horizon. The sun winked over the crust of ice, melting it like an avenging force. Henry's army burned the fields and buildings as they marched across France.

Drem swore under his breath. "Bloody hell, they are going deeper into the beast."

"Think the French have pushed them back?" Erick asked.

"'Fraid so," Drem said over his shoulder. He examined three paths in the melting frost. One separated from the two.

"Nothing missing to tell of," Godwin reported.

"Think you well enough to take the carts and search out our men?"

"'Tis only my gut, Sir Drem." He drew back his shoulders. "I serve our king and England. Erick and I will manage."

"Good." Drem nodded, keeping his eyes on the vanishing trail. "Head for our men."

He glanced up. The men watched him. Did they question him? "Horses are too valuable to lose. I'm going after the horse thief."

* * *

Alexandre pushed Brigitte toward the horse. The pathetic animal barely looked strong enough to carry them. Too bad he was unable to bring out the knight's destrier. Steal his horse as well as the woman? That would have taken the stupid man's pride down to the level where it belonged. He had heard the rumors. The knight's father was a traitor. Alexandre found it amusing and snorted. No wonder the English king nearly had lost the siege at Harfleur. He glanced at his protégée's pinched face.

She did not know it . . . yet . . . but he had many plans for her. He'd use her for ransom. There was money to be made. There were people in power willing to pay him to keep their secrets. He liked that idea: a reward to keep her hidden or a reward for finding her. It all depended on the Count of Nevers and his brother, the Duke of Burgundy. He intended to meet with them. An idea sprouted. What better way than to stop them as they rode to the battlefield? He had seen their numbers, vastly outmanning the English army. The victorious brothers would have full pockets after killing off the English. Ransoms would be paid. The thought of so much gold made his mouth water.

"Mount up," he snapped, dragging her forward. "You first . . . my lady." The title of respect made his stomach turn. Mayhap he would decide whether to explain to her who had abandoned her in the ditches of Harfleur. If not for his interference, she would have been drowned in a river, like an unwanted cur. "Calais awaits."

She cradled her hands to ease the pressure. The rope twisted around her wrists, making her skin raw. Blood pulsed into her fingers. *Too tight. Too tight.*

"You intend to make me ride into Calais like a captured thief?" Brigitte snagged the horse's mane with her fingertips and tried to pull her body into the saddle. If she moved swiftly, she could escape. *Pull up. Keep your skirts out of reach. Grab the reins.*

Alexandre sighed and cupped his hands. He motioned for her to mount the horse.

She fumbled to keep her balance as she placed her foot in his palms. *Face close. Kick it. Then ride. Hard.*

Alexandre guessed her intention and grabbed her leg. He shook his head. "You've lost your talent, little bird." He tossed her up. Tightening the rope to the saddle, he picked up the reins.

He hooked his foot in the saddle and swung up on the old horse. The beast's back sagged under his weight. "Never fear," he said, catching her with the edge of his cane. "I'll make sure you remember everything I taught you."

She turned her palms, wiggling her fingers, slipping them under the folds of her skirt. They were still as nimble as when she had been lifting coin purses off the traveling merchants. She picked at the material, pulling until the woolen thread began to loosen. One of Alexandre's many rules: Get the target talking, distracted by the weight of their own importance.

"We'll have another Nest in Calais?"

He rode behind her. The cane pressed deeper into her stomach.

"We are going to Calais, are we not?" she asked.

"I have bigger plans for you." He chuckled, ruffling the hair on the back of her neck.

Her stomach twisted. The madness had overtaken the master once again. "We are not going to Calais, are we?"

"*Oui.* Soon enough. First, though, we ride to your sire and uncle."

Chapter 25

Brigitte turned to stare at Alexandre. She studied him, looking for signs that revealed his lies. "What sire and uncle? You know I have no family."

"Ah, but that is where you are misinformed."

His smirk made her shiver. Something was not right. Arrogance replaced his anger. Emotion shimmered under the surface.

"My *maman* is dead."

"*Oui.*" He shrugged.

"I think someone has played you for a fool, my dear Alexandre."

"Your sire is nearby. I shall take you to him."

Eyes narrowed, she watched his jaw clench. "*Merci*, but I go to Calais. Maman always spoke of it so fondly."

She eyed the distance to the ground. *Jump. Leap. Run.*

"Mayhap he will give me a reward," he continued. "Sit still. You do not wish to fly."

She scanned the countryside. Black smoke billowed across the gray, blustery sky. "This is not the way to Calais. You've made a wrong turn. We must go to the west."

The cane tightened against her stomach.

"Or your uncle, the duke, will pay me handsomely to keep you away. He's done it before." He nuzzled her neck. "And he has a very, very deep purse."

"You're mad," she muttered. The loose thread in her skirt was now wound around her finger. She broke it off, letting it flutter to the ground. "Maman was many things, but married to nobility was not one of them."

His bark of laughter reverberated against her ear. "Don't be a stupid cow. Of course she was never married. The Count of Nevers has

many paramours. And many bastards. As does most of the nobility."
He gripped her chin, bringing her head to face him.

Her neck ached until she thought he meant to break it. A vision of
sweet Claudette's broken body made her fight against his hand. She
plucked another thread from her skirt and released it. The bit of color
fluttered and tangled in a bush.

"Attend me. I am more than the master of the Nest. I am a master
of gathered information to be sold to the highest bidder."

"You are mad."

"Perhaps. But I will be rewarded." He silenced her with a hard
pinch. "Quiet. I must decide who will pay the most for you to disappear. Your uncle prefers biddable brothers who do as he commands.
Your sire oddly prefers to care for the product of his spilled seed."

"Unlike your sire?" She regretted the words instantly.

His knuckles whitened. The gray of his eyes became like ice. She
shivered despite her efforts to disguise her fear.

Closing her eyes, she focused on the threads. They were looser,
easier to tug on and break off. *Please Drem. Do not give up on us.
Follow me. Please.*

"*Oui,*" he said. He grabbed her hair, forcing her eyes open. "My
sire tossed me on the dung heap as soon as he could. But who needs
a whore and a thief for parents? I got what I needed from both of them.
They taught me to survive. And I beat them at their own game." His
teeth flashed. "'Tis true. Revenge tastes like nectar." He leaned close.
His breath brushed her face. "You become a god. Choosing who lives
and who rots in the ground."

They stopped at the swollen river, its banks overflowing with debris. The bridge that would have carried them across had been destroyed. By whose hand? English or French, it did not matter.

He let her go, nearly unseating her.

Brigitte scratched for a handhold to keep from falling. The thread
she had been about to set loose spun to the ground. She watched it,
fearing what she would see when she looked up at Alexandre.

"My decision is made. We follow the armies. 'Tis certain your father and uncle will attend the battle. Most nobles like to watch the
rest of us die for them, fighting their ridiculous wars."

They followed the river until they came to a narrow passage.
Brigitte tensed as he directed their mount to enter. "It looks deep."
She glanced over her shoulder.

His mouth was set in a firm line. His jaw cracked as he ground his teeth together. He kicked the horse's sagging belly and the beast leaped into the rushing water.

Brigitte opened her mouth to scream. Frigid water ripped the breath from her lungs.

She held on to the beast's neck as it dropped into the depths. Her cloak dragged her down, deeper and deeper, until she thought they could go no farther. It was so cold.

A jolt shook her. Alert, she recognized the cadence. The horse struggled to plow its way to shore. Its hooves struck again . . . again . . . again.

"Wake up," Alexandre roared.

He stood over her, dripping water on her face. Brigitte squinted up at him. The sun, weakened and fading, struggled against the increasing clouds.

She tried to move. Her limbs were numb. The words came out garbled as she attempted to explain.

"Thought I almost lost you." He rolled her out of the cloak and shook it.

Did he care? Had the boy who had befriended her years before returned?

"'Twould be a pity to lose my treasure." He wrung out the water. Squatting beside her, he examined the hole she had been working. "Where'd this come from?" A worried frown formed. He glanced toward the bank where they had entered the river.

Brigitte slid her hands to the hilt of his small sword. The smooth metal felt like fire against her frozen hands. Too late.

He stood. His jaw hardened. His hand curled into a fist and beat out an annoyed rhythm on his thigh.

"You think to betray me? To flee?" He pulled her up by the front of her dress. "To steal the money owed to me? I've earned every gold coin by harboring you in my Nest. And you and the bastard knight ruined it for me."

"Alexandre—" Shivering, she stumbled on numb legs.

"Another storm is coming." His cruel mouth twisted before he released her and bent to retrieve her cloak. It dangled between them.

"*Merci*," she said through gritted teeth.

"See if you feel bold enough to run away from me now," he said, tossing the cloak in the bushes.

* * *

Drem drew his cloak tight against his body and pulled the hood over his head. His shoulders slumped, taking the brunt of the wind. The trail disappeared soon after he found an abandoned cottage. He had failed in his mission to prove his loyalty to the king and the brotherhood, and that he could be trusted.

Instead, here he was, riding into a storm away from the king and his brothers. They were in need of his service and he had failed them. He had lost much more than a mission.

He tried to shake off the hopelessness. Why did the tests continue to come?

The woman had stolen his king's horse. Didn't she know what would have to be done? Severe punishment would be expected. But even so, he could not bring himself to set his hand against her. In truth, he did not give a damn about the cart horse. He needed to find her. They had more to say to each other.

Each time they lay together brought them closer. 'Twas only the night before that he had bared his feelings. Told her some of his secrets. No wonder it had been easy for her to forgive. She never meant the words she spoke. He should have known she would run from him the first chance she got.

Fool that he is, he thought they would never part. What could he do but give chase? The thief had stolen his heart.

His heart ached until he thought he might lose the last crust of dried bread he had eaten.

Aeron stumbled. Ice crusted underfoot. Pellets clanged against metal. No quiet, stealthy movement for this lonely soldier. If the enemy were about, he would be an easy target.

The horse's ever-alert ears twitched.

"Stay strong, Aeron." He smoothed his glove over the charger's withers. Frost clung to its dark coat and mane.

Drem glanced at the shrubs and trees. He prayed the rest of France was hunkered down by a hearth to stay warm until the storm passed. By the time they crawled out of their huts, he already would have joined the English army.

A bit of gold caught his eye. It fluttered against a shrub. He caught it before the wind took it. The woolen thread slid over his leather gauntlet.

Blood began to pound in his head. A war drum, thumping, challenging the weary to find the strength and courage to push on.

Not far down the path, another thread clung to a tree branch. Drem nudge his mount to a gallop. The cadence of the drum increased. She'd left him a trail to find her. Why?

Alert to ever-pressing dangers as he rode closer to the enemy, he searched for more signs. *Tell me where you are.*

The trail stopped at the riverbank. He nudged Aeron toward the water. The horse's ears twitched back in a warning.

"Clever boy," Drem said.

He rode to another portion of the river. Though wider, he could tell it to be shallower. The water raced past the engorged banks. They would have to ride fast and hard to reach the other side.

After ensuring his weapons were secure, he spurred the horse on. The destrier charged the river just like the Welsh god of battle Aeron had been named after. His hooves struck the rock. The impact jarred Drem's teeth. He rose in the stirrups and leaned over the steed's powerful neck.

Relief rushed over Drem as they reached the other side. He leaped from the saddle and wiped the stallion dry. While inspecting Aeron's hooves, he noticed imprints dug into the ice-crusted mud. Three sets. A smaller horse. And two made by humans. One quite diminutive compared to the larger one.

He searched the edges of the clearing for signs of the direction in which they'd headed. A woman's cloak hung in the shrubs, tangled by thorns and grasping branches. Drawing his sword, he hacked through the dense thicket until he could reach it.

She would need the cloak when he found her. Hope and fear mingled until they swirled into a storm raging inside his head. He was on the correct trail. She was alive. But for how long without protection from the early winter? He had to reach her in time.

Snow began to fall, coating the meadow that emerged from a grove of trees. Following his instincts, he rode the shadowy trail. It took him farther into the heart of France. But that was where Brigitte must be.

Drem drew back on the reins.

The bits of thread had stopped.

* * *

Brigitte had never felt so cold. Her teeth clattered, aching from the constant impact. Each muscle in her body burned from shivering violently. "P-p-please."

Her head bobbed against the horse's shoulder. How could Alexandre be so cruel? He was a demon.

He had stripped her of the cloak and slung her over the beast. At least her stomach had stopped aching. She no longer felt the pressure of the saddle's bridge digging into her flesh. She pressed her cheek into the animal's warmth.

Sleep. Dreams of sitting by a hearth. Children, playing at her feet.

"Drem," she whispered. If only he would come for her. Find the bits she had left. If only. Was that his voice?

She reached for him. Her body jerked as she began to tumble, falling into a dark cavern.

Alexandre looked down at the stupid woman lying across the horse. He braced his cane on her back, keeping a firm hold on her. The wench would not get away from him. He thanked God she had stopped struggling. All the chattering teeth had started to get on his nerves. Like dragging steel against a stone. The bitch had a powerful bite. His hand still ached from where she'd tried to take a chunk out of his flesh. Ah, to ride in peace and quiet.

He pulled his cloak close and hoped he was right. His fingers were cold. He needed to find shelter before the sun set.

"That's a good birdie," he crooned. "We'll find the army soon."

Getting no response, he nudged her shoulder. A layer of snow fell away. Her dress, stiff and unyielding, stuck to the saddle. Icicles had formed in her hair. He brushed it from her face. "*Merde.*" Her lips were purple.

He halted and dragged Brigitte off the horse. "*Merde*, Bee, you're no help. No help a'tall." He released her, and she fell. . .

Alexandre could do nothing but stare at her. She had long been a pain in the arse. And once again she'd stolen from him. One of those spoiled nobles would have paid good coin for her.

He rubbed his mouth. *Think. Damn you.*

That ugly broken necklace. People paid for information just as easily as for a body. Always a good commodity to have. Easier too. No mouths to feed. No one to whine and complain. Bitch and moan. And bite.

After searching her bodice, he lifted her stiff skirt. A little pouch, sewn into the lining, bulged with treasure. He tore it away, then rolled Brigitte's body under a bush.

Dusting off his hands, he remounted. Taking a deep breath, Alexandre began to count the money he would make.

Sadness tried to raise its head. Should he have buried her? He looked over his shoulder.

"Bee."

After tipping his cane at her in a salute, the regret vanished like early morning dew. No one would notice one more dead soul.

Chapter 26

Drem led Aeron to the river and let him drink. Then he brushed the snow off the horse's thick neck.

He held out a handful of oats. "Not much, I know."

The destrier nickered, blowing clouds from his velvet nose and ate greedily.

Daylight was fading. Soon Drem would have to decide when to find his king and abandon the hunt for Brigitte. But not yet.

He swung up into the saddle to return to the trail. After a time, the argument in his head became too much. Going back to the inn made little sense. Earlier, he had seen the signs of smoke. The men were marching to the south. If he crossed over, cut to the southwest, he would intersect with them. Something called to him, urging him on.

Drem nudged the destrier. The beast needed no further encouragement and leaped into a gallop. He'd never had the talent like his sister: night visions. They said she dreamed of him and would never give up until she found him. A determined, courageous woman. He had thought the same of Brigitte when he first saw her outside Harfleur's wall. Their hearts came from a place of pride and passion. The two women in his life would be good friends when they met.

Aeron's ears twitched, listening to the sounds of nature. The beast tensed, muscles bunching.

Drem watched him. The battle-trained stallion did not know fear. They entered a thick grove of trees. He nearly missed it. An imprint of hooves had cut into the dirt. Recently. The snow had yet to cover the indentation.

He prayed those sounds were not from the French army. Alone and exposed, he might not last through a skirmish, but he vowed to take down as many as God gave him. The protection of his sword arm was meant for Brigitte and his king.

Shadows grew longer and deeper. They covered the dirt road. Bits of debris from the storm skipped across his path. Something buried under the bushes, fluttered, throwing light and darkness. The trail had disappeared.

He recalled the stories he had heard from his mother and sisters, of the wee people in the woods. Faeries and elves, wood sprites and trolls. Sorcery. His frozen brain brought him things to see that were not there. He shook his head free of the thought.

Aeron balked as they trotted past.

"Steady, my friend," Drem murmured.

He unsheathed his sword. He swiped off the crystals covering his lashes. Was it another cloak? Caught on a bramble, it flapped against the branches. A good thing to wrap around his freezing bones. Unless there was a dead body attached to it. He had already ridden past many a dead soul and did not have the stomach for another.

Dismounting, he crept toward the still form. Snow iced the golden material with a coating of pure white.

His heart twisted. "No."

'Twas a woman with dark hair the color of midnight, lit by a million stars. He had found her. But he was too late.

"Brigitte." He sank to his knees.

Her dress had frozen to the unforgiving ground. He pulled her into his lap. Cradling her to his body, he wrapped his cloak around them, sharing his heat.

"My love," he whispered. His hand trembled as he smoothed her hair from her face. Her lips were blue against the pallor of her skin. Drem rubbed his hands over her body, her arms and legs. Heat radiated from his palms as he lay them on her neck. He held her, refusing to let her go. "I've found you," he chanted as he rocked her, kissing her face, her mouth. So cold.

Aeron stood beside them, as if knowing to block the wind with his body. He nuzzled Brigitte's neck, lipping her hair, warming her with his breath.

Drem could not give up. He would not. Not now. Not ever.

Pressing his ear to her chest, he listened for a heartbeat. A breath. *Please.* Was something there?

The grove of trees stood like soldiers, watching in silence. Aeron stamped his hooves.

Frustration and fear began to boil inside. Another test?

"She doesn't deserve to be punished so cruelly."

Drem closed his eyes. He could not look upon her broken body, devoid of passion and pride. He pressed his lips over hers.

Were they warmer? He rubbed his hands over her limbs again. Resting her slender neck in his palms, he caressed her skin and felt for signs of life.

A faint pulse beat against his fingers.

"Brigitte." Grasping her arms, he shook with hope. "Wake up. My love. Breathe. Open your eyes."

Wrapping the cloak closer, he continued to cradle her. Then he heard the most wonderful gasp and felt her chest press into his body.

Dark lashes fluttered over pale cheeks. And then she opened her eyes. Though glazed, they were the most luscious sable brown he had ever seen.

"Drem." Her teeth began to clack together. Muscles contracted as the rest of her body awakened from the deep sleep of the dead.

He rose, holding her tight. "Aye, 'tis me." He rained kisses over her and let the tears fall.

She rested her palm to his jaw. Pain filled her gaze. "*Merci.* But you should not have come for me."

Drem blinked. Was she not pleased that he had found her? "'Tis nothing a good knight wouldn't do." His jaw clenched, fighting the hurt that followed the betrayal. "I thought to have the king's horse returned."

Her chin rose. Pride warred with a broken spirit. He had to learn what had made her run from him. Why had she cared so little about herself and so much for Calais?

He set her on Aeron's back and fetched her cloak. It had thawed and would offer one more layer of protection from the elements. He mounted behind her. Wrapping his arms around her, he shielded her from whatever might come from the shadows. In time, her back rested against his chest. He listened to her breathe, finding reassurance that she still lived under his care.

The wind swirled the snow over them, relentlessly sticking to their clothes as they rode out of the meadow. The darkest of nights fell. A moonless sky. Clouds covered the stars. The temperature dropped.

Drem searched for winking lights, signs of life. He shivered in tandem with Brigitte. If he did not find shelter soon, they would both be dead by morning.

They rode past a low stone wall. Encouraged, he directed Aeron to carry them closer. There had to be an opening. Shadowy structures stood out from the trees. No light. No smoke spiraling into the night sky. But there would be a barrier between them and the elements.

"Stay with me," he said. "God has led us to safety for the night."

"*Oui.*" Her body shook and she grasped his gauntlet. "We must talk."

"Aye. When we are warm, there will be time to talk."

Brigitte sat near the hearth in the center of the room and warmed by the fire Drem lit earlier She listened to rustling below the floor. The timbre of Drem's voice as he murmured to Aeron, settling the beast in for the rest of the night.

It had been a peasant's humble home. A place for animals to stay warm during the winter months. Their earthy scent still lingered. A bed and rough-cut table and chairs stood in the corner, close to the fire. The thatched roof shuddered against the wind.

They were safe. Unless Alexandre was nearby. Or they found themselves caught between the warring armies.

Tremors shook her until her muscles ached clear to her bones. Would she ever be warm again?

Drem climbed up the ladder, squeezing his broad shoulders through the opening. He tossed his satchel to the floor, then glanced around the room, his gaze stopping when he caught her staring at him. His hair stuck out at wild angles. Auburn brows arched as he crawled farther into the loft. He ducked his head to keep from hitting the low rafters.

Heat flamed up her neck. She couldn't help smiling at him. Never had she seen a more welcoming sight than when she'd awoken to his handsome face.

"'Tis a small space." He tugged on his leather jerkin to drag it over his head.

Brigitte pushed up to help. "Let me," she said.

Their hands touched as they fought for purchase. Lightning seemed to pass between their fingertips. They did not move, just touched, connected by the tips of their fingers.

Drem released his hold and bent, letting the thick leather slide off his back. Then the padded gambeson. Brigitte hung it on a hook near the fire. She turned as he drew his linen shirt over his head.

Tiny gasps of air slipped through her lips as she admired the muscles playing over his rib cage. The waist of his leggings had settled low on his hips. She recalled the feel of his skin. Like an ermine fur her mother had coveted until Monsieur le Faire had given in to her pleas. She licked her lips. The taste of his skin, the strong, supple muscles. She had missed him the moment she climbed out of the bed at the inn.

His hand hovered over the ties holding up his leggings. He tipped his chin in her direction. "When you're done ogling, you'll want to take off your own sodden bits so they can dry."

"I am not ogling."

His brows arched higher.

"I am merely ensuring that you . . ." She fluttered her hand toward his groin. She blinked. Had she seen Maman do that? "That you were not injured in your . . . um, ride."

He toed off his boots and stood in nothing but his leggings. Rocking on the balls of his feet, he braced his hands on his strong hips and waited. The green of his eyes glittered back at her, challenging her to ignore his orders.

"No, sweetness. My stones are hale and hearty. As well as the rest of me." He glanced down. "See for yourself."

Brigitte tried not to accept his baited challenge. But she clearly recalled how she had admired his male . . . appendage, which grew under her gaze.

" 'Tis my heart you damaged."

The velvet of his voice slid over her. Slicing into her consciousness. If only she could find the words to tell him how she felt. Explain her actions. Would he want to listen?

" 'Twas not my intention." Did he truly care for her? Her mind was raw from the damage Alexandre had wrought. Her body ached as warmth returned.

"The French and English armies are converging. We ride to them." He strode toward her and lifted her hair from her shoulders. "You'll want dry clothes to keep you warm."

Nodding, she fumbled with the ties at her sides. Tears came unbidden.

He brushed her hands out of the way. The ribbons fell away, freeing her from the damp woolen bodice. She clasped it to her chest.

He brought her around until she was facing him. A scowl drew his brows together as he focused on his task of releasing the skirt.

She stared at his hands. Strong fingers plucked at the knot. The hair on the back of his hand glistened like fine threads of gold. Those same hands once had brought her a pleasure she never knew existed. She shifted, hungering to be touched again with passion and tenderness.

Taking the blanket from his satchel, he held it out to her. "We leave before dawn."

"A moment. I have something that is yours." Brigitte searched her skirt. Her hand came away empty. "*Merde*."

She spun on her heel. Rage thrummed through her veins, melting any ice the vermin had tried to put there. "I will kill him," she vowed. "The next time I see him, I will run him through with his damned cane."

Drem took a step back. "Your friend? Alexandre?"

"He is no friend of mine." She threw the skirt over the back of the chair. "He took my purse and left me for dead."

When he didn't respond, she added, to clarify her outrage, "It held my mother's necklace." She waved the air. "Yes, the ugly one."

"Your word, sweetheart. Not mine."

"A person would have to be blind not to notice just how misshapen and ugly the piece is. But it was my property."

"I'm sorry. I cannot promise you we will find another just like it. Mayhap you can let it go?"

"*Oui*? Really? And would you suggest that if you knew what else was in that little purse?" She waited, grinding her teeth.

Drem sighed. "And what might that be?"

"All your money, which I lifted from your leather purse." She folded her arms across her chest. "Now you understand why I want to run him through with his cane."

"I would have done it simply because he wished you harm."

Drem sat across from her. His satchel lay across his thighs. He kept it there to cover the growing tent in his leggings. Damn the thief. She still had his heart. And it hurt all the more to know he didn't want it back. But what did the woman want?

Drem cleared his throat. "The cot is naught but rotted rope."

She tilted her head. The blanket slid off her shoulders as she watched him with haunted eyes. "So I noticed. No matter. I have slept on worse." She tested the ropes. Strands of dried hemp broke into dust. "It appears our host has been gone for some time."

"Aye. The hay below is moldered and filled with rats."

Her glance darted about the loft. "I can stomach many things, but not rats. They were everywhere in Harfleur."

Drem grinned and vowed to remember that bit of information. He spread his arms and motioned her to come where it was safe.

Brigitte took a hesitant step closer. "Do you think that chair will hold us both?"

His grin fell and his arms dropped. Where did they go from here? Neither one of them knew whether they could trust anymore.

He rose and spread out his cloak on the floor. Grabbing her hand before she could turn away, he pulled her down with him. His back braced against the hearth, he enjoyed the feel of her, alive, in his lap.

Hooking his satchel, he dragged it closer. The boiled leather had kept the last crust of bread dry. The wineskin he'd bought from the innkeeper was still half full. "This will keep us until we reach Henry's caravan of soldiers."

He nudged the crust into Brigitte's mouth. Then motioned to the wine. "'Tis safe."

"*Oui*," she whispered. "I know this in my heart."

Drem took a sip from the bottle and handed it to her. The wine slid down his throat, warming his chest. "Tell me how we made love all night and then you left with another."

She had a look about her that told him that her secrets were dear to her. Her shoulders hunched. "Why? 'Tis the question I keep asking myself. What do I have to offer?"

He rubbed her back, sliding his hand up to her neck. "You give me purpose, a will to survive. The passion to fight for what is mine. The reason to fight and return from battle."

"Your king will never allow our union."

"We will find a way."

She lowered her head, "You do not understand. I am worse than no one." Her hands twisted the blanket. "I am a bastard." She stopped. "*Merde.* 'Tis why Alexandre wanted me. Tricked me into going with him to Calais."

His hand stilled. "Your sire?"

"*Oui.*" She dropped her head into her hands. "According to Alexandre, I am one of many illegitimate children of the man my mother called Monsieur le Faire."

"'Tis common among—"

"Nobility," she finished.

Drem shifted but made certain she could not escape his embrace. "He wished to ransom you?"

"Given the opportunity, the master of the Nest would sell anyone." She hunched further in the blanket. "Or murder them."

"He thinks you dead." Drem straightened, pulling her shoulders into his body until she rested against him. "'Tis a good thing for us. Easier to catch him with his guard down."

"But why take Maman's brooch?"

"Mayhap he thinks 'tis proof his information can be trusted."

Drem stroked her neck. Slender and graceful. A noble's neck. Illegitimate or not, there was a bigger reason for someone to care about her whereabouts.

"Do you recall how you came to Harfleur? Did the vermin speak of anyone?" If he had a name, he could take it to the brotherhood. The connection to the items in Dunstable Priory was becoming clearer.

"But of course. The Count of Nevers and the Duke of Burgundy were mentioned. He spoke of them as my sire and uncle." She thought for a bit and added, "Uncles. He mentioned more than one uncle. But why does that matter? Maman never married. So as I said, I am no one."

Chapter 27

Drem shook free of the fear that he might lose her after all. "We make quite the pair."

Brigitte offered her first true smile since Alexandre had left her to die. "How so? Because I am a bastard thief and you are the king's trusted knight?"

"Ah, but you are the most beautiful and skilled thief I have ever met." He wiggled his brows. "Or made love to."

"Then what could be better than that?"

Her laughter warmed his heart. He vowed to make her laugh more often. Another reason to come back alive from the battlefield.

He brought her hand to his lips. "I am the son of a man wanted for treason." He kissed each knuckle with a skill learned from too many years with the king. "And you are a nobleman's daughter." He paused, a flash of memory freezing his thoughts. "Did you say the Count of Nevers?"

"*Oui*. Do you know him?"

"I heard he was at court not long ago. Trying to forge the king's marriage agreement."

"It didn't go well?"

"I believe there was a disagreement between the brothers." Drem lifted her hair, enjoying the way it cascaded through his fingers. "Your uncle, the duke, is a very powerful man. One who does not like to be crossed or disobeyed."

"A pity. He is about to learn that a thief cares for it even less."

Drem saw his passionate lady's eyes sparkle and come to life. "We will speak no more about it tonight." He lifted her from his lap and lay her on the cloak. Stretching out next to her, he cradled his head in his arms.

Rolling to her side, she slid the blanket from her shoulders and lay it across both of them. Her smile grew as she reached for him.

Drem breathed in deeply, praying she would not have a change of heart.

Brigitte closed the gap between them. "To conserve heat."

"Oh, aye, 'tis a grand idea. A very smart one." Rolling on his back, he wrapped his hands around her waist and pulled her to his chest. He caught the chemise with his fingers and dipped into her cleavage.

"You must rest. Regain your strength." He stroked her neck, soothing the tension from aching muscles.

"I am much better now that you found me." She stifled a long yawn. "You saved my life."

"'Tis what a knight does."

Fighting sleep, she closed her eyes. "Tell me of your childhood. Why did your king take you from your family?"

His fingers stilled.

She opened her eyes, propping her chin on the back of her hand. Shadows and regret had deepened his frown. "You do not wish to speak of it." Shifting, she placed a kiss over his heart. "And I do not wish to cause you pain."

His fingers returned their stroking. He drew patterns over her skin. Tiny tremors traveled through her body.

"Six years ago I was a lad of fifteen. I met Henry while my sister and I searched for lost lambs." He paused, snuggling deeper under the blanket. "He was still Prince of Wales then. We battled side by side and then became friends."

"You must miss your family."

"Aye. Much has changed since the day they took me away."

She rose, bracing on her arms. "*They* took you?"

"Conscription into the English army is common. Especially if one has a certain skill, as I did, with a longbow." He nudged her shoulder. "Come back. You're letting in the chill."

Sadness for his lost youth washed over her. Memories could not replace family. That she understood.

"I saw my sister Terrwyn not long ago. She's a grown, wedded woman now."

"The one you sent Piers to?"

His nod rocked her body as she rested on top of him. The heat warmed her, made her sleepy as they talked.

"She's one of four sisters."

"I always wanted brothers and sisters. But it was not to be. I think Maman died of a broken heart when her Monsieur le Faire disappeared from our lives."

"We'll find out what happened to keep him away."

"*Merci*, but that would not return Maman to me."

"You're right. It will not bring her back. We both have lost parents through betrayal. I cannot ignore my father's actions. Nor can you ignore the actions of your father or the duke."

Brigitte reflected that he had a point. But what could they do? "Alexandre has the swan. Without it, I can prove nothing."

"The swan brooch," Drem continued. "The one on the chain. Have you seen another like it?"

"*Absolument*. The man . . ."

"Your father, the count."

Brigitte tried to let that sink in, but how could she call him father? "This Count of Nevers. Do you know his given name?"

"If memory serves, he is called Philip."

"Mayhap if I was to see his face. I would know for certain."

"'Tis certain he will join forces with the French."

She frowned. "Then we would be on the other side. Enemies, *n'est-ce pas?*"

Drem cupped her chin. "I would be standing with King Henry. You will not be anywhere near the battleground. If I had any say in the matter, I would take you back to Harfleur."

"Because you do not, I am telling you I will be by your side. I will never return to Harfleur."

His jaw popped from clenching it so hard. She wished to smooth it away, but how else to stand firm on her decision to never return to Harfleur?

"And if I am ordered there?"

"Why borrow trouble we know nothing about? Mayhap we will reach Calais without a battle."

"Perhaps. If King Charles concedes defeat and agrees to terms." He moved his thumb over her bottom lip, stroking across it as if memorizing its shape. "How is it that you are able to read?"

Brigitte blinked at the question. "'Twas a skill my *maman* insisted I learn. She said her father demanded it of her." She sat up. The blanket trailed after her. "'Tis not a common skill for a paramour, is it?"

"Or a thief."

She grinned. "Alexandre always said, 'information is power.'"

"My thoughts exactly." He sat up with her, propping his wrist on one knee. The corner of the blanket barely covered his aroused member. Coiled hair sprinkled over his chest and strong legs glistened in the firelight. He looked like a powerful god. One who intended to wreak havoc on those who had wronged her.

Drem knelt before her. She rose, her loins wet with anticipation.

"Are you able to ride come morning?" He slid his fingers through her hair.

She could not turn from the beauty of his form, his strength. She ran a finger over his skin. The planes of his chest, muscles formed from years of use, were powerful. Yet under all that power beat a caring heart. She saw the tenderness he had for both man and beast. His word was his bond. She touched the satiny skin stretched over his hips, where his legs joined his body.

He would protect her and she would do her best to protect him. Whether he liked it or not.

She placed her hands on his shoulders. "I would ride with you to the end of the earth."

Proving her point, she leaned into him until they were belly to belly. His chest rose and fell, as if preparing to dive into a pool. Then she touched his heavy flesh, moving against her mons. Its engorged head, velvet smooth, dripped nectar in anticipation. His heat made her core flare. Smoldering embers burst into flame like a forest fire.

The chemise slid off one shoulder, exposing her breast to his view. He reminded her of a little boy, looking at all the confections at the patisserie. And then he tasted her.

"Hmm." His tongue danced, encircling her nipple.

The chemise fell, pooling at her knees. Cool air hit her damp skin. She arched her back, allowing him access to all he sought. "Oh," she keened. Little tremors shook her body.

"There is much more we can do before we must leave our little castle."

"Show me." She gasped as he swirled his finger over the nub between her legs. "Teach me."

"So wet and sweet." Their thighs met. Rolling to his back, he carried her with him.

She spread her legs, straddling his hips, knees hugging him close.

A hunger, more powerful than she had felt when she had been on the streets, urged her on. She lifted her hips and sank onto his powerful rod. He filled her until she could take no more. And then, by God's grace, her muscles contracted and released and took in more of him.

They rode together until they carried each other over the edge. Their voices mingled as they cried out their pleasure.

Collapsing, panting, they curled together. Drem's cock nestled between her bottom cheeks. Brigitte snuggled her back against his chest and reveled in the passion they had shared. A pleasured exhaustion soon took over, turning her limbs to liquid. A warm breath caressed her neck. His arm draped over her waist.

Drawing the blanket over them, she closed her eyes and tried not to think of Drem entering the battlefield. She never wanted to lose him again. Turning, she lay her head on his chest and listened to the beating of his heart.

"I think I might love you," she whispered.

Drem awoke to the sound of Aeron, standing below the loft, stamping his hooves.

"Christ's bones, but the animal is a noisy one," he muttered.

The little thatch cottage shook as if from thunder. He groaned. Another day of storms.

Rolling over, he untangled his deadened arm from Brigitte's hair. The raven strands wound around his fingers. It shimmered, cascading in a waterfall from his hands.

She turned onto her back and smiled up at him. "Good morning."

Ah, a happy riser. This bode well for them. He tasted her lips. She had the flavor of a woman well loved. His cock jumped at the thought of more to come.

" 'Tis time we rise."

A frown creased her brow. "I would that we stayed here."

Lifting her hand, he kissed each finger. "But I must attend my king. Our king."

She pursed her lips. "I don't want to lose you."

Ah, so that was what was turning her mood sour. Darrick's warning of strapping a woman to his side returned. Guilt that he might leave her behind should he not return nipped at his conscience. He lay his palm over her flat, smooth belly. Would there be a swelling there soon, growing with life? Sweat ran down his back.

He cleared his throat to get out the words. "Nor I you."

He rose and held out his hand. She reluctantly took it.

Thunder shook the building again. Bits of thatch rained down on their heads. Aeron whinnied, alerting them to danger.

Holding Brigitte's hand, he gathered their clothing and dropped into the stable below.

"What is it?" she cried.

"'Tis the sound of many men. An army of men. Hurry." His sword unsheathed, he led the way.

Chapter 28

An army of Frenchmen swarmed the meadows. Despite the wet, gray skies, their armor shone. Thousands of well-rested knights rode past. Infantry and wagons followed in their trail of mud.

Each horse flew its banner high. Their colors waved and fluttered like exotic birds. The tramping of hooves and the shaking of bridles usually brought a thrill running through his veins. But before he had been in the midst of it. Shouting orders, taking command of the archers.

Brigitte grabbed Drem's arm, pulling on him to wait. The ground shook under their feet. She shut the door, barring him from leaving the cottage. "You are but one man."

"I'm skilled and ready. This is what and who I am. Trust that I will return."

"Your sword arm is no help to your king if you are dead."

He waited, glowering, his arms folding across his chest. "Aye, but we must inform them that the nobles have decided to leave the warmth of their castles."

"This we will do." She reached out. His gauntlet-covered forearms twitched under her hands. "Without drawing attention."

He took a deep breath. She was right. Charging after a horde of French soldiers would bring them to destruction. He touched her lips, running his thumb over the plump flesh.

There was more than the king to consider. He had seen the plunder and destruction. Those of the lower class and women were powerless against enraged knights. They would not consider whether she were friend or foe. They would take until she had nothing left. He could not allow it.

"You are right. We will wait and then blend in. If they are anything compared to English knights, they won't know everyone who serves them.

Brigitte held up their blanket. "Put this under Aeron's saddle."

"Wise woman," he said. "It'll cover the markings."

"*Oui*," She passed him his cloak. "Turn them inside out. The weather cooperates. We pull our hoods low. Keep our faces hidden." Concern knitted her brows. She nibbled her lip. "But how do we disguise that I ride with you?"

"We don't," he said. "If anyone questions . . . you are my leman."

After making a few adjustments to his gambeson, he pulled on the leather jerkin. The white jupon given to every man under Henry's command lay hidden at the bottom of his satchel. He prayed no one would ask to search it.

The carts rolling by changed the tone of the thunder. They needed to make their move.

Lifting Brigitte onto the saddle, he opened the door and led Aeron. "You'll need to ride behind me. I need my sword arm free."

A battalion of soldiers marched past. Their numbers were mixed, some men-at-arms, mounted and walking. Time for them to blend into the masses.

Drem sucked in a breath. A blue flag waved over their heads, leading the way. A dancing lion graced its surface. He felt Brigitte tense. Her chest slammed into his back.

"Steady," he warned. Keeping pace with the soldiers, he rode up to the men and saluted.

A few grim-faced boys looked him over, then turned their sights to their comrade before them.

Brigitte began to relax her hold around his waist. But her fingers continually moved, fidgeting with the edge of the cloak. Was this the way she had managed to leave him a trail? He glanced over his shoulder. Was she doing the same for someone else?

She stared at the men riding past. Her hands had stopped moving and were now pressed together in a desperate prayer. Lowering her head, she kept the hood pulled over her face and buried her hands into the folds of her skirt.

Who was his fearless thief afraid of? What made her as tense as a rabbit in springtime? Glancing over the men, he searched for faces he might recognize. If not now, when they came face to face on the battle-field.

A head of flaxen gold caught the sun. The man rode past them, his whining complaints heard by all, none of whom seemed to care for his plight. His pinched mouth revealed he was unhappy with life, more so when his partner snubbed him by riding away.

When the horse twitched its tail, Drem recognized it. He had spent enough time behind that arse to know it was the stolen cart horse.

Master Alexandre. Drem itched to unsheathe his sword and run it through the spineless creature. He looked down. Brigitte linked her fingers around his wrist and slowly shook her head.

When had he unstrapped the thong? His sword was ready to come out to play with the man's innards.

The need to speak with Brigitte in private grew. Had she recognized the banners? Or was it just because she had seen the master of the Nest riding beside a man Drem was certain could not be her father? The Count of Nevers was too young. He would have had to sire her at the age of six.

The ribbon of soldiers marched around the river bend. They dropped into the valley below. 'Twas time for him to break from the pack.

"Bloody hell, woman," he shouted loud enough for the men around him to hear. He spoke in French. "What's that you say? Again?"

He glowered at the man on his right. "She thinks the world is her privy. Stop and piss every chance we get."

"*Oui.*" The soldier nodded in sympathy. "Women are only good for a romp." He rubbed the dirt-stained corners of his mouth. "Wouldn't mind sharing her with me, would you?"

Drem touched the underside of Brigitte's arm. She tensed but held her tongue.

"Mayhap later. When we have defeated the goddamn English, we will celebrate."

"Heard they crossed over the Somme. Going north." He grinned, revealing blackened teeth. His stench resembled the ditches in London. "We have them on the run. We are the hunters of the little English fox. Won't be long now."

The cloud laden skies opened, drenching them from head to toe. Rain streamed off the men. The sodden ground turned into mud.

Drem grimaced and saluted him. "Viva la France."

Wheeling the destrier to the left, he kept the reins loose, his hand close to his sword. "Hold tight, my *caru*."

The wooded grove stretched out before him. Aeron stepped over felled trees, dodged branches, their leaves heavy with rain. Drem stopped to see if anyone had noticed their hasty departure.

God had smiled on them. The French did not care about a single man riding away from the army. They kept their heads down and concentrated on putting one boot in front of the other.

The mire of mud had begun to slow their march to a boot-sucking crawl.

"This is how you move unnoticed?" she asked. Leaning into him, she added, "You would make a terrible thief."

Drem snapped the reins. "Not everyone can have every skill."

"And how many do you have, my knight?"

He grinned. The thrill of the hunt. The challenge of overcoming obstacles. His blood pumped, roaring, demanding more excitement. He moved a leg over the saddle bridge so he could see her lovely face.

"Too many to count." Surprising her with a kiss, he reveled in the splendor of her lips. Her gasp pleased him, but not nearly as much as when she returned his passion.

Giving her one more peck on the cheek, he turned in the saddle. "Hold tight. You are about to experience my impressive riding skills. We must reach Henry before that massive army does."

As promised, they rode in a northwesterly direction, toward Calais. Steep, hilly terrain slowed them down. Streams, swollen from the snow and rain, made crossing difficult. Bitter winds slapped the air from their lungs. Rest would come after they reached King Henry's army.

Each step brought them closer to Calais. Brigitte should have felt joy and excitement. To finally reach the city Maman had spoken of with a gleam in her eye. Was that not her plan all along?

The French armies were converging, outnumbering the starved and weary English. The chance Drem could be injured or worse terrified her. She wanted to curse and scream, to demand that they turn away from the madness. They were no one of importance. Why not disappear, make their luck where they found it?

Brigitte inhaled the familiar scent of the man riding in front of her. His back and shoulders strained forward, as if willing Aeron to fly. She tightened her hold around his waist as if to never let him go. *No, we will not turn back; we will charge forward into the fray.*

And they rode through the day and into the night. Through the stinging rain and bitter winds.

Brigitte's arms ached. She feared her bones would shatter. Her bottom pounded into Aeron's back until she realized she should move with the horse. The undulating motion brought memories of the night before. And the time before that.

The trail of destruction, the *chevauchée*, had diminished as the army marched toward Calais. The French were hot on their heels. Hunting them down like prey. The gathering had commenced.

They slowed down to collect information in one of the many hamlets. The ring of hammer against anvil brought their attention.

"I'll see what I can find for us to eat. What news we may find," Drem said.

He returned from the blacksmith. "A handful of grain for Aeron. A loaf of bread and a pheasant leg to share." He looked up at her, touching her ankle. "Many have come this way." His frown deepened. Rain streamed down his face as he scowled at the sky. "We are close. Less than a day's ride."

Rain continued to pour from the heavens. Aeron's steps were sometimes unsure now.

Drem doggedly pushed through the mire. They moved faster than a caravan of knights in heavy armor.

They rode west, through villages smaller than the one from which Alexandre had kidnapped her.

Until finally, rounding a knoll, they saw before them a sea of humanity. Soaked to the skin, their clothes tattered and torn from the march. Many soldiers stood barefoot in the mud, sinking up to their shins.

The banners of the Blessed Virgin and St. George flew overhead, announcing to all to fear the wrath of God. Protected by God, the king of England marched through France and refused retreat.

Aeron wheeled toward the handful of tents. Wagons were gathered together as they waited out the rain that seemed to never stop.

Squires ran out to see what the commotion was about. They fled on foot, carrying news of their arrival. Before Drem could dismount they were surrounded, swords drawn.

"'Tis I, Sir Drem."

Darrick and Nathan strode toward him. They nudged aside the men.

"Good to see you are here in time for the dance," Nathan said. Green eyes like a feral cat's stared at her. Waiting to pounce on his prey. "I see you brought your French thief with you."

Darrick motioned to them. "Get down. We talk in my tent. Now." He did not wait for Drem to acknowledge his order but marched to the far end of the camp.

"Do as he says," Drem muttered under his breath. "Stay by my right side."

Brigitte nodded and stepped on his boot as he set her down. Sir Nathan grabbed her as soon as her feet touched the ground.

"Let's not misplace you this time," he said.

"Unhand her," Drem called. He jumped from his destrier's back. Aeron grunted as if to be relieved of the load.

Nathan replaced his arm with a small sword. He shrugged. "Apologies. There is much to discuss."

Brigitte squeaked. Eyes wide, she blinked at him, waiting for him to respond. What could Drem do but comply?

"You there. 'Tis Young John?"

Drem recognized the emotions playing across the lad's face. He knew firsthand that the boy had seen things done to other human beings no one should ever have to see.

"Please take care of Aeron." He held out the reins. "He's carried us a great distance. He requires food and drink. A good brushing too."

"Aye, sir." Wide-eyed, Young John led the towering destrier away.

"Sheath your sword, Nathan," Drem said. He turned and hooked his arm for Brigitte to take hold. "My lady, shall we away?"

Soldiers kept guard over them as they walked through the rain-sodden camp. Mud stuck to their boots. Some had taken to wearing their leggings rolled up past their knees and wore no shoes at all.

The priests made their way through the soldiers, making the sign of the cross and offering prayers of protection.

Drem slowed.

A tall, thin man with snowy white hair wore the robes of the church. He bent over an archer. A large wooden cross swung away from his robe. Was that the priest from Dunstable? Father Timothy?

Drem stopped to stare, but the man of the cloth had turned away. The priests worked their way through the camp like crows, waiting to pick up refuse.

One of the boys waved his hand in a salute. The commander of the ditchdiggers swatted the back of his head. Shouting an order, he pointed him back to work.

Drem unfurled his fists. The provisions had reached the soldiers in time. "The boy and Godwin? How do they fare?"

Nathan followed his gaze. "Erick will be fine. He's strengthening his muscles." He clapped his hand on Drem's shoulder. Stepping over a puddle, he motioned for them to follow. "'Twas good of you to send the men on ahead of you."

They stopped at what was little more than canvas stretched over branches. Nathan stripped off his cloak and threw it on the back of a chair. He shook out his hair like a shaggy dog. Water sprayed, hitting everything in its way. He grinned. "Home and hearth never felt so good."

"Where are the others?"

A chestnut-colored brow arched. "They'll be here soon enough." Folding his arms across his chest, he braced his body in the doorway, closing off all means of escape. "What news have you?"

"I share it with the king or not at all."

"You leave us little choice but to arrest you."

"You need every sword arm you can get."

A thick man, clothed in burlap, stood at the entrance. "God is with us." He spoke quietly, his voice deep and strong.

Drem knew him by his stature. He would not give up his pretense until his king said otherwise. "Sir, I have seen them." He pointed to Brigitte. "She has seen them."

"'Tis true," she added. "Their numbers are vast."

"We have overcome obstacles greater than a few men waiting to bash in our heads. God will send us victory."

"There is one who comes this way. The Count of Nevers and his army are behind us. They are but one of many we have passed."

"We have seen nothing of the French nobles," Nathan scoffed. "They are soft and sit on their arses. Sucking on their mother's tits."

"My lord." Brigitte stepped away and left Drem's side.

Nathan and Drem lunged to catch her, but they were stopped by the king's hand.

"Let her speak," Henry said.

She knelt before the king of England. "'Tis true. We have ridden hard to tell you. They are but a day away. Maybe two, if this rain continues. Their wheels are sinking in the mud, but they will come."

"Aye," Henry said. He reached out to place his palm over her head. "The ground is not fit. Rise." Rubbing his chin, he studied her face. "Eyes the color of warm chestnuts. Midnight hair." His searching gaze dropped to her body. "'Tis a pretty French bird you've captured, Drem." He nodded. "Best not give her reason to fly."

Drem warred with trusting his king. What mood was his liege in this day? Word had come that they had hanged a boy for stealing a church relic. What would he do with a horse thief and pickpocket? Drem prayed his king remembered his vow of chastity on this quest for France.

"You remind me of someone." Henry continued, tapping his lips. "I love a puzzle to untangle. Don't I, Drem?"

"Aye, my king." His stomach twisted in worry.

Darrick ducked into the shelter. "We've received word from our patrols. The scouts report the French have amassed, many thousands strong. They are but three miles across the river."

Drem let go the breath he'd been holding.

"Give the orders to break camp. We must cross the river," Henry said." Drem, Darrick, and Nathan, take three other knights with you. Find where 'tis unguarded and safe to cross."

Chapter 29

Brigitte listened to the men bark out orders. Chaos reigned until the shouts to mount up echoed down the lines. They sat atop their horses and wagons. The archers and foot soldiers lifted their weapons. All ages, boys to old men. Maces, pikes, axes, and arrows were piled in the wagons. Archers carried poles on their shoulders. They waited. Tension grew.

She put her hands to work, loading their meager supplies, wrapping armor, steel plates, and swords in blankets.

Two of the camp followers came to join her by the supplies. A young woman, rosy-cheeked and fair of face, offered Brigitte a shy smile. "Name's Agatha." She tossed the fawn-colored braid over her shoulder as she bent to pick up a lance. "My man is an archer. Over there." She gestured. "Can shoot a squirrel out of a tree. Dead shot aim. One arrow."

"I'm Brigitte." She paused long enough to press the small of her back.

The women looked at each other as they set worked.

"We know who you are," the other woman said. "You're Sir Drem's woman. 'Tis a fine specimen of a man."

Brigitte felt her face flame, her neck turn hot. When she realized they had not come to judge her, she smiled back at them. She recalled the claim Drem had placed on her during the night. "*Oui*. He is mine."

At first glance, the other woman looked older than her friend. "I'm called Mari," she said, her face, haggard from long marches, little food, and unrelenting weather. Then she smiled and the years fell away. "Mam always said busy hands make calm minds."

"And a happy man." Agatha grinned.

They tittered together, nervous laughter spreading like wildfire.

Sweat dripped down Brigitte's spine. She did not know if that was true. Her mind was as busy as her hands.

Peace was out of reach. What if Drem was captured? Or worse? She stood, once again pressing her hands to her lower back.

The soldiers were watching. Their heavy glances let her know they had yet to think of her as one of them. If the tides turned, they would consider her an enemy.

Drem and the other knights returned with alacrity. Their destriers pounded out a path, cutting through mud and ankle-deep puddles.

The bridge at Blangy was clear. The caravan of soldiers and followers, women and surgeons and men of God, moved in a wave, the sound of their drums pounding out the warning that the righteous were coming.

Her skin prickled. How did they know they were God's anointed? Did not the French think the same?

She watched for signs of Drem. To offer a smile, perhaps steal a kiss. She hungered for his arms wrapped around her, shielding her from harm.

His warhorse's shining black coat merged with the other destriers. 'Twas a sea of white jupons, the red cross marked upon the knights' backs. Sacrificial doves.

They crossed over the river without incident. Alexandre's constant explanations of why one should blend in echoed in her mind. She looked over her shoulder, wary of an attack from behind.

Instead of stealth, they marched with riotous excitement. Finally, they would come up against the French, defeat them, and then go home to their blessed England. Ignoring the rain flooding the ruts in the road, they marched on. The horses, men, and wagons negotiated the steep hill.

They mounted the crest, the English king in the lead. A hush fell over the men. The drummer's incessant pounding on his war drum stilled. The English army flowed out over the plateau, spilling over the hill.

Brigitte gasped. A whisper of curses filled the air from those who feared this was to be their last view.

The French army flowed into the valley to their right. Pennons flying, the soldiers took their positions. Their defensive posts paralleled the road to Calais. This was not the small army she and Drem had outraced. Their numbers were greater than Brigitte could imagine. Thousands upon thousands stood in the field. They had answered the call to arms, prepared to defend and die.

She stood in the wagon, searching for Drem. The wind whipped her hair, plastering it against her damp cheeks. *Where are you?*

Drem wheeled Aeron around. Rain dripped off his helm and ran under his chain mail. The sodden wool gambeson prickled his skin. All the archers had taken off their boots and hung them over their shoulders. They protected the tools of their trade, their bows, and arrows, by any means possible. Blankets, old shirts taken from the dead. Anything to keep the arrows' fletches dry. A wet fletch was an untrustworthy piece of weaponry. Like a cannon without stones.

French warriors stood parallel to the road. Their numbers, too great to count, covered the narrow valley below. The newly turned soil a dark strip, a line drawn in the field. The measure of their force too much to contemplate. 'Twas simple: The English were outmanned. Each house of nobility waved their standard high. Drem had yet to locate the Count of Nevers. Nor the Duke of Burgundy. That meant there were more on the way.

Nathan sat beside him. His face grim, he leaned his forearm on the saddle. "The king wishes to speak to the men, encourage them to stand strong."

Drem noted the priests were doing a brisk business in the Lord, hearing confessions as they all prepared for heaven. "They are asking the men to swear an oath for pilgrimage if they live to talk about this day."

"Think I'll place my trust in my sword instead," Nathan said.

They waited, side by side, brothers in arms and Knights of the Swan. The gray skies continued to weep. Hours went by and the daylight faded.

"What are they waiting for?" Nathan grumbled.

"They know we have had little food to eat. Our supplies are low," Drem said. "So they wait, watching to see who falls away first. Hunger is a cruel weapon. One that does not waste their bolts or tire their sword arms."

"They think we will fall back and try to escape? Turn on our commander, the king?"

"Aye, 'tis a game pitting the mind against the body."

"The longer we wait the more chance they will bring in more reinforcements. Look there." Drem pointed. "Another army has arrived."

Darrick cantered up on his destrier. The horse stamped its powerful hooves, its nostrils flaring in anticipation of battle. "Make it known we are to hold our position."

"For how long?" Nathan scowled. "The men grow weary, standing in battle order."

"Worse," Drem added, "we'll lose all light and won't be able to see the enemy should they advance in a surprise attack."

"Nonetheless, we stand strong."

The French were so close Drem could hear their conversations. His archers stood rigid, barefoot in the mud, their shirts little more than rags.

Pride welled in his chest, for the men of England did not move when the smells of campfires drifted over. The French prepared their meals and settled into camp for the night.

When his men refused to shift their line, their enemy changed tactics by jeering.

"Order," Drem hissed to his archers.

Henry strode between the ranks. "Silence. We do not want to give them an opportunity to strike in a surprise raid."

"Your Majesty," Darrick said, "there are lodgings in the village. 'Tis safe for the night."

Henry acquiesced with a nod and waved him off. He finished exhorting the men-at-arms and rode his little gray horse toward Drem. "Take your woman to shelter. See that she is out of harm's way."

"My liege . . ."

"Do as you are told." He reined in his mount, giving him a knowing look. "'Tis time you spoke with a priest. Prepare for your future. Your family."

Drem could not ignore the call that had been at him all day. He turned, searching out Brigitte. She stood by the wagon. Watching him. Waiting.

Her soft smile tilted the corners of her sweet mouth. She raised her hand.

Despite the rain and bitter wind, Drem warmed from the inside out.

"Good. Good," the king said. He slapped his gauntlet on his leg. "By God, this is good!" He waved Darrick over. "Set the prisoners from our march free. Whatever their rank."

"My king . . ."

"We have precious few resources. I'll not have them turn on us, attacking our flanks. Have them swear an oath they will return to me should I win. But if I should lose in this God-ordained battle—an unlikely thing if God is on your side, is it not?" He grinned. "Then they may consider themselves pardoned and at liberty to hie themselves back to their homes and families.

"Well, Drem? What are you waiting for? Settle your woman away from the battlefield. Mayhap she can be of use to the surgeons." He twitched the reins. "I have a feeling we will keep them busy come the morrow."

"The French will be busier."

"God willing." Henry narrowed his gaze, peering into the dark of night. "Would that they chose to lay down their weapons and release the crown that is mine."

Drem bent low over Aeron's withers. He bit his tongue and kept the questions to himself. To march this far with prisoners and let them go? Some who thought to line their pockets with ransom would not take the news well.

He waited for his king to move on to the men-at-arms before taking his leave. Poor weather had been their fiercest enemy thus far. The fletchers and bowyers were hard at work repairing the tattered army. The armorers scrubbed at the rust formed on steel plates. Others attempted to sharpen their dull swords.

Aeron nickered as they approached Brigitte. He chuckled. "Appears someone has lost his heart."

She shoved damp tendrils from her pale face. Fatigue darkened the wells under her eyes.

"And what of you, Sir Drem?"

He held out his gauntlet-covered arm. "Take hold." Two women stood their ground as if to protect her. "Orders from the king," he said. Nothing more need be said.

She wrapped her fingers around his wrist. "This is Mari and Agatha. They need shelter as well."

Too weary to argue, Drem grunted. "Come. We must ready for what comes in the morning."

The women followed like meek lambs. He prayed they were prepared for the horrors that tomorrow would bring.

* * *

Drem bent low and caught Brigitte around the waist. Warmth seeped into her chilled body, bringing life back to her chilled bones. Would there ever be a time when she stopped dreading the cold?

"We have but a moment before I must return," Drem whispered in her ear.

"'Tis a blessing. One that I am unwilling to release."

They rode to a nearby village in silence while the women behind them chattered like magpies. The village was positioned far enough away to stay out of the battle line but close enough to aid those in need.

Too tired to speak, they settled in the comfort of each other's company. Brigitte rested her cheek against his back. She wanted to tell him of her love for him, but to do so . . . what if he turned her away? His relationship with the king was closer than she had realized. Knights came to him for suggestions. The commanders of the brigade of archers searched out his thoughts.

And she was naught but a thief with no family. Many feared she spied for the enemy. Her love would bring him down. She sealed away her secret love, protecting her heart until the battle was fought.

And what if he did not return? She refused to think on it.

Drem dismounted and helped her down. She wrapped her fingers around his arms. They were merely there to guide her, his strength enough to hold her longer than necessary. Lips pressed together, catching a kiss before everyone. Branding her as his woman.

Brigitte's new friends leaned together, sighing when he released her.

"I must see to the men," Drem said. "If I am able, I'll return before battle."

She smoothed her hand over his whiskered jaw. "See that you return to me healthy and whole."

He brought his lips down. The crazed frenzy of the camp disappeared the moment they touched. Just the two of them. A man and a woman in need of reassurance, in hope that all would be well. Brigitte clung to him. How could she let him go?

Breaking away, he set her aside, gently leaving her with Agatha and Mari.

Brigitte watched him leap onto Aeron's back. She could not look away. Strong thighs and arms. Back straight, his head held high, he rode into the storm.

"Ah, my lady," Flanners hailed. "'Tis good to see you."

The surgeon approached her. His leather apron already in place, he opened his arms.

She smiled and bit her lip, her eyes following past his shoulder to where Drem rode toward the battlefield. "Though I pray one day it will be away from this."

"I have great news," he said. "Wonderful news."

Brigitte drew her attention away from the heartache. She must keep busy or go mad with fear. "And what blessed news has you bursting with joy?"

"The brew you and your Claudette gave me is working on the men with dysentery." He grinned. "They grow strong."

Brigitte wrinkled her nose.

Seeing her confusion, he added, "'Twas told it is called the Four Thieves." He waved in her direction. "And you . . ." He shrugged. His cheeks grew red.

"*Oui.*" She held out her hand. "And I am a reformed thief."

He grasped her shoulders. "No. You are more than that. You are a lady to whom we owe our gratitude."

Brigitte rose on tiptoe and kissed his bearded cheek. "*Merci.*"

Chapter 30

Drem rode through the village. The night was miserable, but his lot was better than most. His thoughts turned to Brigitte and how things would be between them once this battle was over. He would have her to warm him with her kiss. He could still taste her on his tongue.

He needed to find a way to protect her should he fall by sword or hammer. He allowed Aeron to have his head, the beast seeming to know of his worries, and led him to the place where he had thought he saw the priest from Dunstable.

The man stooping over in prayer had the same head of gray hair Drem recalled. Though thinner, more haggard, like the rest of the men who made up this tattered army. Solace came not from the man of the cloth, but from the woman he had left with the surgeon. There was still time to be with her.

Drem turned, feeling as if he was being watched. His skin prickled. The old man straightened his back and stared at him.

Drem wheeled Aeron back to the surgeon's tent. A woman walked toward him. Her pace quickened, splattering water from the mud puddles. She ran to him, her arms open wide.

His breath caught. Lungs squeezed his chest. 'Twas his Brigitte.

Aeron recognized his lady and trotted forward. His massive hooves pounding the earth.

Drem bent down, scooping her into his arms. Angled on his lap, she pressed her body close.

Nudging his mount, they sped across the village to the little hut that had been assigned to them for the night.

* * *

Brigitte wound her arms around his waist. Now that she had him alone, fear raised its head. She would show him, sharing with her body.

His fingers danced over her hips, sending waves of fire spiraling through her veins. Her core wept for his touch.

"Drem, I—"

"'Tis only stolen moments that we have." He found her neck, nipping the tender skin, rendering her senseless. "We have until dawn. And then . . ."

Time rushed past her like a mighty swollen river, its waves ripping them apart.

"No." She gripped his arms, holding on to what they had. "This is not good-bye. I refuse. I want more time with you."

He picked her up, cradling her in his arms. Their kiss, deep and long, carried them to the bed.

They lay together. Touching. Tasting. Memorizing. Never letting go for fear it would be their last time.

Drem lifted his head, scowling at the incessant pounding on the door. He pulled up his chausses, tugged on his linen shirt.

A man stood silent in the doorway. He held out his palm. A metal disc, with the swan emblazoned on its surface, caught the firelight. "You are to come. Now."

Brigitte rose from their makeshift bed, her hair a raven cloud surrounding her head. Her love-swollen lips trembled. "Drem?"

He pulled on his gambeson and heard her move about the cramped room. When he looked up, she stood with his jerkin.

"Let me help you," she said. He bent for her as she lifted the stiff leather shirt over his head. She smoothed her hand over his heart.

Catching her fingers, he kissed them, wishing he had said more than how beautiful she was. "My *caru*," he said, his voice deep with emotion. "I will return," he promised once again.

She stood in the doorway, swathed in candlelight. Wind wound through the village, making her hair dance around her head. She caught the door before it flew off the hinges and doused the light.

Five other horsemen left the shadows and rode up beside him. "Good to see you've found a few moments of enjoyment," Darrick said.

A flash of teeth told him his friend Nathan had joined them. Drem peered through the dark. The others he did not recognize.

Six riders in all. Their destriers announced they were knights. They held out their gloved hands. Each held a swan coin. The last to join them was the gray-haired priest.

"Henry desires us to scout the battlefield," Darrick said.

Drem looked up at the darkened sky. The drizzle had returned. "Best to do so while the moon is still with us."

They rode to the field where the battle would take place. As they moved closer, their ride became more hazardous. Their horses' hooves were sucked into the mud. One of the knights had to get down and lead his mount out of the mire. The heavy rains that had made their lives miserable for days may have turned the tides. They would find a way to utilize God's gift to their advantage.

Father Timothy lifted his face to the sky. "Thank you, Lord above," he whispered to the heavens.

This time Drem agreed. They turned to report what they had seen.

"A word," the priest said.

"What is it?" Drem watched the other knights ride off. He wanted to be there when they gave the king their news. And yet he needed to know why the priest was there. Had the man recognized him from the priory? How many men had been knocked unconscious under his watchful eye?

The priest motioned for him to follow. They rode quietly together. "Did you discover the owner of the brooch?"

"Aye," he growled. "And now 'twas stolen by the man they call Master Alexandre."

His gray brows rose. "Why would someone want to steal it?"

"Mayhap you can tell me. Alexandre, the man who stole it, is a thief." Drem's palm itched to take the chance of going to hell and unseating the little man. "Perhaps to sell it. He gains power by selling information."

The priest ignored his plea and asked, "And have you determined the girl's sire?"

"Alexandre told Brigitte her sire is Philip, Count of Nevers."

The priest slapped his knee. His shoulders jiggled under the heavy layers of his cloak. He shook his head. "No. That one would have been but a boy still in the nursery when she was born. Her mother may have been many things, but desiring little boys was not one of them."

"You knew her mother?"

"Only upon times of confession. 'Twas many years ago. Before the old duke of Burgundy passed away."

"The old man, Philip the Bold? He was her father?"

"Who knows for certain?" He tapped his nose. "I had my suspicions. And when those of the House of Valois began asking questions instead of remaining set on the task of discussing alliances . . . we thought it best to find her."

Drem caught the front of the priest's garment. He fisted the material and prayed to God for control. He did not wish to ask forgiveness just as he set foot on the battlefield. "If you knew these things, why send me on this wild chase?"

"A quest is a test, is it not?"

"I should run you through for leaving her in the hands of Alexandre."

He jerked out of Drem's hold. "We had need of information. To find the girl." He shrugged his thin shoulders. "You were ready for the challenge. Two birds. One Stone. You are a hunter." He straightened his clothing. "Knew you could do it too."

"The other half of the brooch?"

"Tucked away. Safe in God's hands."

"Shite." He stared at the man. "What manner of man are you?"

"One who serves both king and God." The infuriating toad of a man continued, "As such, I must encourage you to wed the woman." He held out his hand to stop the flow of curses. "Handfast her if you must. In the eyes of God, be her protector. Put a jupon on her. Give her a kiss for good measure."

"I'm being ordered to marry her?" Could it be as easy as that? "The king has given his blessing?"

"What if she already carries your child? Do you wish illegitimacy for your children? Marry her. Protect her with your name."

"I have nothing but my horse and armor."

"You have your good name. Your strong arm." Father Timothy held out his palm. The swan coin winked between them in the amber light of dawn. "And the Knights of the Swan to watch your back. What more do you need?"

The horns blew.

"'Tis time," Drem said. He glanced toward the building where he and Brigitte had last made love. Thoughts of a life after the battle tempted the fates. But to ignore what his heart and head whispered? That he could no longer do.

"Come with me, Father."

Brigitte paced the little cottage. How could she sleep when Drem was soon to go into battle? Possibly in danger at this moment? Had the knights intended to attack him in the middle of the night?

She stubbed her toe against his armor. Dragging it out of the canvas bag, she pulled out plates of steel and began polishing his chest plate. Stroking the metal, she imagined how it would protect his heart. She frowned. No matter how hard she rubbed, the stains would not come off. Rust had formed over the many days and nights of damp weather. The demon, eating away at the metal, weakened it. She needed sand, but there was none to be found in the little peasant's cottage. Throughout the night, she worked on the armor and fretted that it would not be able to keep Drem safe. Despite her efforts, many of the joints were frozen. Those that she did unstick were slow and would be unwieldy in battle.

She tossed her rag to the floor, dropping her head into her hands.

The sound of rain had ceased. The tearing winds had calmed and no longer rattled the door and shutters.

Horns cut through the quiet morning. Blowing out the candles, she opened the shutter and peeked out. Scurrying footsteps approached.

The door swung open. Drem paused, staring at the pieces of armor scattered over the floor. His brows arched and rose. "We go to battle." His frown deepened. "I must hurry."

"The armor," she said, rushing into his arms. "Do not wear the armor. The helm and your chain mail? *Oui*. The heavy plates of armor over your body? No." She gripped his sleeve. "Drem, 'tis fresh-tilled earth. The rains have soaked the field. Please listen. The clay in the battlefield will claim you if you wear your armor."

"*Caru*. It will soon be over."

"You ask a great deal from a knight, to go into battle unprotected," the little priest said. He peered over Drem's shoulder.

Brigitte frowned. When had he entered? Had she seen him before? "Do I know you?"

His gaze slipped as he rubbed a raw knuckle across his nose. "I think not. Unless you have been to my priory."

"In England? No. I have never been away from France."

"I see." The priest cast a glance toward Drem. "'Tis time, brother."

Drem placed Brigitte's hands on his heart. "We spoke of this once before. 'Tis been on my heart ever since. My *caru*. My love. Will you wed me, Brigitte de Marneir?"

The horns blew again. She flinched. Her fingers curled. Why had he asked now?

Too stunned to speak, she glanced at the holy man. "But I am no one. A thief."

"Not in the eyes of God." He smiled and made the sign of the cross. "What better way to celebrate Saint Crispin and Crispinian on their feast day than with a wedding."

"I much prefer a wedding night to follow," Drem said.

Brigitte folded her arms across her chest and dared to hope she was correct in her opinion. "Then do not make me a widow on the same day. Do as I say and do not wear the rusted plates of armor. "

He swept her into his arms. "As you wish, my *caru*."

The icy grasp of fear still chilled her to her soul, but she cupped his jaw and memorized every plane on his face, the fire in his eyes, the gentle promises in his smile. "*Oui*. I will be your wife."

Father Timothy cleared his throat. "We must hurry. There is little time."

Brigitte stumbled to the surgeon's tent alongside the little priest. She carried the jupon Drem had handed her before he left under her arm. Should the battle turn for the worse and overflow into the village, she was to don the shirt with the red cross so the English would not think her the enemy and kill her.

Were they truly wed? What would the king say when he learned one of his knights had married without his knowledge? And if they lost this war against France, would anyone care? Their last few words together had been spoken in a rush. The agreement for husband and wife, to honor and cherish. He had called her his love. But had he said he loved her?

Her shoe slipped in the mud. She could not recall whether she had said any words of love herself. Her heart ached with a pain that stole

her breath and made her dizzy. Tears stung her eyes. She had never
had a chance to tell him of her love for him.

The battle raged. Shouts. Screams. The ground shook under
Brigitte's feet. The whistle of a flock of arrows. Metal clanging
with deathblows. The English horses had been kept away from the
battlefield. The king had ordered everyone to fight on foot. Those too
infirm or too young had been told to stay with the wagons and supplies.

Everyone turned to look as horses cantered out of the melee.
Their riders missing from their saddles. Blood coated their legs like
stockings of red.

The soldiers' damaged bodies would soon arrive.

Agatha and Mari huddled together as Brigitte paced the surgeon's
tent.

"Where are the wounded?" she muttered. "Surely someone has
news."

"Many nobles have fallen." Father Timothy walked toward her,
his wooden cross clutched in his fist. Heartache glazed his expression.
"The tides are turning, my dear," He kissed the holy cross. "I fear we
are grievously outnumbered. Should we fail, do not don the jupon.
Admit you are French." His eyes darted to the flanks of the battlefield. "Though he has yet to appear, you must search for the duke of
Burgundy."

She brushed the priest's last comment away. The man believed to
be her father did not enter into her thoughts. "I pray for all of them,
Father." One, in particular, came to mind. "Do not lose hope."

"Yes, my lady." He squeezed her hand and then scurried back toward the battlefield to seek out the latest news.

Soon the wounded would come. And she continued to pray.

Brigitte looked up from the fire that she had kept going during the
hours of battle. The priest returned. He ran with his gown hiked high
above his knees.

"'Tis a miracle," he called. "The French are defeated. They are
falling by the hundreds. Thousands. Never have I seen such bold and
fearless Englishmen."

She caught his wrist. "Drem, Father Timothy. Did you see him?"

Chapter 31

For three hours the fighting continued.

Brigitte had not seen Drem since he had made her his wife and left for the battlefield. The wounded began to trickle in. As did prisoners of war. Those who had survived would be ransomed. Soon there would be more captured enemies then they could guard.

A lanky man, with locks the color of straw, stumbled along the path. Alexandre? Never would he have willingly gone onto the battlefield.

Suddenly Brigitte heard a voice she had been aching to hear. All thought of the strangeness of seeing Alexandre were replaced with the need to see Drem. To touch him. Ensure that he had returned, safe from all harm.

Three men approached the surgeon's tent staggering under the weight of the wounded. The one in the middle required help to walk. They had left the carnage behind them, a trail of gore in every tottering step.

Where to start? Where to mend him?

A deep cut to his shoulder bled, the blood seeping down his leather jerkin. A few more inches and they would have cleaved off his head. The torn jupon, stained, was held by a single strip of cloth. One of his beautiful moss green eyes was swollen. Bruises and cuts covered his body. But he was alive.

"Drem," she cried, running to his aid. She locked her arms around his waist until she heard his hiss of pain.

"Come," she said, leading the way to the cottage, where they had left his sewing kit.

The men hesitated.

"I am skilled in healing. I can clean him better there."

They nodded.

Drem's head bobbed in agreement. "She's my wife," he said. "The most beautiful woman in the land."

At that, he collapsed, sagging between his brothers. Brigitte applied pressure to his neck as they carried him to the cottage.

She cleared the table. "Lay him here," she commanded. Rummaging through his satchel, she found the tools she needed. "Ask Father Timothy to fetch some eggs." When they didn't move, she shouted, "Go."

Brigitte found the remnants of the bottle of wine they had shared days earlier. There was enough left to cleanse the blood and gore from the wound.

"Sleep, my love," she whispered, fighting back her fear and the need to rage at the carnage that mankind had wrought. After threading the bone needle, she began sewing up his wound. The blood ceased to flow.

And still he slept the sleep of one who neared the veil between life and death.

She looked up as footsteps approached their door, jumping when it slammed open. Darrick and Nathan stood in the entrance.

"Dear God, are you injured as well?"

Bewildered, they looked down at their bloodstained clothes.

Darrick was the first to enter and speak. "Nothing that won't heal. We heard of Drem's injuries."

Nathan followed suit. "Here." He held out an egg

Brigitte clasped it in her hands. "'Tis a blessing. *Merci*." She stood on tiptoe and kissed their cheeks. "Nothing more valuable than this."

Cracking the shell, she carefully spread the egg white over the wound, sealing it shut. She sat back, suddenly so weary she didn't know whether she could lift a finger. The yolk she would cook to give him nourishment when he awakened.

"We will return soon," Darrick muttered.

"Many prisoners." Nathan glanced at Darrick. "Pray no one attempts to escape or attack us."

"*Oui, bon ami.*"

Nathan held out his arms. "Welcome to our little family."

Brigitte entered his embrace. Cautious. *Family?* "The king?"

"Victorious." Darrick nudged Nathan aside. "Thanks to Drem, he is well." He pointed to his neck. "'Twas intended for our king." He grasped Nathan and shoved him to the door. "We shall return as soon as we are able."

Her eyes watered. Family. For so many years she had dreamed of a family. The Nest had been a twisted family, its branches unhealthy and dying. She placed her hand on Drem's chest, felt the steady beat of his heart. But this one he offered was strong, healthy, built on honor and love.

She lay her head near his shoulder, watching him breathe and waiting for him to return to her. Healthy and whole.

This time, she would say the words.

"*Je t'aime*, my *caru*," she whispered.

Long fingers caressed her scalp. She leaned into them like a cat wanting attention.

Lifting her head, she smiled at the man who had captured her heart.

The corner of his mouth lifted. "*Je t'aime*, my *caru*," he croaked.

They repeated the words together. His arms wrapped around her, drawing her closer.

"I love you madly, Wife."

She cradled his jaw, dropping tears on his face. "And I love you too, my darling husband."

A shadow darkened his gaze. "I failed you. Can you forgive me?"

"Failed me?" She shook her head in wonder. "No. You are here. Alive. 'Tis all I need."

"Your *maman*'s necklace. I did not find it." His fingers curled around hers. "The proof that you are from the House of Valois has vanished."

Brigitte smiled, pushing back the auburn locks that always fascinated her. "'Tis of no consequence. As you say, we are wed. I carry your name now." Her palm slid over her abdomen. She would keep the secret until she knew for certain. "We are all the family I desire."

"Aye. That we are. You have stolen my heart, *caru*. Promise you will never return it."

Drem led her lips to his. And there they united. France. England. They were one.

Chapter 32

Calais

They finally arrived in Calais and settled into their new home. Drem sank into a chair beside the hearth and watched his wife move carefully around the room. The grace in her steps told the tale of her upbringing. She was at home on the grand property King Henry had given him for saving his life.

Ah, but there was always a price to be paid. He was to stay and help hold the city.

England had its victory, but at what cost? And for how long? Until another came and proclaimed God's will that it was theirs. Only God knew His Divine plan.

Drem touched the place where a sword had come near to taking off his head. The fear of never seeing Brigitte again, holding her in his arms, telling her every day that he loved her, had kept him on his feet in that field of death.

Brigitte placed her hand on her belly. She had yet to tell him, but he knew her body. Her breasts were lush and full. Indeed, more so than he ever could have imagined. And she was fraught with emotion.

"Sir Drem, you have visitors—" the servant began.

They barely had been announced at the door when a young boy, taller than when they last had seen him, raced into the room. He barreled into Brigitte's arms and hugged her tight.

Drem leaned back in the great chair, smiling at the two people who gave him hope.

"Piers, lad," she cried. "'Tis good to see you."

"Terrwyn. James." Drem stood to greet his sister and brother by marriage. His injuries ached from the cold winter weather that seemed to have no end.

"Brother." James pounded him on the back. "'Tis good to see you alive and well."

Terrwyn leaped into Drem's arms, nearly taking him off his feet. "I thought never to see you again." She held him away from herself, examining him. "I dreamed of you. So much blood and thundering terror."

"I'm in one piece, Terrwyn," Drem said. "Thanks to my *caru*'s care."

He held out his hand for his beloved Brigitte, motioning her to join them. Piers followed like a puppy, trailing in her steps. "Come. 'Tis my sister Terrwyn and her husband, James."

"Ah, the beautiful and talented Brigitte," Terrwyn said. She turned, enfolding her in her arms. "Forgive me if I am too bold in my affection. 'Tis a delight to finally meet the enchanting Bee."

Wide-eyed, Brigitte blushed prettily. "'No, I—I am thrilled to meet Drem's family."

Drem rescued her from his sister's hold and tucked her by his side. Brigitte's cold fingers tightened around his. Why had she trembled?

Terrwyn waved her hand. "We are just the crust of the pie. Wait until you meet the rest of our family." Her expression clouded. "Well, not all, mind you."

Drem tensed and caught James's eye. "You've received word about our father?"

"He still lives," Terrwyn said. "He is said to have left France and now hides with Owain Glyndŵr."

"Though we have yet to discover the secret behind Piers's past, he has told us many great tales," James interjected.

Drem ruffled the boy's head of golden curls. "I intend to keep my promise, Piers, and find your family."

Terrwyn leaned in. "And he may stay with us until we do."

Drem vowed to thank James for this escape from thoughts of Dafydd ap Hew. He and Brigitte had much to overcome. He vowed they would succeed. Together. Without his father causing any more harm.

James turned to Brigitte. "If you are willing, I would like to sketch your *maman*. Those who brought you to Harfleur."

"And the mysterious Monsieur le Faire," Terrwyn added.

"*Oui.*" Brigitte blanched and nodded. "I shall do my best. But 'twas many years ago."

"Have no fear." Terrwyn tipped her head and whispered, "'Tis James's gift. He is the king's most talented artist."

Brigitte caught her lip between pearly teeth. "I may not recall . . ."

She leaned into Drem's embrace, claiming the spot where she belonged.

"Is there word of Master Alexandre? Did he survive the battle in Agincourt?" James asked.

"'Tis reported he was never seen after the battle." Drem said.

Brigitte's gaze never left his. Worry creased her brow. The same worry that woke him in the middle of the night. The one they whispered to each other. What if irrefutable proof that she was Philip the Bold's illegitimate daughter was discovered? Would she once again become a pawn in the game of power? He thanked God that Father Timothy had vowed to return the other half of the swan brooch to the Dunstable Priory for safekeeping.

Drem fisted his hands. Never would he allow her to be taken from his side.

He looked down as Brigitte caressed his knuckles, helping him to unfurl his fingers and release the anger. "Perhaps. One day the details will come back to her," he said. "Who is to say when?"

"*Oui.* Who is to say?" She shrugged. "Mayhap never."

Terrwyn tucked her hand into her husband's, smiled that radiant smile Drem had come to recognize in his lady wife. "'Tis time," she whispered, her eyes sparkling like a sun-kissed ocean.

"Yes, my sweet." Frowning, James dragged his attention from Drem's sister. "Brother, new Sister. We are ordered to deliver a message from our king." He withdrew a rolled parchment from the folds of his surcoat.

"Aye?" Drem began to itch under their perusal. Their countenances had become stern. He searched for Brigitte's hand. "I will not let her go," he growled.

Piers carried a tray with silver pitcher and cups into the room. Smiling at the boy, Terrwyn urged him to come closer. She filled and passed out the cups as James ceremoniously unrolled the document.

"Terrwyn—" Drem said. The itch had become unnerving. "What are you about?"

Ignoring his plea, his stubborn sister smirked and lifted her cup, touching it to James's. Together, they said, "This comes from our friend. Words of wisdom to carry you through life."

James cleared his throat and began to read, "'May there be someone to hold 'til the wee hours of the morn.'"

Terrwyn stepped closer, entwining her arm through James's, and added, "'Someone to love us despite our faults.'"

James raised his voice and cup higher. "'Someone to care whether we live or die.'"

Together, they finished the words. "'And may that someone be ours to love throughout eternity.'"

"Does that mean what I think it does?" Brigitte whispered in Drem's ear. Tears glittered before sliding down her cheeks.

"Aye." Shaking with relief, Drem caught his beloved, drawing her close. "'Tis Henry's blessing." He caught her mouth, tasting the salt on her lips. He lifted his head. "We are safe. Our king has given us his blessing."

"James, we nearly forgot the rest. Tell him the news." Terrwyn bounced on her feet like a child, reminding Drem of a Michaelmas long ago.

James tilted his head. He straightened, his blue-gray eyes snapping with life. "You are to return to Wales in the late spring," he said. "To your family's holdings. They are returned to you. There you will serve until you are called again."

Drem could hardly take it in. Spring. Brigitte would be round with their child. Their growing family would once again be on Welsh soil. His vows to Brigitte and his king would be fulfilled. Indeed, he would protect them with his life.

Brigitte rose up to cup the back of his head, drawing him down until their lips touched.

"I love you, my *caru*," he said, nibbling on the spot behind her ear, which drove her wild with passion. His palm slid over hers as they cradled the new life growing within.

Smiling a sweet, contented smile, she tilted her head, turning to catch his mouth. "And I love you. Forevermore. Forevermore."

Please turn the page for a thrilling sneak peek of

C.C. Wiley's next book in

her exciting KNIGHTS OF THE SWAN series

KNIGHT TREASURES

Coming in November 2017.

It is Sir Darrick of Lockwood's romance!

Chapter 1

The biting wind, heavy with moisture from an approaching storm, tore at Sabine's hair. She swiped at the bits of dried vegetation stuck to her cheek and drew the bundle closer to her chest. As she wove her way through the stand of trees, she prayed the thin woolen cloak would muffle the babe's cry.

Fear that she had waited too long deepened with every step that brought her closer to the hermit's cottage. Lady Elizabeth must have led Vincent DePierce's mercenaries to the tiny island. How else would they have found this deserted pile of rocks hidden off England's shores?

Sabine stopped in front of the gnarled bushes. There, in the shadows, hidden by brambles and twisting branches, stood the entrance to the cottage she had called her home for nearly a year.

She waited in the storm, listening for a careless hunter's footsteps, and checked the many traps set around the building. After making certain she was not being watched, she slipped inside and kicked the door shut.

Exhaustion turned her trembling legs to water and she slid down the door.

How had it happened so quickly? The men must have known Elizabeth was there and lay in wait, stalking the new mother until she was alone.

Sabine rubbed her forehead. She should have followed closer. Found a way to stop them.

The scene exploded behind her eyelids. A flash of lightning. Shadows reaching from behind. A cry for help. And then the babe's mother disappeared over the cliffs.

Despite the slippery footing, Sabine had tried to see over the edge. The crashing waves had pummeled the shore below. Watching for signs of life. No matter how long she stared into the blackness, the rocks and water refused to release their hold. Elizabeth was gone. And the newborn baby remained hidden in the brush, out of sight and protected from DePierce's mercenaries.

Sabine pressed her palm to her forehead and tried to erase the horrid memory to no avail. Her thoughts returned to the cliffs and the lives that had been altered in an instant.

Sir Darrick of Lockwood bunched his fists in frustration. Their travels from France to England's southwest coast had cost them precious time. He had prayed that when he arrived at the cottage near Balforth Castle, Elizabeth would run out to greet them, her laughter ringing out at the lark she had played on her older brother. 'Twas as their mother feared: His sister had disappeared somewhere between Lockwood lands and Balforth Castle. His heart clenched. Elizabeth was in trouble.

He stared down at the injured man lying on the bed. The villagers said the clergyman called himself Rhys, and they placed little trust in the man of the cloth. Although there were few signs that he'd been beaten, he had yet to stir from his deep sleep, not even waking when Darrick and his soldiers rode in that morning. But his mother, Lady Camilla of Lockwood, was confident Rhys had vital information.

The longer they waited, the colder the trail.

Darrick swatted his gauntlets against his thigh. He needed the answers to Elizabeth's disappearance. How was he to awaken the clergyman from his deep sleep?

Darrick turned as Sir Nathan Staves entered the musty room. Nathan's massive body, formed from years swinging a battle sword for King Henry, blocked what little light the torch produced. He bent, narrowly missing the low wooden beam hidden in the thatched ceiling.

"Sir Vincent DePierce, Lord of Balforth, insists Elizabeth never arrived at his castle gate," Nathan said. "He professes that his men scoured the countryside, searching for signs of his nephew's wife. Claims they returned emptyhanded. She has simply vanished."

Darrick grunted, not bothering to voice his disgust with DePierce's ridiculous theory. Instead, he lay out his own report. "A few of the servants hiding on the neighboring lands say that when Hugh left for France, he took with him a vast number of soldiers still riding under the old Lockwood banner."

"That would leave Lockwood and Elizabeth virtually unprotected."

"Unprotected and without an heir. I'm told a recent missive reported Sir Hugh's disappearance from his command."

"And there were orders from Hugh that should harm befall him, Elizabeth was to make haste to Balforth. To his uncle, DePierce," Nathan added.

"Someone used Hugh's death as bait to draw Elizabeth from Lockwood's safety?" Darrick nodded as if answering his own question. "We find the one who did this, we find Elizabeth. Then we grind him into the ground."

Nathan's green eyes shimmered with vengeance. Darrick could almost see the plans forming inside his friend's head. He would do well to keep his tall friend out of trouble and still manage to find his sister.

"What of the runner we intercepted?" Nathan asked.

Darrick placed a hand over his heart, quoting the missive they had taken from the messenger. " 'After a lengthy search, it is with our deepest regret that we failed to find the remains of Sir Hugh DePierce, Lord of Lockwood.' " He paced the confining cottage. "My God! Vincent DePierce's nephew, Hugh, now Lord of Lockwood. Indeed, it still burns my throat to speak of another man's name attached to my ancestor's home."

"I fear it will not bode well for the servant who misplaced his lordship's body."

"A man of Hugh's ilk will turn up, whether you like it or not," Darrick said with a thin smile.

"You doubt his death?"

"Until I see his body, I advise we embrace caution while we travel upon these lands."

Nathan nodded at the wizened lump lying motionless in the bed. "What of that one? Have you been able to shake him awake? Question him about what he knows?"

Darrick straightened his shoulders. " 'Tis useless. For now, we'll put the hounds on the trail again."

Nathan scrubbed at the stray whiskers on his jaw. "Did you note the fear in the villagers' eyes? None would mention your sister's name. Perhaps if I speak with them without the lord of Balforth by my side, we will discover where he has hidden Elizabeth."

" 'Tis imperative we find her. Without Elizabeth to claim Lockwood from the king, DePierce may stand to receive all the lands held in Hugh's name."

"You're in Henry's good graces. Surely Elizabeth's rights as heir to Lockwood will hold."

"Unless DePierce claims Elizabeth as his latest wife and declares Lockwood as his own," Darrick said.

He leaned forward and pressed his ear close to Rhys. Nothing more than the sound of labored breathing came from the clergyman's cracked lips. Darrick spoke over his shoulder as he continued to watch the little man. "Would that I could leave this bedside and join you, Nathan. Once again, I must ask you to put yourself in danger and see what you can learn from the people of Balforth."

Nathan flexed his shoulders. Restless, he strode to the window and looked out. "You know I stand for you. Have done so since we were children playing knights protecting our king."

"In truth, you are part of my family," Darrick said. "More so than those of my blood."

Nathan nodded. "Knights of the Swans until the day we die."

Darrick's gaze shuttered. "Perhaps those are memories left for another time. You know the consequences."

"Let us away from these lands," Nathan said. "Ignore those who've turned their backs on you! An eye for an eye. Turn away from the lot of them."

"You know I could never do that," Darrick said. " 'Tis certain DePierce has drawn Elizabeth into his greedy clutches. I am honor bound to find her and ensure her safety. Try as I might, I cannot ignore my family's call for help. No longer can I let the threat to Lockwood run free."

"So be it," Nathan relented. "I honor your decision."

Darrick frowned. "Be safe, my friend," he warned.

Nathan moved to carry out his orders. He paused in the doorway. His indecision was apparent, as he wrestled with his thoughts. "You know Elizabeth already may have succumbed to his treachery."

"We must continue to hold the hope that she will be found alive and well," Darrick said. "I'll have the men prepare to ride as soon as we learn anything new." He paused when he felt a tug on his sleeve.

"I must know," Rhys whispered, his voice as hoarse as flint scraping across a rock. "In truth, do you intend to help the Lady Elizabeth?"

Awash with relief, Darrick leaned forward and pulled the little man upright. "Tell me what you know!"

Rhys's beady crow like eyes stared into his face. "I see now that you, too, have your father's eyes. The bards didn't exaggerate their tale when they likened them to the strength of steel." He stopped his efforts to pry Darrick's hands from his clothes. "Be a good soul. Pour me a drink from yon jar. See there. Sitting on the shelf . . ."

Darrick unlocked his fingers and let Rhys fall back to the straw mattress. He snatched the jar with one hand, grabbing the wooden vessel that stood beside it with the other. Thrusting it into Rhys's hands, he waited impatiently for the man to continue.

After sipping the elixir from the wooden cup, Rhys spoke slowly. "I arrived at Balforth after I left your father's side. They had need of both healer and clergy at the castle."

Darrick waited as Rhys took another slow, laborious swallow. The little man made a show of letting the soothing liquid trickle down his parched throat. Testing Darrick's patience further, he took another drink before continuing.

"Unfortunately, the wives of Lord Balforth have been beset by poor health."

"Plague?" Darrick asked.

Rhys looked up from under a ragged hank of hair. He took a deep, rattling breath, and added, "Nay," he said. "The marriage bed."

"You forget, old man, Elizabeth is not Lord Balforth's wife."

"Not yet," Rhys mumbled under his breath. "When I heard your sister was widowed and traveling to Balforth, I tried to watch over her. As a favor to your father."

Nathan returned to the cot. "How did you know of Hugh's death so soon? 'Tis only recently that official notice was delivered."

Rhys glanced back at Darrick. Shrugging, he waved aside Nathan's question with a pale hand. " 'Tis of no importance. Perhaps a loyal retainer came with the report. I don't recall."

"Quickly, old man, where is she?" Darrick asked.

"Vincent DePierce was most displeased when your sister arrived at Balforth Castle. You see—"

"You saw her?" Nathan pressed closer. "She arrived at Balforth?" He turned to Darrick. "I knew it. We'll tear Balforth apart."

"Please continue with your tale. Where is my sister?"

"She hides on a small island off the west coast. Few people know of its existence." Rhys hesitated before continuing. "Should have found safety there. Until today. No one knew where she was. Save myself and the maiden I sent with her to tend to her needs."

Darrick cursed the delays he and his men had met with every step of their journey. "Continue," he ordered.

Rhys bowed his head. "May God forgive her. The serving girl did not stay as instructed. Fears of the old hermit hiding on the island were too much for her. She deserted your sister to fend for herself."

"Where's the servant now?" Darrick asked.

Rhys's gaze rose from his lap. He studied the men before giving them his answer. "She was reported missing at the same time as Lady Elizabeth. The DePierce mercenaries were waiting. Her arrest came as soon as she returned home."

Darrick searched the man's face for truth. "Damn it, man! How is this possible?"

"You must understand! The soldiers of Balforth are very efficient. The maid did not have a chance." Rhys's eyes shifted away. "Even now, I fear they are on their way to ferret out the safekeeping of the two women and end their lives."

Darrick leaned over, his face close enough to smell the pungent odor of wild onions on Rhys's breath. "Are your brains addled? You just said the other woman is no more."

A flash of impatience burned in Rhys's eyes before he hid them behind heavy lids. "Nay, 'tis true!"

"There is another?" Darrick asked.

The thin blanket bunched under Rhys's gnarled fingers. His voice continued to rise in agitation. "Aye, the stubborn wench. Too headstrong for her own good." He wiped the spittle from his mouth and motioned toward the door. "You tarry long enough. Leave tonight for the island. I pray you are not too late."

Nathan grabbed Darrick by the front of his gambeson. "You cannot mean to go there alone."

Darrick shrugged free. "I am capable of handling two women. 'Tis you who enters into Balforth's den of vipers. Don't draw attention until we station more men." He nodded toward the rumpled clergyman. "Watch him closely."

"Hear me, Rhys," Darrick called from the doorway. "If what you say is true, I owe you a debt of gratitude. To be paid upon my return. However, should you play me false, know that I'll be on your trail. And I will find you."

Acknowledgments

I am grateful for so many wonderful people who support me in this wild writing life.

Raisa Allison, my sister, I thank you for being you. Your strength inspires me.

And to Cindy Jackson, my lifelong friend, and warrior, I thank you for giving me courage to reach beyond the stars.

Once again, a huge thank you goes to my friend and super beta reader, Susie Fourt. And many thanks to my critique partner, Kimberley Troutte, who always talks me through the crisis. Thanks for reminding me to breathe.

Last, but certainly not least, to my darling husband, knight in shining armor, and best friend, I thank you for helping me to believe. PS: I love you more today than I did the day before.

C.C. Wiley is a longstanding member of the Romance Writers of America, and a published author. She lives in Salt Lake City with her high school sweetheart of over thirty-five years and their four wacky dogs. When given a choice, she prefers a yummy, well-written, historical or contemporary romance that is chock-full of hope, love, and a Happy Ever After. She believes there are wonderful courageous characters waiting for someone to tell their story. It's her hope that each adventurous romance she writes will touch the reader and carry them away to another place and time, where hopes and dreams abound.